EN

Route

CASSIE GARZA

ISBN: 979-8-9939623-1-3

Edited by Austin Dewar and Paige Lawson

Cover art by Lex Salazar

To Nathan,

Thanks for the inspiration, you little shit. Sorry you aren't around to read this, but I probably wouldn't have let you anyway.

Author's Note

Dear Reader,

Thank you so much for taking the time to read my debut novel, *Love En Route*. While I hope the adventures of Cameron, Rook, and Maverick are as fun to read as they were to write, I would like to touch on a few themes that may be triggering.

This novel is my attempt to create an authentic portrayal of grief for those who are also navigating transitions in identity, relationships, and career. It contains allusions to alcoholism and child neglect, along with explicit references to a fatal car accident (not depicted onstage). I approached these topics through the lens of my own experience and neuroscience research, which I reference throughout Cameron's journey, and I often use humor to balance the emotionally laden themes of grief and loss, though they remain central to this story.

Best,
Cassie Garza

Part One

Following the death of a loved one, you may find yourself avoiding thoughts, emotions, locations, and situations that remind you of them. This strategy is known as *avoidance*.[1-2]

Creative name, I know.

If you're using avoidance to cope, you might seem perfectly fine on the outside. Fine enough to go grocery shopping, pick up your kids, or flirt with that coworker you have oddly sexual tension with. So while you can pass for a healthy, functioning person, what you've really done is shoved that shit down.

—Cameron Loredo, Blog Post #22, *Six Feet Above*

Chapter One

It's not often that I attend a birthday party for my dead brother, but when I do, I bring a plus-one.

A plus-one who is currently fixing my smudged eyeliner and poking at my waterline on the porch of my childhood home. Leave it to my best friend Vivian to fixate on my aesthetic choices at a time like this.

I sigh, swatting her away as she frowns for the umpteenth time. "Quit it. I know I'm a lost cause."

She steps back to evaluate her handiwork. "You've got that sort of haunted, sleep-deprived thing going on. Grief never looked so hot."

Between her red curls, corset-style top, and trademark smirk, Vivian is both infinitely cooler than I am and also infinitely less likely to lose her shit tonight. Granted, she'd only met my brother a few times over the last five years. Once I left Texas for California, my college roommate and my brother weren't exactly destined to cross paths. But she spent enough time with him to know how he filled every room he strutted into, some of which were in the single-story, mildly unkempt house before us. My parents never claimed to be horticulturists, but the weeds creeping over the edges of the porch are more aggressive than I remember.

I blink a few times, destroying any progress Vivian made with my sleep-deprived grief grunge look. "Are you sure this isn't too weird for you?"

"Please. You know I'd never miss a chance to party with the Loredos," she says, pointedly tapping her purse. Based on the clinking sounds it made while I drove us over here, it contains multiple alcoholic drinks of an unknown concentration.

"I don't know if it qualifies as a 'party.' More like a small gathering of blood relatives with shrinking hippocampi and a severe lack of hobbies." Besides the occasional morning Sudoku or crochet project, I have no idea what my parents have been up to in the eleven months since The Accident. Based on the state of our front yard, this is the first time they've had company since settling into early retirement.

"You're gonna have to save the nerdy shit until I'm at least one glass in." Vivian tilts her head at me as footsteps sound on the other side of the door. More than a couple of footsteps, actually, along with a song that's a few decibels louder than my parents' average leisurely listening.

Headlights frame our shadows against the front door, and I instinctively stare directly into the light before shielding my eyes.

"How many blood relatives do you have?" Vivian asks as the car parks against the curb, right in front of three other cars. I must've been too distracted by the small liquor store rolling around my passenger side floorboards when we arrived to notice how packed the street is, especially when my old parking spot was open in the driveway.

"That are currently in this state? Two, as far as I know," I say, ringing the doorbell as the headlights flicker off behind us. When my parents first suggested that I visit them to celebrate Maverick's birthday, I counter-suggested at least three different locations. They've never made a fuss about my requests to meet at coffee shops, restaurants, or even the bookstore-bar I've been working at for almost a year. But tonight, they insisted I be here.

Home.

I take a deep breath, steeling myself against the nausea that's already starting to set in as the door swings open, revealing my overalls-clad mother. She smiles, light blue eyes crinkling at the corners, and clasps her hands together with a *smack*. It's the same gesture she makes when one of her theater students has a particularly powerful delivery or finishes painting a backdrop. Like Maverick, she emotes rather loudly. "Girls! You made it."

"Of course," Vivian says, elbowing me in the ribs when I take too long to echo her. It's not my fault that my cognitive processes are lagging. That tends to happen when the rest of your energy is directed toward not throwing up. I haven't stood on this porch in months, and the last time I did . . .

Well, the circumstances weren't as celebratory.

"Wouldn't miss it," I add unconvincingly, throwing myself into a side hug when my mother's smile wavers. Vivian does the same, and I pause on the doorstep to collect myself.

Despite my best efforts at pitching other venues, I will have to enter this house and socialize for at least a few minutes. And while it looks like my parents have invited at least half of the population of Rustin, Texas, into our home, things could be worse—I could run into Maverick's best friend. Luckily, the odds of that are approximately 0.0 percent.

Laughter floats down from somewhere past my mother's head, and she ushers us in. I must make a conscious effort to relax and an even more conscious effort not to sprint back to the car. Who knows? Maybe Maverick's postmortem birthday party is the perfect time to subject myself to whatever memories are trapped in these walls. Between Vivian's booze bag lightly ramming into my right hip and the small disco ball hanging in the entryway, all signs point to a festive, non-traumatic evening. In fact, maybe it's time to let loose. Maybe I *can* be a carefree, social person for one night.

That sounds better than a burnt-out pre-med with boy problems and a dead brother.

• • •

Bacon. Cheese. Hash browns. By the smell of it, I have stepped into an alternate reality—or an alternate time zone, at the very least.

"Before you ask, yes, I'll be having just egg whites instead of the good stuff." A voice sounds from just out of my line of sight. I turn to find my father, who is smiling under an increasingly gray, increasingly Mario-esque mustache. While I didn't inherit the facial hair, I did end up with his dark eyes and nearly black hair. And his love of cholesterol-spiking foods.

I raise my hands up, edging closer to the dining room wall as someone I vaguely recognize makes a beeline for the bacon. "Hey, it's not my fault that heart conditions are disproportionately represented in male mortality—"

I pause as the faux pas registers. Statistics haven't exactly been my friend lately, not when male mortality has been disproportionately represented in our immediate family. It was highly improbable that Mav would stay out so late the night before one of his shows, and even more improbable that someone would run a red light while he was in the middle of an intersection.

But here we are. Celebrating his 25th birthday without him.

I clear my throat, avoiding the empathy in my father's eyes in favor of scanning the breakfast-for-dinner spread. Our dining room table is filled to the brim with chocolate chip waffles, scrambled eggs (with a slightly smaller portion of egg whites), hash browns, and an absurd amount of bacon. The chairs are nowhere to be found—I suspect they're in the next room, where chatter buzzes under the music.

"We traditionally do Italian for his birthday, but as you know, Linguini's has been repurposed," my mother explains in her singsong way, entering the dining room with Vivian trailing closely behind her. As my fellow sales associate at Plot Twist, the bookstore-bar formerly known as Linguini's, Vivian is well aware of the establishment's Italian roots. "We made do with his second favorite," Mom says.

"Speaking of favorites," Vivian says, reaching into her bulging purse, "I heard you two love champagne."

"Love a mimosa even more," my mom says, accepting the first bottle with a smile before grabbing the orange juice from the end of the table. If I weren't focused on maintaining emotional equilibrium, I'd be wondering how she concocted five mimosas in two seconds. Maybe she took up mixology instead of gardening.

When Vivian procures not one but two more bottles, my father lets out a low whistle. "Now it's a party."

"What do you mean *now*? You invited half the town," I say with a wave at the vaguely familiar stranger still lingering by the bacon.

My mother *tsk*s at me, shaking her head while I stack waffles on a paper plate. "I told you they're running *Cats* in the city, didn't I? I simply had to invite the cast. You know your brother would've celebrated with them, anyway."

"So we've been infiltrated by the thespians," I mumble, frowning at my small tower of waffles. They looked a lot more appetizing before guilt started worming its way into my esophagus. I've put off talking to Maverick's theater friends for . . . Well, for almost eleven months now.

But now that she's revealed the invite list, I do recognize the one other person in the room that I'm not related to or roommates with. I shuffle over a few paces and peek around the corner, where a curly-haired cast member flails his arms in front of the floor-to-ceiling bookcase in the living room. The others shout at him while he continues to windmill in what appears to be a lively game of charades.

Unfortunately, the limb-flailing does nothing to distract me from the bookcase itself. Aside from actual books, it displays a framed excerpt of my first research publication, my brother's high school lacrosse trophies, and a small shrine of theater programs, which my mother has collected since Maverick sang his first solfège—

"Do. Like a female deer, not a dying one," Maverick says, *aggressively pushing the buttons of his Nintendo DS from where he lies on the couch. Weeks of practicing, and I still sound like a mortally wounded animal.*

"Mom's gonna kill me." I rearrange the sheet music on the living room carpet. I should be crying over math homework like the rest of my friends. Instead, I finish math early and cry over scales while my brother judges me from the sidelines.

Middle school is off to a great start.

Mav sits upright, couch creaking as he squints at me under the shaggy hair he's refused to get cut for months now. "You don't need a lead role. Just be a tree or something."

I shake my head, eyeing the Beauty and the Beast *pamphlet on the bookshelf. Easy for him to say when he lands the lead role in literally everything he auditions for. "No. Not good enough."*

He sets down his game. "Look, we both know you suck."

"Rude."

"Truth hurts." He sighs, sounding about a million years older than thirteen, when my shoulders drop. "You don't even like performing. Do your own thing. Mom knows her theater legacy is safe while I'm around."

"Would you like to go the backyard, honey?" Mom asks. "You're looking a little overheated."

The words yank me into the present moment, where my mother's cool hand is pressed against my forehead. I blink a few times, dispelling the image of adolescent Mav as Mom's pinched eyes come into focus.

Between the music, limb-flailing, and mild hallucination, I'm starting to remember why I didn't want to be near this house tonight— or any other night. If Vivian hadn't already started chatting up a blonde by the charades game, I could fake a spontaneous fever and drag her to the car, where it's a short drive back to Aunt Brandi's guest house.

I take a step back, lowering my plate in one hand while I fan myself with the other. "You're right. I'm feeling feverish. I should probably head out before I infect someone."

"You only just got here." Mom fans me with her empty plate and frowns. "And you can't leave yet. We're still waiting on one more."

On cue, the doorbell rings, and every head in the dining room swivels in unison. It would be comical if not for the growing sense of unease in my already turbulent stomach. Aside from the cast of *Cats*, it doesn't sound like Mom invited any other randos. Maverick's closest relatives (plus Vivian) are already here, and I know for a fact that Aunt Brandi will be in Japan through the end of the month for her latest marketing campaign. Which leaves—

"Sorry I'm late." In a rush of warm summer air, dark waves, and broad shoulders, Rook Everett Hale strides through the door. I freeze as he greets my parents, giving my mother a quick hug and shaking my father's hand, before turning his attention to me.

Not too long ago, the sight of him would've sent me into cardiac arrest. Years of unrequited pining for your older brother's best friend will do that to you.

While my stupid, weak-willed hormones might be circulating fast enough to make my heart pound, I know better now. Rook is no knight in shining armor—he's the prick who didn't bother showing up to his best friend's funeral.

Chapter Two

Maybe I'd feel better if he looked different. But besides the sleeker frames of his glasses, he looks exactly the same. Same tanned, high cheekbones. Same hazel eyes with enough burning green to make blood rush to your face in an impressive feat of vasodilation. Same stubble around his jaw that never quite goes away.

Nothing to indicate his newfound lack of a soul.

"Shit." The word slips out before my prefrontal cortex can kick into gear. In my peripheral vision, my mother covers her face with her hands.

He merely raises an eyebrow, a half-smile on his full lips. "Actually, it's pronounced 'Rook.'"

I grab a mimosa from the table, swishing the bubbling orange liquid around as I sift through conversation starters. *How's work been? Anything interesting happen since my brother became another routine call? It's sure looking like it'll be a dry summer—busy season is right around the corner!*

"So, Rook," I say, willing myself not to flinch when our eyes meet again, "to what do we owe the pleasure?"

He takes a step toward me. When I scowl, he pauses, then says, "It's Maverick's birthday. I was invited."

"Huh." As I recall, he was also invited to Maverick's funeral. Must've had a scheduling conflict. That, or he regretted our night together so much that he couldn't show his face.

And continued to not show his face for the next eleven months.

As much as I'd love to call him out in front of everyone, the only person who's privy to that particular backstory is Vivian, and she's still loitering around charades. It's probably for the best that she hasn't caught sight of Rook yet—while my parents were all too happy to explain his absence away with *Everyone grieves differently*, she was ready to fight him with her bare hands.

The silence carries long enough to alert my mother that something is Very Wrong Here, and she says, "I think we could all use some fresh air. Why don't we head to the back? Your father fixed the lights." The father in question scurries across the room before the last words are out of her mouth. I can't blame him. He has zero tolerance for confrontation in normal circumstances, much less these ones.

Avoiding Rook's questioning look, I make my way through the living room, raising my drink so that Vivian looks my way—and instantly latches onto the man trailing behind me. Her eyes widen, and a small indentation forms on the floor where her jaw hits it. I manage a tiny nod before she excuses herself and follows our procession.

After a brief struggle with the sliding glass door, we file out onto the back patio and settle into the half-circle of wicker basket chairs on the cement. Fairy lights dangle from the patio cover, illuminating the line where cement meets grass as Vivian sits between me and Rook.

"What's he doing here?" she whispers loudly enough for the three other people near us to clearly hear. As uncomfortable as my father looks, my mother appears to be suffering from a particularly bad flare-up of IBS. Her mouth is puckered, and she's staring at her husband so intensely that a vein pops out on her forehead. This can't be good—her IBS face only comes out when she's hiding something.

When Dad gives her a nod, alarm bells start ringing in the back of my mind. I stay completely still as she pulls a folded paper out of the large pocket on the front of her overalls, and the ringing morphs into tornado sirens.

"He's here to celebrate Maverick's birthday"—she smooths the paper against her knees and reaches over me to hand it to Vivian—"and to help with the talent show."

The blush blooms in my cheeks the same instant that I start choking on my last sip of mimosa. Because it's not just any piece of paper. It's a flyer.

I claw at my cup, but who knows? Maybe I should just let myself choke to death right here.

Before I can succumb to the great beyond, Vivian thumps my back, and Rook rises from his seat with a convincingly concerned divot between his eyebrows. I bat both of them away as the air begins to flow back into my trachea.

The thing about that flyer is, Aunt Brandi made it. Thanks to her status as Girlboss Marketing Hotshot, she's been spreading the word about the talent show-slash-fundraiser-slash-memorial extravaganza we're holding for Maverick. And she's done her job very well.

I, on the other hand, have not.

"What's this?" Vivian asks, examining the flyer. I look away from the microphone and tiny stage with *Maverick Loredo Memorial Talent Show* plastered across the top in bold neon letters. Pretty sure Mav's picture is in the corner, too.

"A fundraiser for theater kids who want to be theater adults." My dad frowns.

I sigh, delivering my next words to the stars overhead. "It's a talent show fundraiser. A tribute to my theatrical brother, who insisted on being the Troy Bolton of Rustin High." There's a sharp intake of air from the chair next to me. My mom, already tearing up. Probably because Mav's love for the dramaturgical started in her classroom. I press on, "Ideally, we'd get enough donations to renovate the community theater that's already in Rustin. He had to drive an hour to rehearse at the one in the city"—and whined about it every time—"but realistically, we'll raise enough money for a few scholarships."

Vivian chews on the inside of her cheek, examining the flyer in her lap. "This says it's a month away." She taps the very bold, very finalized date on the bottom of the flyer.

Rook tries to meet my eye. I pick at a loose wood filament on my armrest. "June seventeenth," I say.

"Which is why Rook's here," my mom says, dabbing her eyes with a handkerchief, which was also stashed in her overalls pocket. My fingers pause mid-fidget. "To help get acts for the show."

The backyard falls silent, waiting to be filled with the wails of my dying ego. After all, I volunteered to scout for acts. In fact, I volunteered to put the whole show together. Back when Mom chose to retire rather than return to the same walls Mav helped her decorate, and Dad . . . Well, my father spent an entire week looking for the last bottle of

Mountain Dew Mav threw away. I wasn't going to make them plan a whole show around their dead son.

This is supposed to be my responsibility. Nobody else's.

"What do you mean? I've had the lineup secured for months," I manage to get out. It's not a complete lie. I've *thought* about who would make a good act for the show. Mav's pals at the inconveniently distant theater, who look to be queuing karaoke lyrics on the living room TV. The improv group he's loved since high school. Maybe even some of his old students, since he started giving voice lessons a couple years ago to supplement his patchy income.

So I've basically secured . . . at least thirty minutes' worth of talent show material.

Fine. It's a complete lie. But I'd rather lie than admit failure.

Rook opens his mouth to reply, but it's my mom who speaks up first. "Cam, honey. We've asked around, and we know that you haven't started getting the acts together yet."

The words hang in the air, suspended in a moment where I can pretend that June seventeenth will never happen, before settling squarely in my auditory cortex. Shit. Shit. *Shit.* She knows. They all know, going by the stomach-flipping amount of pity in their eyes. Even Vivian, who didn't hear about this thing until two seconds ago.

"Who'd you ask?" The words are surprisingly steady for how leaden my tongue feels.

Rook clears his throat. "When I reached out to Sebastian about the party tonight, he said he couldn't make it . . . and when I asked about their act for the talent show, he said he hadn't heard from you."

"Oh." Out of all of his theater friends, Maverick's favorite was Sebastian. I should've known he'd be the one to rat me out, since I haven't gotten around to returning his texts. It's been a busy eleven months of working at Plot Twist, researching for my blog, and attempting to self-administer Cognitive Behavioral Therapy instead of waiting for Rook to magically appear at my door.

I did see Sebastian at the funeral, but that wasn't exactly the best venue for striking up small talk. Especially when he was the last one to see Maverick before The Accident. They had been getting breakfast for dinner, a classic final rehearsal tradition, which turned into a late night out—and a very late drive for Maverick.

I'd rather have Sebastian rat me out a thousand times than face him tonight.

"If it makes you feel any better, I've been looking for an excuse to take the Tennessee Trail," Rook says, casually removing his glasses and cleaning the lenses with the bottom of his shirt. Every blood cell formerly participating in my anxiety spiral reroutes to my cheeks.

"What the hell is a Tennessee Trail?" Vivian asks. I focus on breathing in through my nose, out through my mouth, giving that parasympathetic nervous system a chance to kick in.

Tennessee Trail. Right. Because only a specific type of dork would call it that.

Rook leans back in his chair, watching my mindfulness routine out of the corner of his eye while he answers. "It's a road trip Mav and I take—used to take—to Nashville every year," he explains. The fumble makes something twist in my gut, but I can't afford to pay attention to that right now.

"What does the Tennessee Trail have to do with anything?" I ask the room, since three quarters of them have been conspiring against me.

It was the pinnacle of Mav's year, that trip. A bro trip. A no-way-in-hell-will-my-little-sister-come-along trip.

Rook places his glasses back on the bridge of his nose, meeting my icy gaze with tentative warmth and says, "Mav and I made a lot of interesting friends over the years. I'm sure if I talked to them, they'd come out for the show. Even if they don't perform, they could spread the word . . . "

He trails off as I sink further into my chair, crossing my arms in a decidedly dominant manner. My parents stiffen in their seats—they know what's coming. But Rook is still looking at me with what appears to be genuine curiosity. If I'm lucky, he'll notice the piece of waffle I just spotted in my hair.

"Three things. One, it sounds like Rook has this taken care of, so I appreciate the courtesy notice that I'm no longer needed. Two, don't all of these 'interesting friends'"—I can't begin to imagine who Rook would classify as *interesting*—"have social media? You could just DM or call or whatever. That seems quicker and easier. I mean, the carbon footprint alone . . . Three," I say, pausing for effect, "does this mean we have access to your coworkers? Because I'm sure a sexy firefighter dance sequence would raise a ton of money for the cause." Dad gives a start, his chair scraping against the cement, but Rook remains mostly unfazed. If anything, the corner of his mouth twitches into a semi-smile. A quarter-smile.

It used to be my goal in life to get a reaction like that out of him. Now, I only have the smallest of heart palpitations.

He shrugs. "I'm not big on social media. That was always Mav's thing. Plus, it's harder to say no to someone's face." I open my mouth to object—to his words, his nonchalant demeanor, his ability to say

Maverick's name without crying—and then close it. He's got a point. At Plot Twist, I leverage the awkwardness of saying no to someone's face all the time—it's the best technique for pitching membership programs. He continues, "I'll have to ask about the dancing. We don't currently have a choreographer, but I can double-check."

Vivian snorts, and I kick her under the table. Traitor.

"So Rook goes on the Tennessee Trail, rallies the troops, and reports back to me while I . . . diligently log the lineup on my Notes app?" A familiar ache fills my chest, the one that so graciously lets me know when I'm about to disappoint everyone.

"Oh, we wouldn't send him out alone," Mom says. She reaches across the table and rests a hand on mine. "We'd love for the both of you to take the trip—together."

My parents smile encouragingly at me, emanating support and faith in my ability to emotionally self-regulate, as every synaptic network simultaneously crashes in my mind. Wires cross and fizzle and burn out.

Rook's hand on my leg in a moonlit room.

A borderline sacrilegious graduation cake.

A phone call.

A casket.

Silence.

More silence.

Eleven months of silence.

I fold my hands neatly in front of me, hiding the tremor. Almost. "Thank you so much for the offer, but that won't be necessary. I know it *looks* like I've been putting it off, but really, I've got this under control." I force myself to meet my parents' eyes. Mom squints like if she stares long enough, she'll understand where she went wrong with me. Dad switches between checking my mother's expression and mine. Vivian scowls down at the flyer. When I get to Rook, I can't help but add, "Feel free to hit the road, though."

Mom's hands fly to her collarbone, but Rook merely says, "It's okay." The words fall flat, devoid of sympathy. "Why don't you sleep on it? It'll take a few days to make the trip, even if I shorten it, so travel time would be a factor. But we'd have better odds of recruiting people who would say yes, and the acts would have a wider range than if we searched locally. I know how you feel about a cost-benefit analysis."

Vivian exhales loudly through her nose, and I fight the urge to launch my empty plate at her. It makes no sense for my heart to be kickstarted by a comment like that. After having known each other for over a decade, he was bound to notice my love for data-driven decision-making.

And then deem me not worthy of his presence during the worst eleven months of my life.

"When do I need to give an answer by? When the clock strikes midnight?" I ask dryly.

The corner of his mouth twitches. "How about tomorrow night? I plan to leave by Tuesday at the latest."

I dip my chin once and stand up, gathering any remaining shreds of dignity rather than sit here a moment longer. "Thank you all for the intervention, but I think it's time to head out. Sorry I can't stick around for cake." I gesture for Vivian to get up with me, and we make our round of goodbyes as the cicadas start to chirp.

Voices mutter behind us as we stride through the house, and Vivian stops to say goodbye to the blonde from earlier while I make a break for the car.

It's not like I won't consider Rook's offer. No, I'm more than happy to do my due diligence. Make the drive to Aunt Brandi's guest house. Reflect on the months of unreturned texts and calls and letters I mailed to him like an octogenarian. Wait the appropriate amount of time until I can reasonably say no, I won't need any assistance with Maverick's talent show, thank you very much.

Despite my parents' best intentions, there's no way in hell I'll be trapped in a car with Rook on the road trip of my nightmares.

Chapter Three

"I *knew* you two hooked up."

"Are you kidding me right now?" I hiss, cupping a hand over Vivian's mouth as a customer peruses the shelves one aisle over. She grins under my fingers, entirely unabashed at her outburst in our place of work. As a flipped Italian restaurant, Plot Twist has high ceilings and walls of exposed brick that are gorgeous . . . and also affect the acoustics.

Her next words are muffled under my palm, and I only move my hand away when the customer is halfway to the checkout line. She grins. "This is your fault. You could've explained last night instead of stewing in your room," she says, kneeling to adjust the shelf talker wedged under a book below us.

"I don't *stew*. I analyze." Examine and assess trends, process information until it's categorized into something neat and explainable. So what if I decided to process in the comfort of my own room? It's not every day that the man who broke your heart drops in for your dead brother's birthday party, eats breakfast-for-dinner with your family, and offers to take you on the road trip from hell.

"You could've *analyzed* in the living room. I took out the good wine and everything." Sidestepping her pout, I push the cart of new arrivals toward the neighboring section of romantasies. I adjust a display copy, making sure the sprayed edges are visible before grabbing a few new titles from the cart.

"Oh my God. Wait, turn around again," she says, eyes wide. I do as I'm told, twisting my neck to investigate the seat of my jeans.

"What? What is it?"

She looks me over, taking a step back to evaluate before nodding to herself. "For a second, it looked like the stick up your ass was coming out," she says, laughing as heat rises to my cheeks. I swat at her arm, and she dodges me before planting herself just out of swatting range. "Seriously, though. I don't get it. You'd be killing, like, seven birds with one stone here."

After a brief moment of determining I won't attack again, she leans across the cart between us, counting off on her fingers as she speaks. "You'll get acts lined up for the show, you can take a mini vacation from being Ms. Overachieving Future Doctor"—I roll my eyes, switching a book from the pile in my arms to the nearest shelf—"and you get to torture him for a week."

I pause, the purple-edged hardcover momentarily forgotten as I echo, "Torture?"

"Exactly." Honey-brown eyes stay locked on mine as she says, "So what if you're in the car for a few days? This is your chance to guilt trip him for being such an asshole. He's already halfway to crawling back and begging you for forgiveness—I could see it in his stupid puppy dog eyes."

"Puppy dog eyes?" I laugh. Are we talking about the same person? Tall, dark-haired, willing to ride into the sunset as my life fell apart? "I don't know what you think you saw, but he acted like everything was fine. Like nothing ever happened." Because to him, it was nothing. Obviously. I can still see him twiddling his thumbs on the back patio, completely content to sit there as I suffered three consecutive anxiety attacks in the span of twenty minutes.

I resume my book stacking, taking extra care to line up the middle row as Madame Truffalo watches us from across the floor. My boss, witnessing our glacial restocking pace in real time. I doubt she'll reprimand us, though—Truffalo would rather set a first edition on fire than raise her voice. "You can't be serious right now."

"I absolutely am serious right now." Vivian straightens up, moving the cart until there's nothing but stained carpet between us. "You were in love with this guy forever. Since you no longer want him to propose and be the father of your freakishly smart babies, you might as well take advantage of his car and connections."

A lanky teen stands in my periphery, no doubt working up the courage to ask about the latest fantasy release. In a low voice I say, "I can't make someone come crawling back if they never cared about me in the first place," leaving Vivian to move on to historical fiction while I pivot to the figure loitering next to us.

He fiddles with his leather jacket as I plaster a customer service smile on my face. "How can I help you?"

"Um, do you have *Wayward Pines* by Joel Basswood? It's for my girlfriend," he adds quickly.

"Fantastic choice," I say, only slightly gagging on the words. My mom's a Basswood fan, too. She always could stomach the misogynistic undertones better than me.

I walk him a couple aisles down, leading him to the dedicated Basswood shelf. He grunts a "Thanks" as I return to the cart.

"It's simple," Vivian says, like we were never interrupted by an emo-adjacent teenage boy. "You'll suck it up and tap into those famous Loredo acting skills."

I scrunch my nose, but her I-know-I'm-right-and-also-incredibly-persuasive smirk is already in place. This is the solution? Acting? I have a wide range of wonderful, eclectic skills: Parallel parking, whistling, identifying signs of a stroke—but nothing of the thespian sort.

"You're a natural. You only kind of looked like you wanted to throw up when you talked to that kid."

I frown at her. "The acting genes didn't go to me."

"I know, I know. They went to Maverick. But wouldn't he be proud that you're following in his footsteps?" she asks, eyes full of mirth and something a little too close to concern for my liking. "You heard Asshat. I know you want to do this on your own, but he'd connect you with whoever they met on the Tennessee Trail. You just have to pretend you can tolerate him for a few days. And haven't they been taking that trip forever? They've probably made enough friends to fill up the whole two hours of a show."

"Two and a half hours, with intermission," I correct automatically. I brace my core, pushing the cart around the corner of the next aisle as she walks alongside me. "While I appreciate the blind faith in my acting abilities, I'll pass. Besides, everyone knows emails are the most efficient way to communicate these kinds of events. I compiled a list of Rustin's most talented last night. The email has been optimized for maximum engagement, so we'll have more acts in no time." As long as I don't have to see, speak to, or be in the same room as anyone on that list, I can do this. The email template is typed and ready to go. *To Whom It May Concern: Apologies for the late notice—I've failed spectacularly at getting my shit together. Are you free in approximately three weeks for a pro bono performance at my brother's memorial talent show fundraiser?*

"Right . . . Whatever that means." She sits on the edge of a display table as she levels an exasperated look at me. "Let me say this in a way that might get through to you. It would be more *efficient* to talk to people that actually knew Mav instead of sending emails."

"I'll take that into consideration." I know it would be more efficient to talk to people, and I still have time to do that. But for now, I can't listen to the last voicemail Mav left me, much less chat up potential acts for the show. Emails will work just fine. I might even send a text or two. Anything to avoid breathing the same air as Rook for multiple days in a row. We haven't been alone together since the night before The Accident. It's one thing to go MIA on me, but to miss the funeral?

I hide my wince behind a paperback, and Vivian turns away from me, adjusting the clip holding half her hair up before Truffalo spots us again. "All I'm saying is, you could *optimize* your female rage by showing Mr. Broody Firefighter Man that hooking up meant nothing to you, too."

"Tempting," I mutter, ignoring the customer making her way over to us. It's Vivian's turn to interact with people.

She throws her hands in the air. "Fine. I'll drop it. But let the record show that I think this is the perfect opportunity to make him pay." With that, she begins chatting with the middle-aged woman looking for—surprise—Joel Basswood's latest release.

Make him pay. The phrase ricochets around my skull, rebounding off images from last night. Bubbling mimosas. A flash of hazel eyes. A trace of a smile at my sexy dance sequence joke.

They quickly dissolve in a haze of unanswered calls, teary nights, and pints of Ben and Jerry's.

The only logical conclusion? If I'm going to get the show together myself, I need to stay as far away from Rook as possible. Now's not the time to backslide—especially after spending the better part of a year searching for ways to glue back together the heart he helped obliterate.

I might not be able to act or postpone the show indefinitely, but I can make sure he never has the chance to break it again.

• • •

The streetlights are just flickering on when I pull into the cul-de-sac, illuminating the small fleet of cars in my parents' driveway. With Mav's sedan next to my dad's truck and my mom's car tucked into the garage, my parking spot remains open. The curb is empty, so I can only assume that Rook wasn't invited back for another surprise ambush. Which might help my cause—I'll be able to think more clearly if he's not here while I give my spiel about handling the talent show on my own.

Hauling myself out of the driver's seat, I rehearse my speech to the moths gathering around the garage lights. "I know I've been lying about getting the acts together for the last eleven months, but I'm ready to do it now. I've got a foolproof strategy in place that doesn't require driving across state lines. However, if Rook wants to take the Tennessee Trail for the next, I don't know, three to six months—"

And then I see them, framed between the curtains of the front window, as I pause next to the hood of my car. My parents, sitting at the dining room table. My father at the head, shoveling a small mound of mashed potatoes onto his plate. My mother to his left, straightening the utensils. Dad says something funny enough to make her throw her head back with laughter, and he smiles at the sound. It's all very wholesome, a Norman Rockwell painting come to life.

Until Mom looks left, directly at Mav's empty chair. It's automatic, muscle memory. Like she's waiting for him to join in and share the joke.

In the next few seconds, several things happen:

1) Her face crumples, and her body along with it.

2) My father stands up, coaxing her to lean into his chest as she cries.

3) My stomach twists into a knot, air rushing out of my lungs until I'm stumbling back against my car.

From this angle, I can only see half of my father's face, including his drooping mustache. He holds her until her shoulders stop shaking, and she pulls back from him enough to accept a napkin. His lips move, and she smiles through the tears dampening her cheeks.

I know she'll be fine. Those tears are already releasing stress hormones, and her body's natural painkillers will kick on in a second. The moment will pass, and we'll be free to have dinner like a nice, normal family while I explain my plan to reject Rook's offer.

Except . . . there will be more moments like this. A lifetime of moments like this. And while I can't prevent all of them, I can do everything in my power to make the talent show spectacular. A proper tribute to their son. A memorial worthy of my larger-than-life brother.

As much as I would love to prove otherwise, recruiting people face-to-face would probably be the most effective strategy, especially if we can increase the talent pool with all of Rook's *interesting friends*. Damn him. I know his profession requires him to be good in a crisis situation, but I never wanted to be the cause of one. And the devastation my parents would experience if the show doesn't come together in time? Definitely crisis-worthy.

I push myself off the hood, ducking closer to the garage door before my father can catch sight of me through the window. If I'm going to take the Tennessee Trail, I'll need help packing tonight.

With a couple of swipes, I pull up Vivian's phone number, the call tone ringing loud enough to rattle my teeth. I turn down the volume when she picks up. "How'd the speech—"

"If I hear a single *told you so*, I'm telling Truffalo that you're the one who kept putting the Bible in the historical fiction section." She sputters an unintelligible, vaguely profane phrase, and I turn the volume another notch lower. "I've reassessed, and it turns out I was missing key information in my original analysis. I could A, do nothing and cancel the show, inevitably bringing shame to myself and my family. B, send well-crafted emails to a carefully compiled list of Rustin's entertainers at the risk of nobody responding. Or C, weaponize the thespian abilities I may or may not have while getting acts together on the Tennessee Trail."

"And?"

I peer around the corner, where my parents are still waiting for me on the other side of the window. For them, I can tap into any latent Loredo acting skills that trickled down to me, even if it means sitting next to Rook for multiple days in a row.

"Thespianism it is."

Part Two

For those of us lucky enough to experience traumatic grief, *intrusive memories* are a fact of life.[3-4] One moment, you're taking a stroll down the frozen dessert aisle of your local grocery store. The next, you're watching your dead brother pick out a pint of chocolate ice cream.

You can thank your brain for that. It's trying to work through unprocessed trauma, making you relive memories whether you like it or not.

Intrusive memories are, to put it scientifically, not fun.

—Cameron Loredo, Blog Post #14, *Six Feet Above*

Chapter Four

I don't know what I expected from the start of this week in hell, but it wasn't Rook in a green long-sleeve rolled up to his elbows. No, I'm most definitely focusing on the next few days of emotional turmoil and barren landscape.

Not his forearms. Certainly not how his biceps strain against those cotton sleeves while he drives.

"So," he says, breaking my ogling session and the hour-long silence. "I heard med school is starting up soon."

I turn to face the window, watching my mouth twist into a scowl in the reflection. "Did my parents also tell you about the birthmark on my left ass cheek?"

A flush creeps up my neck before the sentence is fully out. Rook happens to know about that birthmark already.

He seems to realize it, too, clearing his throat before continuing, "Vivian mentioned that she would head back to California when you go to orientation."

Huh. Somewhere between the reappearance of my not-so-true love and my dignity being burned at the stake, I must've missed that part of the conversation.

Keeping my eyes on my bare wrist—where a bracelet that Rook gifted me used to be, once upon a time—I say, "Yes, orientation is in a couple of months. I would've started last year, but . . . "

I couldn't stomach the thought of all that life and death, even in lecture slides. Reminders of the one person I never even had a chance of saving.

"You deferred," he finishes for me. I stifle a flare of annoyance that he bailed me out of that increasingly morbid line of thought.

"Correct. I started working at Plot Twist, mostly for the discount." About ten seconds into meeting Madame Truffalo, the white-haired, owl-eyed, eccentric owner, I was sold. Though technically, Rook was the one who suggested I check it out when it opened up last year. "Come to think of it, I've never seen you there. And I've been working there for, what, ten months?"

I blink innocently as he presses his lips into a tight line. One of the driving factors in my childhood turned young adult turned new adult crush on Rook was a shared love of books, starting with a tattered copy of *Percy Jackson* he forgot in our living room. I may or may not have read it in a single night.

The things we do for unrequited, prepubescent love, am I right?

"I was at the grand opening," he says curtly. I wait a beat for additional commentary. When none comes, I make peace with the fact that we'll have at least another few minutes of silence and stretch my arm along the side door. It's seasonally warm for May, but I still had to do a significant amount of guessing for my packing list. Rook gave me almost nothing to work with besides, *Whatever you're comfortable in.* There's nothing but interstate, flat lands of various grains and crops, and mounds of cow feces.

While Mav was a natural outdoorsman, I don't see any reason for him to be particularly exhilarated by this trip so far. At least, not the route itself. But somehow, in all the years Rook and Mav drove the Tennessee Trail, I was never allowed to know the details. It was all very hush-hush. No Instagram photo dump at the end, no posts on Mav's stories. Social media blackout while he spent time with one of his favorite people in the world. He wouldn't even text me for the week.

Here I am now, taking the Tennessee Trail with the one person who refused to text me for many, many weeks. That has to be an example of some type of irony in Mom's curriculum.

After a half-hour of yellow-brown fields streaking by the window, I can't help but break the silence with, "So am I allowed to know what the first stop is, or . . . ?"

Rook drums his fingers along the wheel, no doubt regretting his attempt at small talk. He practically radiates cognitive dissonance as he decides whether to chat with his best friend's little sister or continue last year's pattern of ignoring me altogether. "We'll be outside."

I sit forward, leaning into air currently devoid of more information. "Seriously? That's all I get?"

He side-eyes my position and sighs. Such an inconvenience, my wanting to know where he's currently driving us. If he'd quit angling the directions on his phone away from me, I wouldn't have to ask. "Look, Maverick swore me to secrecy when we first started this thing."

"He swore you to secrecy when you were *seventeen*. Given the circumstances, I think you're free of that particular oath." He shakes his head. "Can I at least know who we're trying to recruit?"

I've spent the last forty-eight hours drafting and rehearsing my recruitment speech, a combination of my (failed) email campaign and just enough emotion for human interactions. If I have a better idea of the target audience, I can adjust it beforehand. That'll give me something to do rather than sit here and stare out the window like the lead in a depressing music video.

His face brightens, and I blink a few times, willing my heart to slow. All these years, and that expression still gets me. It's almost romantic.

In a fucked up, pitiful kind of way.

"Oh, you'll love Dusty. He has a massive collection of reptiles that he brings to elementary schools on his off days."

"Like a mobile zoo," I offer, and he nods.

"He'll be a great act," he says with a small, faintly lopsided smile. "Trust me."

The words pierce my lower abdomen, and I divert my attention back to the bovine outside the window. A year ago, I wouldn't have questioned trusting Rook. In fact, eleven months ago, I trusted him with my entire heart.

While I'll always appreciate a learning opportunity, I never make the same mistake twice.

• • •

It's times like these that I wish I had inherited whatever made Mav so good with animals. We've been out here for twenty minutes, and the most wildlife action we've gotten is a lizard and some NPC birds.

But it's beautiful. I'm not sure how this pocket of land is still green, but it is. Something to do with temperature changes, precipitation, lack of noise pollution . . . Environmental science was never really my thing. But I can still appreciate the chartreuse of the trees, the sage of the leaves, and a thousand other hues that make up the foliage around the dirt path we're on.

One day, I would love to take my time exploring this Arkansan state park and really savor the cleaner air, greenery, and lack of Texas traffic.

That day will have to be after the memorial talent show extravaganza.

"How much longer would you say—"

The words get lost in the back of Rook's T-shirt, along with the rest of my face. He turns enough to give me a cursory glance, then steps casually to the side, as if he didn't stop directly in front of me with no warning.

"This is the route Mav and I took every time. He's the one who discovered it, actually." He pushes a stray branch to the side, and I hesitate. Whereas the main trail we've taken is a clearly marked dirt path, this appears to be little more than a break in the brush. "Scared of a couple twigs, Loredo?"

"I don't make it a habit to follow strangers on unmarked trails," I say, folding my arms across my chest. "And somehow, I don't see Dusty the Closeted Herpetologist going this direction, either."

"Would you believe me if I told you it's a shortcut to Dusty the Closeted Herpetologist?"

I frown, taking a step back to better scan for poison ivy or reptiles of the non-Dusty variety. The thin, barely-trodden indent in the dirt doesn't sit well with me. Or maybe it's the fact that Maverick contributed to that indent not even a year ago. Following his footsteps—literally—is a little too much to take in at ten in the morning.

Then again, if Rook's telling the truth about the shortcut, we'll be able to recruit Dusty that much faster. We could be a hop, skip, and a jump away from having one stop down on the Tennessee Trail.

Without another word, I maneuver past him, making it a full ten yards before realizing that I have no idea where I'm going. He steps around me with a muttered "Stranger, huh?" I have no choice but to follow. We hike in silence, dodging stray branches and fungi as we go.

When the first whispers of lactic acid start to hit my quadriceps, I hear something other than our footsteps and my labored breathing. Babbling of water. Water on more water. Water on stone. It's a matter of a few more steps and we're out of the thickest of bushes, trees parting to reveal the source of the noise.

A waterfall, not much taller than the surrounding trees. A baby waterfall, then. A secret waterfall. Moss lines the edges, and large-leafed vines cover the wet stone. A small body of water sits patiently at the bottom. Clouds overhead block most of the sun, and a slight breeze cools us off.

It's stunning in a sacred, secluded kind of way. And also in a devoid-of-Dusty kind of way.

"This is the shortcut." Rook nods toward the waterfall, tightening one of the straps on his backpack. "Dusty's got his own outpost about a few miles up the main trail, but it wraps around in a loop up the mountain. If we climb, we'll end up right next to it."

I lean on my heels, taking in the fifteen-foot natural water feature. "And how are we supposed to climb this thing, exactly?"

Without another look my way, he strides over to spot a few yards to the right of the base of the waterfall, where some rocks jut out enough to serve as a small platform. He squats briefly before launching himself onto it—like a box jump, but with a much higher chance of preventable injury. I allow myself a respectable two seconds to admire the view of his ass in those shorts before swinging a leg over the side of the rock.

Once my feet are firmly planted next to his, he turns his attention to the small mountain of stone hovering over us. "It's easier than it looks. There are plenty of handholds, and they're far enough away that water evaporates off the stone before it gets too wet." He leans back, gesturing for me to take the lead.

This is it. The shortcut he promised. Before the trembling in my hands becomes too noticeable, I find purchase on a crevice barely large enough to fit my fingers. With Rook's eyes boring a hole in the back of my head, I haul myself up a couple of feet in a single movement. Maybe this isn't a mountain after all. Only about fifteen feet of slightly damp stone that's sure to send me plummeting to my—

"For once in your life, can you stop running through every possible thing that could go wrong?" Maverick hefts himself another few feet in the air, the wind carrying his reprimand to where I'm white-knuckling the first rung of the ladder twenty feet below.

"Fat chance," I call up, eyeing the flecks of rust showering down each time he finds a new handhold. While I don't particularly enjoy the death trap that is Rustin's water tower, Maverick insists on climbing it every time I'm home from school. "I can feel the tetanus coming on just looking at it."

He halts, releasing his hold from one hand so he can give me a thumbs-down with it.

"Be careful," I shriek as he dangles precariously in the air, smiling as if this is normal. Just another day of tempting fate and spiking my cortisol.

"*Always am,*" he calls back. "*Now climb the possibly tetanus-inducing ladder with your brother.*"

With a final look at the solid, non-rusty ground, I force myself to grab the first rung of the ladder. And then the second. By the third, I barely even feel the vibration of the hundred-and-eighty-pound man climbing above me. It's almost too easy to keep ascending, foot by foot, enjoying the warm summer breeze on my face as I approach the halfway point—

And then I look down. Over six hundred skeletal muscles clench in unison, and the familiar acidity of panic coats my throat. Tearing my eyes away from where my water bottle sits at the base of the tower below, I force myself to draw long enough breaths to get oxygen into my brain.

Because no oxygen means unconsciousness, and unconsciousness means falling. And falling means no med school.

Focusing on the metal in my hands and not the yards of empty air under me, I slowly make my descent. Only once my feet are on solid ground again do I relax enough to breathe properly. With one hand on my water bottle, I rest my back on one of the pillars, closing my eyes until the reptile part of my brain isn't convinced I'm about to plummet to my death.

Like a good, supportive sister, I watch as Maverick makes the rest of the climb, oblivious to my reckoning with mortality. I manage to swallow a scream when he hoists himself over the safety railing at the top. And then again when he bows, the gesture swooping enough that I can clearly see it from down here.

My phone vibrates in my pocket, and Maverick's name lights up the screen (along with the absurdly close closeup he set as his contact picture).

"Yes?"

I know what his next words will be even as he lays down next to the ladder, where I can make out the outline of his body on the grate of the platform. "You looked down again, didn't you?"

I'm silent for long enough that he harrumphs in affirmation. "That's what I thought. One of these days, you'll realize the best stuff is on the other side of fear."

"We're burning daylight, Loredo."

Rook's voice scatters the image like a stone across a pond, and I dig my nails into my palms to ground myself. That's what I need—grounding. Reality. I need to focus on the now, and in the now, there's no way I'll be able to unclench my fists enough to climb up a waterfall.

He takes half a step closer, close enough that each inhale brings his scent of fresh pine and clean laundry. His voice drops lower when he notices how stiff I am. "Everything okay?"

I clear my throat, making an effort to relax my posture before lowering myself enough to slide down the rock and onto the ground. "I just remembered that I'm deathly allergic to limestone."

"This is sandstone." He drops down next to me.

"That's what I said."

I shove down the phantom panic and meet his questioning gaze, daring him to contend my newfound allergy. For all he knows, I developed it within the months he decided that I wasn't worth speaking to.

For a fraction of a second, the groove in his brow makes him look more concerned than annoyed. I hold my ground until the microexpression disappears altogether, and he trudges back the way we came with a "Fine. But I choose the route on the way back."

Chapter Five

Between the two-mile stroll and awkward obligatory head nods we gave fellow hikers on the main trail, I've already expended more social energy than my father does in a full calendar year. I'm ready to take Rook up on his thirtieth offer of trail mix when a small log cabin comes into view, adorned with a weathered wooden sign that reads: *Ranger Station*. It sits beside a fork in the trail in a small clearing with tall, reedier grass bordering the front.

After a final stretch of dirt pathway and zero additional hikers, I skip up the cabin's wooden steps and knock on the door.

Silence.

I knock again, and Rook takes a step closer to squint inside. Precious seconds tick by without the door opening, and there's no sign of movement in the window. In all the scenarios and speeches I ran through in my head, it didn't occur to me that we wouldn't even have an opportunity to speak with someone. We *need* him to be here.

"Perfect. Dusty the Closeted Herpetologist doesn't exist," I say, shoving down the anxiety swirling in the pit of my stomach.

"He does exist. Scout's honor." Rook crosses his heart with a finger before promptly sauntering behind the back of the building. "But his bike is gone. We must've just missed him."

I drop to a crouch on the bottom step, pinching the bridge of my nose between my fingers as I lean my elbows on my knees. If Rook hadn't tried to get me to climb a vertical surface, maybe I could get my shit together for more than five minutes at a time. In fact, maybe if he had told me about his little shortcut on the way over here, I could've mentally prepared to make the climb. And we could've gotten here when the single act we need to recruit was still around.

"Hey, I'm professionally obligated to investigate the smoke coming out of your ears." Rook takes a seat on the step above mine, careful not to touch me accidentally. "He's around here somewhere. If we don't catch him on the way back, there's an information board at the trailhead. We can post a couple of flyers there."

I snort. "Because we drove all this way to post a couple of flyers." I might as well have just sent out emails. Instead, I couldn't get my own brain under control, and we're doomed to state park information board marketing.

He straightens next to me. "It's better than nothing."

"Barely," I mumble, tracing circles in the dirt with a stick. But he does have a point. If we don't have a way to contact Dusty, then flyers are the best we can do.

Except . . . maybe we can contact him.

I let the stick fall to the ground and say, "Why don't we just call him? You must have his number already, if he knows we're visiting." Rook is suddenly intensely focused on retying his left shoe. The blood drains from my face, and I repeat, "You must have his number already, if he knows we're visiting."

"Not exactly." He quits fiddling with an aglet, eyes pinched as they meet mine. "He would've had questions about why we were coming early, and . . . Well, it's not the kind of news you deliver over the phone."

"He's gone, baby." I flinch, closing my eyes against the echo of my father's voice. Logically, I know Rook has a point. While The Accident was certainly news in Rustin and a few counties in Texas, there's no way the news about Maverick made it across state lines. Without Rook telling them ahead of time, there's no reason anyone we encounter on this road trip would know about it. And if I had the choice between hearing those words through a phone call or in person, I would choose the latter.

"Right." I rub my eyes, warding off the headache I feel brewing in the distance. This is the Rook I've known for most of my life. Considerate Rook. Kind Rook. Doing what he thinks is right, in his severely misguided, suffer-in-silence way.

I should not be empathizing with someone who hasn't done the same for me, but I also don't like the pained look on his face. So instead of leaving him to suffer, I ask, "What was that you said about the route back?"

The frown melts into a smirk, and his eyes brighten. "This way." With that, he turns into the brush directly behind the empty ranger station. Complete and utter disregard for any ticks hiding out in the brush.

It quickly becomes clear that he was telling the truth about the shortcut. In less than five minutes of trekking through vegetation, I hear the babbling of the waterfall. In another couple of minutes, the rocky outcropping opens onto a plateau, and the initial drop of the waterfall is in full view.

Rook approaches the edge, nudging a small stone over it with his toe. It hits the water a couple of seconds later, the sound of the *plop* covered entirely by the sound of the waterfall itself.

"Thank you for the physics demonstration. Can we head back now?"

He stands there, arms crossed over his distractingly broad chest, and looks pointedly back at the edge. "This is the shortcut. It's even faster on the way down."

I produce a dry *ha*, looking over his shoulder for a secret staircase, slide, or perhaps an elevator. But he stands there as if he didn't politely request that I jump off a small cliff.

"I know it's a leap of faith"—his mouth twitches when I glare— "but I'm prepared. Waterproof backpack and everything." He pats his compact, athletic backpack for emphasis. While I'm sure that he did his research before investing in this singular piece of gear, my chest constricts at the thought of my phone getting waterlogged. Besides years' worth of random notes and text messages, Mav's last voicemail is in there, waiting for me to finally listen.

Which I'll never be able to do if the backpack isn't as waterproof as Rook thinks.

"Maverick was the one who found this place. Jumped right off before I could get a word in," he says.

"Sounds about right," I allow, backing up a couple of steps. No need to give Rook the impression that I'm considering doing this. "He's more of an act-now, think-about-the-consequences-later kind of guy." Was. Was that kind of guy. I hug myself tighter at the thought. "I won't be jumping from here, and the water looks shallow, anyway."

He dips his chin in a silent *please.* "We've been doing this for years. Plus, I'm a certified paramedic—if you concuss yourself, you have a guaranteed first responder."

"Calm down, *Chicago Fire*," I say. His eyes flash, the corner of his mouth ticking up, and I ignore the thrill it sends up my spine. "And I'd like to think I could treat my own head wound, thank you very much."

My words lack the bite I'd like, partially because he's taken a step closer to me and partially because he has a point. If they've jumped off this thing for years, then it's deep enough, sparing us the awkwardness of me drowning at the first stop of our trip. Though I wonder, would Rook tell my parents right away, or would he wait eleven months to do that, too?

"Exactly. You can save yourself if something goes wrong, and we'll get to the car quicker." He takes yet another step closer to me—close enough that I can clearly see the faint reflection of my own face in his glasses.

Too close. He's too close to me right now.

"Have fun with all that," I say, waving over my shoulder as I backtrack to the main path. "I'll catch up with you."

"Cameron." I jolt to a stop, the sound of my name on his lips setting my cheeks on fire. Damn him and his effect on my hormones. If I could get through the day without my endocrine system betraying me, it'd be a miracle. "I have an idea."

Footsteps approach from behind, and I sense more than see him stand next to me. "If we go a little further down that path right there"— he nods at a barely visible break in the brush to the left of the water— "there's another ledge. You'd only have to jump half as far."

My stomach flips, but not as violently as it did at the prospect of jumping from here. Halfway down . . . I could manage that, if it means we'll get to the car and then the next stop sooner. Unfortunately, he's made another good point.

Rather than giving him the satisfaction of admitting that out loud, I merely hand him my phone and head for the area he had nodded at, which opens up from a barely visible break in the brush to a barely visible zigzag down the hillside. We don't speak as I reverse bear crawl down. It's a strategic move—this way, I can focus on earth and stone under my hands and feet and not how far the drop would be if I tripped. Rook follows suit, far enough above me that he's not kicking dirt or stray pebbles into my face.

When my feet find purchase on a stable surface, I continue hugging the earth as Rook plants himself next to me.

"This is it," he says, presumably so I turn around and prepare to launch myself over the edge. If I don't consider the possibility of hitting the water wrong and losing brain cells I'll need for med school, maybe it'll be easier to do so. In fact, maybe I should consider possibilities of what could go right. Maybe this pool of water has magical properties that will cure all the maladies I've accumulated in the last twenty-three years. Or completely reverse the trauma I've experienced in the last eleven months. Or stop my leg hair from growing back so fast.

"Alright. On three," he prompts, and I suck in a breath to steady myself before turning. Once I've successfully repositioned myself, I say through gritted teeth, "One."

"Two," he says, body tensing next to me as he crouches slightly.

"Three." Before I can revisit the list of reasons this is a terrible idea, we leap over the edge, launching ourselves into the air. In a whirl of blue sky, green leaves, and my own scream, we hit the water at the same time.

I bob back up, flailing like a kid in a swimming pool as the cool water shocks my system. A couple of feet away from me, Rook resurfaces, though he appears to be preparing for a role in a cologne commercial. The good ones, where nothing makes sense and there's at least one well-groomed, dark-featured man in boxer briefs.

Because Rook is hot. Objectively. Like, model hot. Probably does pole dancing for cardio in the firehouse. Since we're in a commercial, he also has to do the whole dive-under-water-and-run-your-hands-through-your-wet-hair-as-you-come-up-for-air thing.

"Was that so bad?" Somewhere between our conversation at the top of the waterfall and here, he must've stashed his glasses in his backpack. I have a clear view of his eyes, alight with a boyish joy that tugs at my heart. Fifteen-year-old Cameron would be losing her mind right now.

I scowl at him through the fluttering in my stomach. "You couldn't have told me to pack a swimsuit?"

"We'll air dry." With that, he paddles to the edge of the water, and I follow behind. When he wades into the shallower water, his shirt clinging to his chest and shoulders, I instinctively suck in a breath. To exactly no one's surprise, my body betrays me. That nagging part of my brain begs to close the distance between us, to dig my fingers into the hard muscle of his shoulders and arms as he—

I shake my head like a cartoon character trying to dissipate a dirty thought bubble, forcing myself to freestyle to a spot a few feet away from him. It doesn't matter if he has a cologne commercial physique.

Thanks to my far-below-average swimming pace, I have time to review the data:

1) So far, our plan is to rely on a handful of flyers to get acts for the show.

2) Once we reach the shore, our clothes will be soaking wet for the hike back to the car.

3) All the waterproof backpacks in the world won't change the fact that he abandoned me and skipped out on his best friend's funeral.

All around, not stellar results—for my heart or the show.

• • •

The return trip effect is in full force when we approach the beginning of the trail, clothes dripping a spotted trail of their own. A giant information board comes into view, as does a man clad in a campaign hat, grey shirt, and green trousers. He squints at us, waving enthusiastically when he catches sight of Rook's face.

Rook returns the wave. When we're within earshot, he says, "I was hoping we'd catch you."

"You aren't due for another couple weeks," the Park Ranger™ says, pulling Rook into one of those hugs where men grunt and slap each other heartily across the back. I take the moment to scan the information board we must've passed earlier. Two of its three panels are dedicated to information relevant to the park—trail names, maps, animals you may get maimed by—but the third is full of community events. The talent show should fit in nicely with the posted camps, concerts, and tours in neighboring towns.

"There was a change of plans." Rook pulls away from the far too wholesomely enthusiastic greeting and steps aside, putting me in full view. "This is Cameron, Maverick's sister. Cameron, this is Dusty, a park ranger who has an impressive, completely legal collection of reptiles."

"Hey, that's Ranger Dusty to you. And I'll show you the permits right now if I have to." He faux-glares at Rook before shaking my hand, teeth white under his salt-and-pepper beard. "It's a pleasure to meet you, Cameron."

"Likewise."

"Besides pretending that you two swam somewhere that's actually open to the public"—he steps back, looking pointedly at our soaking clothes—"what can I do for you?"

This is it. This is my time to declare the carefully drafted and rehearsed speech I've saved for just this moment:

As I'm sure you know, Maverick loved nothing more than being a theater kid and supporting the arts. He always dreamed of renovating the theater in our hometown rather than driving two counties over for theaters with more funding. Which is why we're hosting the first annual Maverick Loredo Talent Show right in Rustin, Texas. We want to make his dream a reality by raising funds for our very own performing arts theater, and we want you *to supply the talent.*

Except . . . nowhere in that speech do I talk about The Accident, which Dusty has almost certainly not heard of. Which means I'll have to work it in. Right now.

But there's no harm in starting out with what I already prepared, especially since a cloud of panic has settled into my chest. Slapping a customer service smile on my face, I say, "As I'm sure you know, the only thing M—"

I clear my throat, fixing the smile back on my lips as Rook's forehead crinkles in my periphery. If I could get through a year of biochemistry, I can say my brother's name out loud. "The only thing M—"

The word falters on my tongue as my lungs shrivel to a size incapable of intaking oxygen. Dusty's eyes flit nervously between me and Rook, who is fully leaning in to inspect my face. Maybe I *did* smack my head on the water and forgot already due to water-smacking amnesia, or I contracted a brain-eating amoeba. That would explain the static sound filling my ears, loud enough to block out Dusty's next words. Based on his expression, it was something along the lines of, *Are you okay?*

"Excuse me." I make a break for the car, barely registering the small metal object Rook presses into my palm until I'm halfway across the lot.

Keys. He gave me the car key.

Throwing the door open, I collapse into the backseat, landing amongst the sports drinks (Rook's), trail mix (Rook's), and Crunch bars (mine) we stocked up on at the gas station. I breathe, focusing on the sensation of the belt buckle digging into my back. Anything to block out the insistent, all-encompassing *thing* trying to destroy me from the inside out. All because I tried to say Maverick's name.

It's a matter of seconds before the static dissipates, and another couple of minutes before my breathing is back to regular intervals. Once my respiratory system is nice and out of hyperventilation range, I force myself into an upright position. By the time Rook opens the driver's side door, I'm firmly in the passenger seat.

He scans me, taking in my flushed face and semi-dry clothes, before settling behind the wheel. I meet his eye, daring him to say something about my little episode.

Maybe he can tell I don't want to talk about it. Maybe he doesn't care. If he has any grievances with my abrupt departure, he doesn't voice them.

Instead, he says, "Dusty's bringing snakes," and shifts the gear into drive.

Chapter Six

"What the hell is a jellyhole? And why does it sound so suggestive?" I ask. At least three separate shops have proudly advertised these things. Must be an Arkansas exclusive.

While I've successfully parried most of Rook's concerned glances over the last two hours of driving, I can't avoid the look he gives me at that comment. His side eye would make a lesser woman quake in her waterlogged shoes.

It's me. I'm a lesser woman.

"They're jelly-filled donut holes."

"Ah. I see why y'all liked this place, then. Jellyholes *and* possum pie," I say, inhaling deeply enough to scatter the butterflies in my stomach. While that combination of food doesn't sound particularly appealing to me, I can see how Mav would go for that—he'd eat anything.

The families outside seem to have a similar affinity for food. Jelly-faced kids roam the hot asphalt, pastries in hand. Their parents linger around a flea market that offers shade under various pop-up canopies. This town might not be the largest, but it does have a respectable amount of shopping and eateries.

"He loved it," Rook agrees, the words impressively neutral while he runs a hand through his damp hair. Again, with the neutrality. I don't know if I'll ever get used to referring to Mav in the past tense, but it's not a problem for Rook. Despite his behavior at our first stop, he obviously cauterized the parts of his heart that had to do with grief. Anyone that skips out on their best friend's funeral would have to . . . even if they were confusingly sweet in suggesting a shortcut for the shortcut and then proceeded to recruit an act all on their own.

After a few minutes of people-watching on my end and silence on Rook's, we pull into the parking lot of a quaint motel, all red brick and multicolored doors.

"At least buy me dinner first," I say, taking in the motel's large neon sign. It's automatic, an offhand comment I'd say to Vivian and *not* the man parking this car.

"A Crunch bar doesn't count?" he throws back, the corner of his mouth ticking up. I squirm under the sparks it sends up my spine and shove the door open so he doesn't see evidence of the rush of norepinephrine in my system.

Vivian would've liked that line. Damn him.

We gather our bags and wet clothes out of the backseat and make our way to the motel's arched entryway. Aside from the outdated beige carpets, this place looks fairly modern and mostly free of furniture with questionable stains and chewed gum. Altogether, it's surprisingly good quality for a random town in Arkansas.

"Welcome in." A light-haired, heart-faced woman pops up from behind the service counter. "Do you have a reservation?"

My perusal of the counter's snack selection grinds to a halt. Of all the trips I've helped plan for my family and Vivian, I've been the one to book these things. With the twenty-four-hour turnaround, I didn't think about planning those parts of the itinerary for this one. Odds are they aren't fully booked, but maybe we stumbled into their prime tourist season. Was there enough time for him to make a reservation? What the hell are we supposed to do if he didn't call ahead? The reception is already iffy at best, and who knows how far away the next motel is—

"Yes, under Rook Hale," he answers and sets our bags down at his feet. He leans over the counter. "Should be two rooms."

I must be showing my relief more outwardly than intended. He turns to me and says under his breath, "Figured it's for the best."

Just like that, the relief sours into something significantly less appealing. *For the best?* It's not like we haven't shared a room—and a bed—before. He must've realized that being in a car with me was more than enough time spent in forced proximity. I mean, it's one thing for *me* to not want to be trapped with him for hours at a time, but for him to specifically request two rooms on such short notice? Who knows how much extra he spent to make that happen. Probably requested rooms on different floors while he was at it.

The nice employee is busy tapping away at the keyboard, but she does look up at those words. Glances between the two of us. Goes back to typing.

I plaster a smile on my face. "Couldn't agree more."

His brow furrows at my tone, but she's already handing him our key cards.

"Have a nice evening," she says with an enviable amount of professionalism. Rook dips his head in acknowledgement. By the time he's stashed the keys in his pocket, I'm already halfway to the elevator.

For the best. What a convenient way to explain away every choice he's made in the last eleven months.

In a few strides, he's caught up with me. We step into the elevator, shoulder to shoulder but not quite touching. Any contact is solely through proprioception.

"What's the plan for tonight?" I ask once the elevator lurches upward. He looks at me cautiously, measuring the plummeting temperature of my tone, then directs his attention above us. Like the safety hatch overhead might be worth a shot.

"We're going into town," he says after a second, slipping a room key into my palm. A diplomatic answer. No commitment to any particular venue, which checks out—he hasn't been one for commitment thus far.

"Sounds great," I say with a close-lipped smile.

Ding. I step out of the elevator, flipping wet hair over my shoulder as I head for my room that is, in fact, on the floor below his.

"What time should I be ready?" I adjust my grip on my luggage.

"Is an hour long enough?" he asks. I nod. That should be more than enough time to shave every square inch of my body, blow-dry my hair, and emotionally recover from the first half of the day. Sure.

"See you in a bit," I say, heading down the hall before he can see how rapidly my chest is moving. I toss my bags aside the moment I'm through the door, and they land somewhere around the vicinity of the desk.

It's not like I was planning on sharing a bed with him. But the last time we did, he said he couldn't get enough of me.

Gone. That version of Rook is gone.

I slide against the wall to the floor, willing my pathetic lungs to get a grip. I now have a whopping fifty-five minutes to get ready for . . . whatever it is we're doing. I'm sure once I let my hair down and take off my nonexistent glasses, I'll be ready to face the treachery ahead. Think 90's transformation montage, except it's me in a motel bathroom.

Who knows? Maybe we'll recruit enough acts tonight to be able to head home early, and it'll all be over by this time tomorrow.

A girl can dream.

• • •

The bar smells of cigarette smoke, beer, and single Southern men with an abundance of facial hair. A loud neon light proclaims the establishment as the *Bar Owl*. The Bible Belt never fails to deliver, does it?

I almost say so out loud when I turn to find Rook already looking at me. Well, looking strictly at my face. He doesn't let his eyes wander down the deep V of the black jumpsuit I'm wearing tonight. Based on the alarmingly impish smile Vivian gave me before I left this morning, I don't even want to know what other outfits she stuffed into my suitcase—I barely scraped the top layer to find this.

The hefty wooden door shuts behind us, and I force myself to look away from the sign overhead at the swarm of people below. This place is impressively busy for a Tuesday night in a random town.

I swallow hard, trying to ignore the unease in my gut. My two-second encounter with Dusty was embarrassing enough. This is a place where Mav used to talk to people, drink with them, and use his Mav-charm to make them love him. Who knows how many in that swarm are locals? Or how many will remember him and have questions?

Which is why we need to narrow our focus as soon as possible and get the hell out of here. So far, the only promising talent appears to be the bartenders themselves, who are moving at warp speed to serve the crowd of multigenerational clientele. I catch glimpses of a blonde ponytail and a black bun through the shoulder-to-shoulder patrons.

"While I'm sure the marg towers would be a hit"—I look pointedly at one side of the bar, where a small group is pouring themselves generous amounts of fluorescent pink slush—"we were actually planning on having a dry talent show. I don't know if mixologists are a feasible act."

"Wouldn't dream of it." Rook's delivery is sharp as he comes to a halt at my side, the neon blue owl overhead casting shadows on his angular cheeks. Dark lashes brush those cheeks as he frowns at me, and I wince at the oversight. Of course he wouldn't dream of it—not after the years of drunken assholery his father put him through. Rook was always Mav's designated driver for a reason.

Before I can muster up an apology, he pivots away from the bar, directing his attention somewhere across the room. I follow, blinking at the residual burning light from the sign. As I adjust to the low bar lighting, it becomes clear that not everyone looks like an extra in *Yellowstone*. There's quite the mix of twentysomethings puffing cigarettes and vapes in dark corners, thirtysomethings having a tasteful beer at the pool tables, and middle-aged groups cackling over marg towers. Older folks are scattered at the high-top tables, all positioned toward a TV screen mounted to the wall that reads *Trivia Night*.

I frown. "We're scouting for a show, not an academic decathlon." Before the sentence is fully out, the rest of space comes into focus: the small stage, the singular microphone, and the standing keyboard off to the side.

"Which is why we'll stay for karaoke. The owner has a band and usually closes the place down, but I figured we could scout for other vocalists in the meantime," Rook says. I bite the inside of my cheek, taking another cursory look at the room for signs of potential talent. Aside from possible pool sharks, the stage to our left does look the most promising.

I sigh in resignation. "Did we have to come early enough for trivia?"

"It's tradition," he says simply, as if that's reason enough to throw away hours of possible recruitment time. For all I know, our motel hosts karaoke two hours before this one does. I open my mouth to protest further, but he cuts me off. "I'll grab drinks, and you can find a table. Just make sure it's nowhere near stage right—Petunia gets handsy after about ten-thirty."

Indeed, as he leaves for the bar and I claim a table close to stage left, I spot an older woman with large glasses and a light pink cardigan smiling broadly in his direction.

Not that I can blame her. Between the fit of his jeans and the muscle barely concealed under his T-shirt, Rook is annoyingly hot. Especially when he leans over the bar to order, that shirt lifting high enough to show the outline of his abs—

"Pay attention, Cambo. What were you looking at, anyway?" I choke on my sip of water, spraying droplets over the tiled kitchen countertop. Maverick blocks both the sliding glass door and my view of Rook. Mav's best friend has been coming over more and more over the past couple of years, first with his mother, and then by himself. When he is here, he likes

to help out around the house. Which is why he's currently pulling weeds in our backyard.

Shirtlessly.

I wipe the droplets off my mouth. "What do you want."

Mav gapes at me, his neon orange braces making the expression all the more dramatic. "I've said this, like, fifty times—you need to get your crap off the table so Mom can finish my costume."

Of all the moments Mom could've worked on his Beauty and the Beast *costume, she had to choose this one. There has to be a scientific term for when the exact thing you don't want to happen happens.*

I set my glass down with a smack. "It's not crap. *I'm practicing my manual dexterity." At least, that's what I said to convince Dad to buy me a bracelet-making kit last week. Between the ten bracelets I already made and the five more I plan on making today, I'm basically able to suture already.*

The sliding glass door opens behind Mav, and Rook steps around him to head to the kitchen cabinet.

Mav watches him as he gets water from the sink before glaring at me again. "I don't care. Move it," he says and stomps off.

"Move it," I mimic under my breath, and Rook chuckles. When I look up at where he leans against the counter to drink, he's smiling a smile that doesn't show his teeth.

I don't know why—I'm sure he has a nice smile. Though I'm more focused on ignoring his shirtlessness with little to no success.

He sets his nearly empty cup down next to mine and says, "What're you doing with the bracelets?"

"Um," I stall, trying to stay calm. I didn't realize he had noticed me making them in the first place. Heat rushes to my cheeks, and I say, "It's

mostly for practice, but I guess I can give them to Mom's class. Maybe it'll be good luck for the show." I hadn't thought of that before this moment, but it sounds legitimate. See? I can stay cool under pressure. Totally cool and not at all freaking out.

He nods, adjusting the glasses he started wearing a few months ago when my dad noticed him squinting at the TV subtitles. "You like green, right?"

Only since you showed up.

"Yes," I say, but it comes out as a question more than an answer.

"That's what I thought." He does his special no-teeth smile and heads for the backyard, carefully closing the sliding door behind him.

The rest of the day is uneventful—I move my bracelet-making station to the living room and help Dad make dinner while Mom and Maverick bicker over the sewing machine. Rook takes the bus home since his mother stopped picking him up from here last year.

It's not until I head to my room for the night that I notice something out of the ordinary. A glimpse of a color lighter than the copper handle of my bedroom door. I crouch closer to examine the non-handle material, and my heart skips a beat. Two beats.

It's a green bracelet, braided in a pattern different from the one I've been practicing all day. Rook must've done it quietly while I was helping with dinner, planting it here before heading home.

I tug it over the handle and over my wrist, tightening the ends until it fits snugly. It'll have to be snug if I'm going to wear it for the rest of my life.

A lucky bracelet. Green, just for me.

"Staring is generally considered rude, you know," a low voice quietly chastises in my ear. I jump about two feet off my seat, managing to spring *into* Rook. As in, now I'm in a position where I can feel every inch of him through the thin fabric of this jumpsuit, the toned muscle barely concealed under his T-shirt and leather jacket.

I jab a finger at his chest and hiss, "Don't sneak up on me."

He only raises an eyebrow, clearly amused. Then his eyes are on mine, trailing down to my lips. In the space between us, the air becomes supercharged, thrumming to the rhythm of my heart in my chest as he leans in . . .

And reaches behind me, where he sets our drinks on the table. "Don't be so easy to sneak up on," he says with a straight face, engulfing me in his fresh laundry and pine scent as he slides onto his seat. His leg knocks into mine, and I take the opportunity to slide my chair back a few inches.

I sip my individual, non-tower margarita, which is admittedly delicious, and stew as Rook pulls up the trivia code listed on the TV. This is *not* how the night is supposed to go. We are not here to dawdle or lackadaisically sit and sip while time ticks away.

"Is the marg that bad? I told him to lay off the lime." I follow the unfamiliar voice to the most symmetrical, Southern Belle-looking woman I've ever seen. She maneuvers effortlessly around the tables, coming to a halt in front of ours.

I nearly choke, setting the glass down as I sputter, "No, it's great." She doesn't look convinced as she leans in to give Rook a hug, her blonde ponytail bobbing behind her.

"And I know Rookie here won't complain about an IPA," she says, pulling away as he raises his bottle in a silent cheers. She turns her attention back to me, smiling as she scans my face. "I'm Jocelyn, and you must be Maverick's sister. Heard a lot about you over the years." Her eyes flit to Rook as he presses the bottle to his lips. "She's even prettier than you said."

It's his turn to sputter, and she thumps his back heartily while I smother the warmth flooding my system. Of course Rook had to find me attractive at one point—and then promptly decide one night was all I was good for.

Which is why I grin, willing my blush to be more of a rosy, unbothered glow. "Rookie's always had a bit of a communication problem."

He narrows his eyes, and I tilt my head, daring him to disagree. We maintain the stare down until Jocelyn laughs nervously, tightening her ponytail as she takes inventory of the bar. "I'll go relieve Sam so he can get trivia started. It was nice to meet you, Cameron." She gives me a side hug squeeze, leaving Rook with, "We'll catch up later about that thing you wanted to talk about."

My heart jumpstarts as he dips his chin in acknowledgement. So we're putting off the conversation until the very end of the night, giving ample time to anticipate all the possible reactions she could have. All the possible reactions I could have, for that matter. Who knows if I'll be able to keep it together long enough to deliver the news this time? Not being able to listen to Mav's voicemail is one thing, but not being able to say his name is another level of pitiful.

"'Rookie'? Seriously?" Rook says, breaking me of my reverie with a handful of casual words.

"Hey, she said it first." I watch as Jocelyn moves behind the bar, mixing drinks in a flurry of controlled chaos. "I'm kind of pissed I could've been using that this whole time. Now, I'll have to come up with something clever."

His frown fades into a stern look. "And what, exactly, would you propose as a clever alternative?"

"Hmm." I tap my chin with my forefinger. "Bishop. Knight. Pawn. Gambit."

"Very funny," he says, though his lips twitch. In the next second, his expression is carefully neutral. "Jocelyn's the one with the band—a local bluegrass group, but they have a good following. She's usually the closing set for karaoke. I'll tell her and Sam about Mav after everyone clears out."

Irritation flares in my chest, clawing its way up my throat. I know he had to cover for me with Dusty, but I don't need his sympathy. Especially when I was the one who was supposed to get acts together in the first place. "It's my responsibility—"

"And I'm telling you that it doesn't have to be. Not tonight, anyway." The delivery is matter-of-fact, his attention elsewhere. Specifically on the barrel-chested man currently checking the mic on the stage, his dark hair curling out of the bun on his head. Rook glances my way. "I would drop the Excel face, though. You're scaring our teammates."

I huff. Mav coined my *Excel face* years ago whenever I was overthinking. Said I was *formulating*.

But Rook is right. Somewhere between interacting with Jocelyn and this moment, three others have joined our round table. I reset my facial expression and follow Rook's lead in introducing myself to them, though I forget their names as soon as they say them. Mostly because I'm distracted by the man's mic check on stage—nothing to do with how Rook's arm brushed against mine as we shook hands with our new teammates. Or how it lingered for a moment longer than necessary after the introductions were over.

"Okay, folks, simmer down." The man onstage beams at us, spreading his arms wide as he says, "Welcome to Bar Owl, where the drinks keep you happy and the trivia keeps you humble." The crowd snickers, and I channel my rising anxiety into tapping my foot against the leg of my chair. "For all you good people who have been here before, bless you. For newcomers, here's the deal: there's three rounds, no more, no less. Each round has eight questions." My stomach clenches. Three rounds could easily stretch into hours, especially when people are willingly slowing their cognitive processing time with alcohol.

Despite my obvious internal distress, Sam continues, "I'll be scoring the answers, so just know that nobody is judging you on your horrible spelling—except for me. Winning team gets free wings. First question starts in two minutes." He fiddles with a handheld tablet for a moment and then wags a finger at us. "Oh, and there's bonus points the faster you answer. We don't tolerate cheaters around here."

I straighten in my seat. If they're rewarding us for playing quickly, maybe we can get to karaoke faster than I thought.

During our two-minute interim, Rook volunteers his phone to submit answers on. We land on the underwhelming team name of *Roadies*. Yet another decision made in the spirit of tradition.

The countdown dwindles to seconds on the screen, and Sam once again takes charge of the mic. "Kicking it off in the first category of general knowledge, we have: what play did Shakespeare write for King James I?"

Easy. Between my mother and Mav's lifelong obsession with all things theater, I've known this one since middle school. I submit the answer, allowing myself a couple of seconds to gloat in the subsequent dopamine hit—right until I catch sight of Rook's face.

"What?"

"This is a *team*," he says, looking pointedly at where the Trio of People Whose Names I Forgot is still squinting at the TV screen on stage.

"And I got bonus points for the *team* by answering quickly. It's a win-win."

He motions for me to hand his phone over, scanning the single word—*Macbeth*—before giving me a stiff nod. "You should at least pretend to let the others help answer."

"But . . . " I don't want to make a long night longer by waiting around for them. Maybe if we answer quickly, the other teams will pick up the pace, too, and we'll be on our merry way to post-karaoke trauma dumping.

He waits, lips pressed into a flat line, as I trail off. When it's clear that I won't be voicing my true motivations aloud, he says, "I'd hate for your hubris to get in the way of our seven-year winning streak."

Damn him and his use of *hubris* in this context. I'd appreciate it more if he wasn't annoying me with his logic and use of literary vocabulary.

"You think I'll make a mistake?" I challenge, the rest of his sentence catching up with me. As if I'd break their streak. I love my brother, but I doubt he was taking on the bulk of the trivia answers.

"I think you're only human," Rook says carefully.

I sip my drink, considering his words. There's nothing outright disrespectful about what he said, even if it makes me feel . . . off-kilter. *Only human.*

With neither the energy nor the will to unpack the emotions swirling around my gut, I scoot back until I'm using the entire seat rather than sitting on the edge of it. "Fine. I'll give everyone a chance to see the answer before submitting," I concede.

"I knew you'd be a good sport." He smiles at my wrinkled nose and raises his beer toward the other half of our team. "Don't get us in too much trouble before we have a chance to recruit. One of our future acts might be at this table."

I scan the trio, who are just now noticing that we already submitted the answer. I offer an apologetic smile to the balding man closest to Rook, and he shrugs back at me before turning back to the other two.

"I doubt that," I say, low enough that only Rook can hear.

"You never know. People might surprise you," he says as the screen changes, and the room falls a degree quieter in anticipation. I watch the reflection of the screen's bouncing question mark graphic on his glasses, but he doesn't look my away again. No, he's busy placing his phone as far away from me as possible, chatting up the shrugger. If I didn't know better, I'd think they'd known each other for years.

People might surprise you, indeed.

Chapter Seven

After an hour of diplomatically working with the rest of the team on general knowledge and pop culture questions, the special category of the night is Band Kid Core. Sam giggled when announcing that one, exchanging a knowing glance with Jocelyn from across the room.

"Question seven: the act of translating notes into a different key signature."

"Transpose," Rook says. Our trio of new friends bob their heads in agreement, even though they admitted they'd never played instruments in their life a few minutes ago.

I roll my eyes. "We get it. You're a piano prodigy who can see sounds or whatever."

"You know," Rook says, readjusting himself to face me after carefully typing in the answer, "for someone who won't stop giving me shit, you sure knew the last six questions in a row."

"I took a couple of music classes for my fine arts requirement," I say, nonchalantly sucking the final drops of my drink when he raises an eyebrow. While I did take an introductory music class, my interest in music theory actually originated in middle school. Coincidentally, it was also the same year Rook started playing the keyboard that had been chucked in our abyss of a garage. And he turned out to be good. Like, really good. As in, being-able-to-hear-a-song-and-play-it, compose-music-on-the-spot kind of good.

He opens his mouth to respond and is promptly cut off by Sam's boisterous, "Here it is, the last question of the night."

As much as I hate to admit it, I do feel a twang of disappointment at those words. It's been nice to sit back and get lost in the questions, to focus on facts rather than all the tables Mav probably sat at while playing the same game. As far as I'm concerned, we did end up shaving off a few minutes. We often answered the questions in a fraction of the time other tables took, and we're finishing up at an hour and a half rather than the two full hours I initially estimated.

"How many movements are in Vivaldi's 'The Four Seasons'?" Sam says.

A collective groan sounds around the room, and I beckon Rook to hand me the phone. "Three. All concertos have three movements."

He raises an eyebrow, not moving an inch otherwise. "It has to be twelve. Each season has a concerto."

"You know what? I don't like your tone." I squint at him, forcing synapses to fire even as the second marg makes my brain fuzzy. "It's three."

His eyes light up. "Want to bet?"

"Sure." I shrug. "What are we betting with? I can get you a membership at Plot Twist, but that's all I can do without liquidating assets."

His shoulders shake in a silent laugh, and he jerks his chin at the stage. "If you're right, I'll sing the first song when it's time for karaoke. But if I'm right, you're up."

"Deal."

It's only another minute until all the teams have their final answers locked in, and Sam waves his tablet around. "Last round's answers are: bass clef, 6/8 time . . . "

I drum my fingers across the edge of the table, mentally checking off each answer as he reads them. Between Rook and I, we're at a hundred percent accuracy so far.

" . . . last but not least, Vivaldi's 'Four Seasons' has not one, not two, but twelve movements total."

My fingers stop, as does my entire heart.

I don't need to look over to know Rook is gloating in his typical, muted way. No evidence other than the upward tick of his mouth and the glint in his eyes.

This is *not* good. Whatever degree of vocal talent was in our gene pool was given to Maverick, not me.

Sam grasps the mic and announces, "Thank you all for participating. Please be on standby as we—and by we, I mean I— calculate the final scores." He swipes the screen once, then says, "Lucky for you, the app does it for me. In third place, we have the Factoids. In second, we have the Brain Breaks. In first, with a whopping ten-point lead—can we get a drumroll please?" The bar erupts into a semi-drunken yet passable drumroll. He smiles proudly and says, "The Roadies."

Applause as I chug a glass of water. Rook graciously waves at the neighboring tables, positively glowing in the face of my imminent peril.

Sam claps, microphone still in hand, and says, "Please claim your wings at the kitchen in the back. To all you losers, thank you so much for playing, and we look forward to seeing you next week."

The applause dies down, and the screen flips from the bright orange backdrop of trivia to the deep purple of karaoke. Sam drops down from the stage and saunters over to our table, pulling up a stool next to us.

"Look at that. Rook Hale, in the flesh." He beams and enthusiastically pats Rook on the shoulder as our teammates disperse, ready to claim their free victory wings. Once the chairs and stools stop screeching around us, Sam redirects his attention to me. "Jocelyn said you brought a new"—brief pause— "friend."

That's my cue. "I'm Cameron."

"Sam." He gives me a salute. "Congrats on the win, though I can't say I'm surprised." He turns to me and manages a stage whisper over the sound of the crowd. "Rook's something of a trivia whizz."

"Cameron held her own . . . Right up until the last question," Rook interjects. "She's really here for the karaoke."

I contain my glare to a small twitch of my left eye as Sam manages to smile even wider. The man is practically levitating out of his artfully worn sneakers. "You really are related to Maverick." He scans the tables around us. "Where is that hellion, anyway? He's usually requested some Broadway song nobody knows by now."

There it is. The other shoe dropping, right down to wherever my stomach just descended to. Rook said he would break the news about Maverick at the very end of the night. He did.

But it should be me, the sister who's supposed to be taking care of all things memorial talent show-related. I shouldn't have to lean on someone else to deliver news like that, especially not someone who's historically proven to be too flimsy to lean on.

I clear my throat, fully prepared to take the opportunity to naturally bring up exactly why we're here, when Rook interrupts me with, "We'll catch up after karaoke." He says it smoothly, like it's inconsequential. Something he's more than willing to put off for another couple of hours. "Cameron was just saying how she can't wait to take the first song."

"Carrying on the family tradition, I see," Sam says with a grin, and I blink back at him. Tradition. As in, I'll be singing the first song on the stage that Maverick traditionally sang the first song on.

My stomach sinks further, and it has almost nothing to do with the rum and coke someone just spilled on my right sandal.

"Speaking of which." Sam angles himself toward Rook. "I haven't been playing lately, but the keys are always ready. I'll even get them warmed up for you."

Rook pales, a flash of pure panic in his eyes before he rearranges his features into a strained smile. "Messed up my wrist climbing earlier, so I don't think I'll play tonight. Thanks for the offer, though."

I eye him curiously as he gathers his two empty bottles from the tabletop. I didn't notice this mysterious wrist injury earlier today. Then again, I was preoccupied with the looming stack of rocks he expected me to climb.

Sam nods sympathetically, giving Rook another consolatory pat before saying, "Well, Cameron, I'll get the song queued up. What will it be tonight?"

And just like that, my hippocampus stalls. All memories of any song I've ever heard, cherished, or sang along to flee the scene.

"Um," I stall, scanning the stage like a perfectly manageable, karaoke-appropriate song will present itself if I stare hard enough.

To my horror, Rook answers before I do. "Dealer's choice. She likes a challenge."

Sam gives me a fist bump. "Respect."

I return the fist bump with a grimace, waiting until Sam has his back to us before flicking Rook's arm. Which, admittedly, hurts me more than him. Damn him and his lean muscle mass. "You're unbelievable."

He shrugs. "Don't blame me. Blame Vivaldi."

Before I can properly scowl, Sam beckons me on stage. I take the set of three stairs as slowly as possible, prolonging the inevitable. Funny, how determined I was to get to this part of the night. Back when I thought I'd be a mere spectator.

With the microphone centered in front of me, a low, thrumming bass starts up, matching the pounding of my heart in my ears. Petunia makes her way to the newly empty spot next to Rook just as "Another One Bites the Dust" starts playing in earnest.

Little too on the nose, that one.

I keep a healthy distance from the mic, boring a hole into the screen as the song title flashes across. Good thing the twenty-second intro is instrumental. It'll give me some time to adjust to the lights up here because *holy shit* they're bright. How did Mav do this?

No, Mav was probably immune to bright lights. He'd only been in them for his entire life.

How the hell am I supposed to focus on the lyrics when Maverick is supposed to be here? It's disgraceful for me to be on this stage when he can't be, fumbling around like a lost, slightly inebriated puppy. I need to focus. I need *space*. Maybe if I back up a step or two or five—

My heel catches on a cord, and there's a whoosh of air under my back. Gasps from the crowd. The clatter of a chair on the ground.

Everything goes black.

• • •

Bright fluorescent overhead lighting. The smell of rubbing alcohol and sterility. An undercurrent of fatigue not entirely covered by beeps and footsteps.

I've spent enough time in a hospital to know when I'm lying in one.

"Ugh," I groan. The lights are so, so bright and my head hurts so, so bad. Scratch that—everything hurts. My head, my body, my pride. Luckily, only a roomful of people was present to witness my fall. A room that included Rook, who's probably on the phone with my parents, insisting that they pick me up from the hospital so he can get the rest of the acts together without me holding him back. Even if I vaguely remember a Rook-like figure scraping me off the floor and slinging me over his shoulder.

I clearly hallucinated some sort of firefighter fan fiction. Must've been the fall on top of whatever alcohol was in my bloodstream. In fact, he's probably on his way to the next stop, whistling to the tune of every song that isn't being DJ'd by me—

A soft snore floats over from somewhere on my right, and I sit up fast enough to make my head pound. Someone placed a piano or anvil or something of equally inconvenient weight on my skull, so I settle for lying on my side.

Rook is in a chair, sitting by the wall closest to the door. His dark hair is disheveled as if he's been running his hands through it. Repeatedly. His head rests back against the wood, neck bent enough for his Adam's apple to be highlighted in the harsh lighting. No lines disrupt his smooth forehead, and there's no tension in his jaw. I take in his lax face, his full lips falling open with each exhale.

Based on the rhythm of his breathing, he's been out for a while. Which means we've been in the hospital for a while. Which means I've managed to ruin the karaoke recruitment night *and* delay our progress for the entire trip.

There isn't a clock anywhere to be found, but my purse is on the tray next to my bed. It's close enough that I can see my fake engagement ring peeking out of the side pocket, five carats of cubic zirconia reserved for whenever Vivian and I got approached by creeps at the college bars. All the more reason to get ahold of my bag while Rook's asleep—there's no way I'm explaining *that* piece of jewelry this trip.

I lean across, ignoring the soreness in my body as I swipe at the tray. While I miss the purse strap, I do manage to knock the TV remote on the floor, where it skids straight into the wall next to Rook.

"Hmmm."

I freeze as he rustles in his seat. One eye opens to a slit, sliding down to my outstretched hand.

"Cameron," he murmurs, and it takes all my coordination not to fall over the side of the bed at his tone. Like my name is something precious, something to be handled with care. Not something associated with someone to be used and discarded on a whim.

"Shh." I withdraw my hand, carefully avoiding the safety bar on the side of the bed, as he settles back into his awkward wall headrest position.

We stay like this—me, on my side, him, head against the wall—until his breathing settles back into an easy, steady rhythm. His features are peaceful, his brow not furrowed in the least when he lets out a final, sighed, "I miss you."

My heart jolts into a sprint, my skin tingling from the IV in my hand to the tips of my toes. Unless I hit my head hard enough to affect my auditory cortex, I heard him correctly.

He said my name. He misses *me*.

A shrill ring rebounds around the room, and his eyes fly open as I launch myself at my purse with renewed vigor, cringing as the noise ricochets around my skull. Damn phone.

Vivian's name lights up the screen, and I flash it at him. He squints at it and rises from the chair, blinking a few times before leaving the room with a mumbled "I'll find some water."

Once he's firmly out of the doorway and into the hall, I accept the call. "Why the hell are you calling me at"—I pull the phone away to check the time—"six-thirty in the morning?"

"I forgot about the time difference," she says with enough alertness to tell me she's been up for at least an hour.

"I'm in Arkansas. We're in the same time zone."

"Shit. You're right." A pause, then, "I couldn't sleep. You weren't responding to my texts, and your parents told me about the hospital. I just wanted to make sure you're okay."

"Oh." I sink further into the pillow, maneuvering myself onto my back as I scroll through my phone.

Two calls from Mom. Three from Dad. An onslaught of texts from Vivian:

Did you really fall at a karaoke bar?? Plz tell me there's a video

Which hospital are you at

You better be asleep rn

If you don't respond in five minutes I'm calling the police

Between the throbbing of my head and Rook's *I miss you*, I haven't had the chance to dwell on the optics of it all. Poor Vivian must've been pacing new indents into the carpet. "I'm fine."

"You sure?"

"Yes."

She lets out a long breath, the relief obvious as the sound wave pummels my left ear drum. "How's dipshit doing?"

"He's actually been . . . " Alarmingly considerate. Dependable. Willing to sleep next to me in a hospital room overnight. " . . . not terrible."

I can practically hear the corners of her mouth turn down. "Don't tell me you're losing your edge already."

"Of course not," I say, eyeing the imprint Rook left on the chair.

"Good. Because I'd hate to have to remind you about the weeks when you waited around for him to call." I bite my tongue, which conveniently distracts me from the residual pounding in my head and chest. Technically, I had my phone out in case anyone called. Ever since The Accident, I promised myself I would never miss a call again. But during those first few weeks after the funeral, I may have been extra aware of another name that wasn't on my screen. "Or of all the texts he didn't answer. Or when he didn't show up for Maverick's—"

"Okay, okay. I get the point," I hiss, closing my eyes. Unfortunately, shutting out the world doesn't blunt the truth. No matter how many sweet words Rook says whilst unconscious, it doesn't change the fact that he wasn't there when I needed him most.

Footsteps approach from down the hall, and I squeak out a quick "Love you, bye" just as Rook appears in the corner of the room.

I attempt to place my purse back on the tray table, but it's still an inch outside of my comfortable grab radius.

"Easy, now," Rook says, handing me a plastic water cup before scooping up my bag.

"I love when you talk to me like I'm a startled horse."

"If you'd stop horsin' around, I wouldn't have to, now would I?"

I blink at him. He isn't quite smiling, but his eyes gleam in a way apparently reserved for dad jokes and jabs at my character.

Tucking my purse under his arm, he settles back down into his chair. "Seriously, though. You managed to get yourself in trouble after I *specifically* requested you not to, what, twenty minutes before?" While everything about his expression and posture says he's joking, there's an undercurrent of genuine concern there.

Or maybe I hit my head hard enough to develop alexithymia.

"What can I say? I'm an overachiever. Always have been." I dismiss him with a wave of my hand and sip the water, counting cracks in the ceiling tiles overhead. One, two, seven, thirty-four. Who knew counting could be so hard when your one-night stand turned road trip buddy is staring at you like you'll disappear if he looks away?

Time to redirect. "So they've got an IV in me," I say, looking pointedly at the tube funneling into the back of my hand. A wristband rests where my braided bracelet used to be. Given that Rook was the one that gifted it to me, it's only right that it'd go missing the same night he started ghosting me. "Seems pretty standard. The Bar Owl-to-ER pipeline must be thriving." I pause to evaluate the throbbing. "My head hurts, but not like I got hit by a bus. More like a Segway."

He nods like the analogy makes perfect sense. Which, after a day in the car with me, it probably does. "Dr. Lane said it's a miracle, but you only have a minor concussion. They wanted to keep you overnight for observation, so here we are." He pops his knuckles, shaking out the tension in his shoulders.

What the hell does he do for PT, anyway? Shoulder press his coworkers?

Not important right now. My eyes are firmly on the ceiling when I say, "Makes sense. They're probably monitoring for a subdural hematoma. Maybe a subarachnoid hemorrhage . . . " I sigh at his amused smirk. "You know I can't help myself, right?"

"Can't help the medical jargon that flies out of your mouth? With all due respect, ma'am, you sound like you ate an anatomy textbook," he says. The delivery is casual, as if he didn't just destroy my ability to form a coherent thought with the word *ma'am*.

I frown as the heart monitor reading spikes next to me. "Yeah, well, it comes with the territory. Future doctor and all." After this stint, I'm not sure I'll have enough brain cells to get me through the next four years.

Or through the rest of the trip, for that matter. Though at the rate we're going, my synapses will crumble of natural causes before we finish recruiting for the talent show.

We barely caught Dusty in time, and I doubt Rook had a chance to talk to Jocelyn about getting her band to play at the show if he was busy carting me off to the hospital.

Here I am, once again, bristling. Frazzled. Supine.

"It's too bad we wasted the night in here. Could've used the stage time to advertise the show," I say. Rather than providing a sense of relief, saying it out loud only compounds the guilt settling into my overactive heart.

Rook leans back in the chair, his face far too relaxed for our current predicament. "I'd rather lose a morning in the hospital than risk a subdural hematoma or, God forbid, a subarachnoid hemorrhage." I try to glare at him, but his crooked smile makes me warm in places that need to be dormant. "And it wasn't a wasted night. Sam felt so bad about your fall that he practically volunteered Jocelyn for a slot."

I push myself onto my elbows. That sounds promising . . . and mortifying that we secured an act as the direct result of my public head injury. "She said yes to a gig in another state?"

"She did." His fingers tap a steady rhythm against his thigh. "Between you and Maverick, she couldn't say no."

I open my mouth to say something exceptionally intelligent and headstrong, but nothing comes out. What am I supposed to say? *Screw you and your niche-but-incredibly-helpful networking abilities.* No, while I was actively concussing myself, he was securing a band for the lineup.

I've never felt so utterly useless and begrudgingly grateful at the exact same time.

Rook notes my expression, pulling himself out of the chair. "You should rest a little longer. I'll see about breakfast and a refill on the water." Without another word, he gathers our empty cups and strides back into the hallway.

This isn't adding up. Even with a head injury, the left side of my brain is operating well enough to notice the inconsistencies. No contact for eleven months, and now he's telling me dorky jokes, fetching me water, and saying he misses me. For all that time, the trend was clear: my confusion about his absence had a negative correlation with his ability to care.

Either these are outliers and he's far better at manipulation than I thought, or I'm missing something entirely. There *has* to be a confounding variable.

Chapter Eight

It's not so bad, this passenger princess business. Not that Rook was going to let me drive at any point on this trip in the first place. Traditionally, either he drove the whole Tennessee Trail or Mav did. And Mav drove last year, so this year would've been his anyway.

Thanks to that tradition and my sleepover at the hospital, I've secured my spot in the passenger seat, which feels . . . unsettling. I need to be *doing* something, like flagging down the singular car that's been on this stretch of road with us for the last fifteen minutes. They very well might have a potential act in the backseat.

"So," Rook says, breaking our rhythm of wheels on asphalt, "when did you become such a sore loser?"

"I don't know what you're talking about." I take a break from vehicular scouting and flip down the sun visor, assessing my combination of mascara, concealer, and bushy ponytail. The overall aesthetic? Minimalist-makeup-meets-squirrel-tail.

"You've barely said anything since breakfast. Since I know you're not hangry"—he looks pointedly at the crumbs I managed to bring in from our latest restock of gas station muffins—"I'm assuming you're still thinking about trivia."

It takes a sizable amount of willpower not to laugh in his face. Eleven months of nothing, and he's asking why *I'm* being silent?

"Have you considered that I'm sitting in mute terror of your driving skills?"

That earns me a chuckle. Unlike the greater population of Texas, Rook does not seem to have an aversion to the function of a blinker. He was more than willing to deal with the stress of staying between the lines of the road and avoiding stray tumbleweeds, which was . . . admittedly nice of him. Since she decided to spend her first year after graduation staying with me in Aunt Brandi's guest house, I've been the one to drive Vivian everywhere. She refused to use her parents' money for a car, even if they'd never notice the charge. Pretty sure their credit line is infinite. So while I'm a huge fan of Vivian working her way up to her own vehicle, it does mean that I'm usually the one behind the wheel—both the honker and the honkee.

All things considered, Rook is a very safe driver. The man loves his rules and routines, which is also how I knew we were getting close to the next mystery destination at our most recent stop for gas. He'll go through the same exact sequence of micro-actions:

First, he'll turn the music down by exactly three notches. He thinks it won't tip me off. (It does.) Besides, we all know that less noise helps you see better when driving. Then, he tells me we need gas. (The tank is three-quarters full.) When we pull over for said gas, I flee the scene to use the bathroom while he parks. He'll pretend to pump gas for five minutes. (Three minutes longer than necessary.) When I'm done braving the gas station toilet, I walk the aisles without buying anything. By the time I come back out, he's fiddling with his phone, angling the screen away so I can't see. (I can, but barely.)

I still don't know *where* we're heading. Between Rook's attempts at concealing his screen, the lingering pounding in my head, and my side mission to peer into the car down the road, I can't tell. From the snippets I've gathered during this go-around, we're heading toward a town that might actually have reception.

"We'll be stopping soon," Rook says with a glance at the clock on the silent radio. We agreed on little to no music today while exiting the hospital parking lot. He insisted that it wouldn't be conducive to my recovery process.

"Do I get any clues about this one?" I ask. Hey, it's worth a shot. I get a glance my way but no divulgence of critical information. "Fantastic. In that case, I'm finding some loud, secular music to aggravate my head injury."

Before he can react, I switch the radio on. Static fills the car as I adjust the dial, finally landing on a channel that's semi-listenable.

"Thank you for joining us at 107.6, The Stix." Rook raises an eyebrow at me, and I shrug while the radio host continues, "Next up, we've got Country Artist of the Year, Chris Spur . . . "

"Please, spare me," I groan from the backseat.

"What's wrong with Chris Spur?" Rook asks, looking at me in the rearview mirror. Those eyes. Ugh. I'm the first to look away.

"Cam has recently decided to be a music snob. Don't worry—it's exclusive to country singers with names that sound like lab equipment," Mav butts in, fixing his hair in the passenger side mirror. He wants to look nice for all the people we'll be sitting in a dark theater with.

"CRISPR's more of a technique than actual equipment, but I'll give it to you," I say. "And I'm only keeping it niche so you can be the snob for every other artist."

"Not every other artist. Rook covers the old white guys missing an ear," he interjects, flicking up the visor. Rook gives him a sidelong look, lip quirking up at the corner.

Oh, to be in the passenger seat while he's behind the wheel. A girl can dream.

"You're mixing up Beethoven and Van Gogh. One was deaf. One was missing an ear. Both were white. Only one played piano professionally," he says. Mav rolls his eyes and exhales dramatically.

"I'd like to highlight that both are technically artists, but that's not the point. The point is, Cam is dying on this hill. A few years in California, and this is what we have to put up with now." He throws his hands up, pleading with the heavens. Or the car ceiling. *"Why couldn't I get a sister who worried about more important things, like finding a Beverly Hills cougar for her brother so he doesn't have to work anymore?"*

I pretend to gag. Which isn't that hard, actually.

"First of all, ew. Second of all, you're a hypocrite. Third of all, there are objectively superior Chrises within the genre. I just can't tolerate his specific brand of pandering," I say. If I hear Spur's newest hit, "Head Over Hooves," again in this lifetime, it'll be too soon. *"Plus, you love your jobs."*

Mav grunts, leaning the seat back far enough to smash my legs into oblivion.

"You're right. I love being an aspiring actor who turns to public school substituting for supplemental income."

My jaw drops. *"You're an aspiring actor? Have I seen you in anything?"*

He makes a show of puffing his chest out and says, *"I was the lead in my local theater's run of* Romeo and Juliet. *Twice."*

This is a bit we've had for a while now. For a couple years longer than I've wanted to be a doctor, Mav has wanted to be an actor. I'm sure the fact that our mother is a theater teacher had nothing to do with it.

"I think we're here," Rook says, interrupting our comedy routine. A red brick theater looms in front of us, and the parking attendant motions for us to pull forward. It's one of the few shows Mav hasn't been selected to perform in, so tonight's scouting mission is entirely to assuage his curiosity about the cast. Besides, nothing says Support the arts! *like driving an hour and paying thirty bucks for parking.*

He thumps the ceiling with his fist. I swear his ratio of Neanderthal to Homo sapiens *is way off.*

"Twenty bucks says they'll let me make a cameo," he says as we turn into a parking spot. If I could roll my eyes any harder, I would. Any interaction with my brother requires an intense workout of the old ocular muscles.

By the time Rook shifts into park, Mav is halfway out of the car. But I linger in the backseat, breathing in Rook's clean, woodsy scent.

Not in a creepy way. More like a platonic, getting-my-head-together-before-three-hours'-of-theater way. The fact that he smells good is an added bonus.

"Ready to go, Loredo?" Rook asks, catching my eye in the mirror again. I swallow the sudden dryness in my throat. That eye contact? Another platonic move. That's all I can let myself believe it is without going into cardiac arrest, anyway.

I sigh, releasing any stray daydreams with the stream of air. "Ready as I'll ever be."

"Don't make me pull over, Loredo." I blink at the hand waving in front of my face. Rook exhales, shoulders slouching with the movement. "You went catatonic for a moment there. I knew they shouldn't have discharged you already."

I straighten in my seat, snapping the sun visor up. "I'm fine. Just . . . recalibrating. Plus, I had a really expensive sleep session last night," I retort.

No response. But he does clench his jaw enough to make the strain apparent. "Thanks to that expensive sleep session, you're here. Alive and well enough to use sarcasm."

I simmer while he checks the next directions on the GPS. I didn't sign up to be lectured about how grateful I should be that I'm *alive and well*. My pride has already been eviscerated enough, if not from the fall off the stage, then from the fact that Rook, of all people, is the one helping me get the acts together. He has no room to chastise me about zoning out or not talking to him for a few minutes when he spent months ignoring me.

His phone screen shifts, alerting him that we're less than five minutes to the next stop. He looks at it for half a second—long enough to note the updated time. When he refocuses on the road, he lets out a slow exhale, tapping his thumb on the steering wheel when he says, "Mav was never any good at the special categories in trivia, either. He covered pop culture for the most part. Which is eventually how we became friends with Sam and Jocelyn—he told her she sounded like Britney Spears if she grew up on a prairie. Whatever that means."

I snort a laugh, and he looks at the GPS again, that damn thumb still tapping the wheel in a barrage of eight notes. Four minutes until we arrive.

Before the eleven-month stint, I'd known Rook to be dependable. Imperturbable. Good in times of crisis, which lined up well with his profession of choice. He's never been one to fidget. And there's no way a single gas station mocha could generate that much hyperactivity.

"The next stop won't involve convoluted pop culture references, will it?" I prod, settling back into my seat to study him. He chews on the inside of his cheek as he changes lanes, looking over his shoulder twice as he does so.

It's twice as many times as usual.

"I can neither confirm nor deny." He fiddles with the tuning dial, sifting through a series of songs before ultimately turning it down to zero. "Don't get too excited, but you might have access to anatomy textbooks."

I wince. "I don't know if I'm ready to hit the books just yet. Doesn't sound *conducive to the recovery process*," I say. I lean against the window to let the stream of artificially cool air hit my face and check his phone again. Two minutes until arrival.

"Good point," he says, the words quiet enough to warrant more than a glance his way. His mouth is pressed into a tight line, and his thumb keeps tapping the wheel as the middle of nowhere transitions into the middle of somewhere. The streets become more populated until eventually we pull into the parking lot of a shopping complex. Rook weaves between cars and trucks, managing to find a parking spot in the front row of the massive store at the center of the development.

We sit with the engine on, and I pretend not to notice how long it's taking him to clean his glasses with his shirt. They can't be that dirty if he's been able to see well enough to drive this far, which means he's stalling.

If this stop could unravel him to the point of wiping each lens seventeen times in a row, who the hell are we here to see?

•••

Framed by the cloudless sky overhead, *Branch O' Books* is painted in long, artsy strokes. Based on the quality of that sign alone, the owners have to have money. Another indication would be the aforementioned overflowing parking lot, though some of these customers might be here for the neighboring craft store. Or fish and game shop. Or adult video store. The developers of this complex really covered all their bases, didn't they?

"They opened four years ago," Rook says, pulling the keys out of the ignition. The car stills, and I examine the storefront through the windshield. Branches wind their way through the glass display next to the entryway doors, and books are propped up on each limb. That would explain the name choice, then.

This stop must've been Rook's idea. If there's anyone who could match my yearly reading goal, it's him.

"Impressed yet?" he says, cracking the driver's side door open enough for warm summer air to drift in.

"So much so that I'm considering stealing company secrets for Plot Twist." I open my own car door as he mumbles, "That seems seriously misguided."

We approach the storefront together, and I successfully ignore how very broad and very chiseled his chest looks in a simple T-shirt as we step in unison. There are more important tasks at hand than admiring his Clark Kent-grade body. For example, we need to recruit an act for the talent show from a bookstore, which traditionally does not supply extroverted employees or clientele.

"What's the angle here? Do they host slam poetry or something?" I ask, and he holds the door open for me. I pass through the narrow doorway, close enough that his clean, faintly woodsy scent scrambles my brain only incrementally less than the concussion did. It's a miracle I got those questions out. If there's even a slight chance of telepathic abilities, I'm screwed. When my head clears enough, I step fully into the store, spinning around like an untrained, hopelessly dirty-minded ballerina as I take in the interior—

Holy hell. There's an actual treehouse in here.

Right in the center of the store, sitting within the sturdy branches of an absolutely massive oak. And by massive, I mean *massive.* The trunk has to be at least three or four feet in diameter, a dendrologist's dream. The darker brown contrasts with the light carpet of the rest of the store, so if your brain doesn't want to acknowledge that an outdoor feature is very much indoors, the color contrast will force it to.

Meanwhile, the treehouse itself is the size of a large shed. Maybe even the size of two small sheds or three even smaller sheds. While I've never claimed to be an expert in spatial reasoning, I'd say it's around two hundred square feet.

As for the decor, it appears that a small community of garden gnomes or sentient woodland creatures took charge. A flower-lined ladder leads from the carpeted floor to the treehouse's tiny wooden deck, and every inch of the boards making up the structure are covered in paintings of natural landscapes. But the whimsical aesthetic doesn't stop there—it extends throughout the store. Natural light streams in through the windows of the front display, and the shelves are arranged in neat rows, short enough for someone of my height to easily reach the top. A metal lattice lies just under the ceiling, an anchor for the vines draping over its sides. Some of those vines hang just short of the shelves, supporting hand-painted (or at least made to look hand-painted) signs for each genre.

It should look messy. But just like the front window display, this is controlled chaos. The kind of charming, controlled chaos that Mav would thrive in.

"Be honest," I say, ignoring the lump forming in my throat. "How many times did he try to swing down from the treehouse on a vine?"

Rook smiles briefly, but his eyes dart around the room, seeking something other than childhood nostalgia-based architecture. "One too many."

He pauses, seeming to get his bearings. "You can climb up to the treehouse, if you want. It has signed copies and special editions, but there should be some back there as well," he says, nodding toward the other side of the room. Nestled in the back right corner is a cozier, floor-bound version of the main attraction.

"We'll have to check it out," I say noncommittally, standing on my toes to get a better look of the layout. Unless Rook is planning on recruiting treehouse enthusiasts, I can't imagine who he had in mind for this stop.

"Rook?" A silver-haired woman, a stack of books wedged under her arm, pops into view from behind a table advertising the newest romances. Customers walk in a steady stream of foot traffic around her, and she shifts the stack onto the table before cutting through them.

"Sarah," Rook says in greeting. Between her bootcut jeans and the floral print blouse draped over her thin frame, she blends in perfectly with the charming, garden-adjacent aesthetic. I wouldn't be surprised if she was the one responsible for the full-scale indoor treehouse idea.

"Oh, honey." Her lips part in muted distress as she steps closer, taking in the bags under his eyes I hadn't noticed until this moment . . . which means this morning's extended coffee stop may have had more intentionality than I suspected. He did stay up with me in the hospital after driving all day yesterday, but I hadn't considered how it'd weigh on him while we're in here.

Sarah stops a couple of feet in front of him, gathering her flowing blouse with one hand while she places the other over her heart. "I'm so sorry about Maverick."

My blood runs cold, the sound of his name in her unfamiliar voice skewering my heart. Yet another person who knew Maverick in a place I never had the chance to visit with him. I can only imagine how animated he must have been, swinging from vines and perusing the books she'd laid out as if he'd actually read them. I can tell she cared about him, if not from the kindness in her eyes than from the look of pure and utter devastation on her face.

But there is a person who doesn't have to imagine, and he's currently frozen at my side. Even when she opens her arms, clearly wanting to hug him, he doesn't budge. Rather, his body stays rigid, eyes glazed over enough to show he's not seeing the woman in front of him at all. At least, not in the moment she's in now.

Maybe it's because he bailed me out of my own deer-caught-in-headlights moment. Maybe it's because part of me is all too familiar with being so overwhelmed that you do nothing at all. Whatever the reason, I slip my hand into his, giving it what I hope is a reassuring squeeze. He starts at the contact, but I don't let go.

Sarah seems to sense that this fugue state is temporary, lowering her arms to her sides as he takes a few controlled breaths. The moment will pass, but your brain doesn't know that when it's actually happening. I give him two more breaths before I squeeze his hand again. This time, he shakes his head enough for a stray lock of hair to flutter across his forehead. With a slight stumble, he lurches forward, dropping my hand as she wraps her arms around him.

I avert my eyes as his stiffness dissolves, leaving him to melt into the hug. It's the kind of hug my mother gave me at the funeral, the Band-Aid-on-a-bullet-hole variety. Even if his actions have indicated otherwise for the better part of year, it's clear that some part of his heart needed the comfort.

It'd be easier to keep hating him if I could ignore that he's just as human as I am.

After another few seconds of pretending to consider purchasing a memoir, I risk a look at them. Rook gently pulls away, and Sarah sniffles before turning her attention to me. Through red, puffy eyes, she says, "Cameron. It's nice to finally meet you. I'm Sarah, partial owner of Branch O' Books." She takes my hand between both of hers. "Your brother was so proud of you. We heard all about your medical school acceptance—congratulations."

"Oh." I blink at the unexpectedly up-to-date comment. Maverick helped celebrate my acceptance when it happened, sure, but I didn't realize he was spreading the word beyond our household. I'd assumed he'd be busy bragging about the latest role he landed, not the fact that I voluntarily committed to four years of hell.

Look at me now. Voluntarily committed to three more days of hell via road trip.

A little too conscious of the weight of Rook's gaze on me, I clear my throat and say, "Thank you, Sarah."

Sarah dips her head, and Rook asks, "Is the Globette still in business?"

"Absolutely. The next show is in ten minutes, so you got here just in time," she says, dabbing her tears with the hem of her blouse. "I'm happy to walk you upstairs."

"Actually, I'll meet you two up there," Rook says. Before I can communicate either my confusion at the term *Globette* or my panic at being left alone with a stranger through eye contact, he makes a beeline across the floor toward the bathrooms.

"It's been a long couple of days," I say by way of explanation. Sarah watches him, concern etched in her brow. Stranger or not, she clearly has a soft spot for him. I don't blame her for worrying.

"Of course." She takes a moment to gather herself, fanning her face until the tears have officially dried to a slight shimmer down one cheek, and we start our trek toward the winding staircase just behind the treehouse. I keep tabs on Rook as he walks through the crowd, managing to not collide with a single customer, which is admittedly impressive for someone built like a professional swimmer. Before he completely disappears around the corner, he flexes his left hand.

The one I held.

Chapter Nine

The Globette's namesake becomes clear when the lights dim on the elevated wooden stage, and puppet renderings of the Montagues and Capulets come into focus. Declarations of thumb-biting are made, and disgruntled puppet servants gesticulate wildly. Within a few minutes, a mini street brawl breaks out, much to the delight of the children in the rows of folding chairs around us.

Thanks to the creepy puppets, I have a few minutes to recover from our warm and slightly traumatic introduction to Branch O' Books.

Not that all puppets are creepy. But when Rook sat down next to me and said Sarah's son was a Shakespeare extraordinaire, I didn't expect his medium of expression would be puppet shows. Apparently, out of the many ways they've tested the waters since the Globette was built, the puppets have had the best response.

It sounds like a win for all parties—families are already on the second floor for the children's section, parents feel like they're raising their kids to be sophisticated little members of society, everyone gets free popcorn so they're buttered up to buy even more books. I can see how Mav would've appreciated the unconventional approach to one of his favorite plays. Whoever Sarah's son is, he's doing a great job of voicing Romeo. Who would've thought a puppet could project so well.

There he is now, facing the crowd in his puppet-sized Romeo attire. With exaggerated jaw movements, he says, "Here's much to do with hate—"

"—but more with love." My mother mouths the words along with Maverick, though he's well beyond the age of needing her help with lines. He is not, however, beyond the age of requiring his entire family to attend every show he's in.

Well, his entire family and Rook, who happens to be sitting directly next to me in our designated front row seats.

The stage lights dim, and Maverick looks into the distance as he carries on about Renaissance-era family feuds. In another few short minutes, he'll openly yearn for Juliet's cousin, Rosaline, before promptly throwing himself at Juliet's feet. For a universally recognizable symbol of romance, Romeo is a pretty shit lover.

Rook bumps me with his knee, and I inhale sharply. Sparks dance along the point of contact, jumping across my skin in true nodes of Ranvier fashion. It's embarrassing how quickly my nerve endings betray me in the dark of the theater. I need to be nonchalant. It was a purely platonic knee bump from my brother's best friend. Nothing to write home about . . . until he leans over, gesturing for me to do the same.

"Do you think he ripped his tights backstage or during the brawl?" he whispers. I follow his gaze to where Maverick is now kneeling on stage right, the rip across his right thigh clearly visible in the spotlight. There's no way Mav would've missed that before coming on stage.

"Brawl," I whisper back, and Rook nods to himself, like this was an extremely pressing question. With most of his days spent inhaling smoke *and lugging hoses around at the fire academy, I would've thought things like the status of Maverick's tights wouldn't be so urgent.*

Perhaps I'm not being urgent enough. Lord knows Maverick will be talking about how he narrowly survived this wardrobe malfunction as soon as the curtains close at the end. Between that and the traffic from the hour-long drive it took to get to this theater, he'll have more than enough complaints to regale us with for the foreseeable future.

For now, I focus on the drama unfolding on stage rather than the possibility that Rook was looking for an excuse to talk to me. I've gotten my hopes up about him too many times before, and I'll be damned if I spiral over an offhand comment about costuming.

I settle back into my seat, propping my elbows on each armrest as the next scenes unfurl before us. I've heard a million iterations of this script over the years, thanks to Mom's work and Maverick's insistence upon performing Shakespearian monologues around the house. But I have to give credit to Mav—he disappears into a role, no matter how overdone the material is. He loves to try out new inflections or adjust his body language to express a new variation of the same emotion. The only one who can rival his affinity to put a new spin on an old character is Sebastian, who has the role of Mercutio for this run.

The familiar scenes come and go with no discernible missteps or disasters, other than the tear on Maverick's leg. Overall, not bad for opening night, though my blood still boils at the preventability of it all. It doesn't matter how many versions of this play I watch—the string of miscommunications that ultimately lead to the lovers' demise gets me every time. Especially since the same letter that caused so much suffering could've resolved all their issues before they really started.

The fuming is also a welcome distraction from being hyperaware of the person sitting next to me. It's not until the end sequence that I let my eyes wander over to Rook, who's sipping wine like the performance arts-supporting sophisticate he is. There's no harm in lingering on the Cupid's bow of his top lip or how his hair curls around his ears. It's purely empirical, these observations.

Until his eyes flicker to mine.

"What do you think?" Rook's voice in my ear startles me enough that popcorn goes flying in approximately three different directions.

"I think you could've told me that we were recruiting a theater kid," I hiss back, setting the plastic container down so I can push the floor popcorn into a small pile with my feet.

He chuckles and kicks a few stray kernels my way. "Would you have believed me?"

I pause. Would I believe that we'd be watching Muppet version of the most beautifully tragic piece of art I've ever consumed?

"Maybe not."

A child shushes us from a couple of rows over, and I quit my attempt at cleaning up my own mess. Conscious of the families around us watching the puppets milling about the stage, Rook whispers, "Oakley's gotten so much better. A few years ago, he couldn't say a single word in front of a crowd."

"Oakley is Sarah's son?" Rook gives me a thumbs-up, and I squint at the lanky, curly-haired teenager currently facilitating a puppet costume change. While the hair couldn't be from his mother, I see her influence in the shape of nose and the freckles scattered across his face. By the way he flits around the stage like a trapped bird, I can't help but think that some of the stage fright stuck around. "I'm guessing Maverick had some tips for him."

"You could say that." We get shushed again—this time, by an adult—and I let the conversation drop. Maverick did his fair share of mentoring over the years, often picking up substitute gigs with theater or choir classes at local schools to buffer his income. It's only to be expected that he would continue the trend in the Shakespearian theater of a tree-themed bookstore.

Rook shifts next to me, and I try not to stare as he rolls his neck in a slow, practiced motion. If the droopiness of his eyelids is any indication, the caffeine is already wearing off. Besides, we're actively in the recruitment process. Letting him doze off wouldn't be the worst thing in the world—that would be watching a Shakespeare play that doesn't feature my brother, knowing he was probably sitting in these chairs last year.

A soft snore fills a break in the action onstage, and Rook jolts himself awake for two milliseconds before closing his eyes again. While the noise does elicit a glare from the gap-toothed boy that shushed us earlier, I leave Rook to sleep off any memories that might be swirling just under the popcorn-covered floorboards. I may not understand why this is the stop that's broken his blasé exterior, but I can allow him this.

Amidst the crowd of cultured children and semi-napping adults, I watch the rest of the family-friendly tragedy unfold in silence.

• • •

"So? How was it?" Sarah asks. The benches have cleared out, and the puppets are returned to . . . wherever puppets go when they aren't scarring children for life.

"It was fantastic. Really loved how he made the language easier to understand. I know Rook would've had a hard time otherwise," I say with a knowing smile at my companion. The left side of his mouth twinges down, and I stifle a laugh.

"Oakley is a genius for making Shakespeare so easy to follow," he agrees, shoving his hands in his pockets. Good sport.

Sarah hums with satisfaction. "So he is. He's heading to university for English this year, you know. I'm sure he'll tell you all about it in a second here." Her eyes shine, overflowing with the same pride my mom's did when I showed her my first research publication. She swipes at them with her sleeve. "I apologize. I just . . . He's so happy now. He struggled for so long."

Rook offers her a napkin leftover from the popcorn, and she accepts it with a watery smile. "We didn't know what to do with all his passion. He's all grown up now, but from the time he was a little boy, he could recite whole scenes from *Macbeth* like that." She snaps her fingers. "His father was traveling so much. Book signings, promotional tours, all those things," she says, but her eyes flicker to her ring finger.

"What'd you say about Dad? Is he here?" Oakley plants himself next to Sarah, head swiveling as he scans the room. Between his slightly disheveled dark hair and gold-rimmed glasses, he's primed to be an English major. No wonder he gets skittish under the spotlight—he's meant to be spending his days in the dark corners of university archives, living off dusty books and thirty-page papers.

Sarah pats his shoulder and says, "No, honey. He said he wouldn't be back for another month, remember?"

"Oh. Right." Oakley wilts, his face falling. He shoves his hands in his pockets, looking for all the world like he wants to slouch into oblivion, when his eyes catch on Rook's watch. He straightens, blinking rapidly as he takes in Rook's amused smile. "When'd you get here?"

"Right before the show. Great job, dude," Rook says, giving him a fist bump. The action seems to revive Oakley's spirits, or at least turn his posture from a dying flower to an alive one. He pushes his glasses up his nose, scrutinizing me before declaring, "You're Maverick's sister."

"I am." Although Mav and I don't look all that much alike— different eye color, hair color, build—we both got wide cheeks from our father, a rounded nose from our mother. I wasn't mentioned in the news article about Mav, but I get the sense that Oakley pays attention to details. He knows.

Too much, apparently. His eyes are heavy when he shifts his attention to Rook. "I sent Maverick a draft, and he never responded. He wouldn't do that." Rook nods silently, and Oakley continues, "I found the article a couple of weeks after it happened, and the flyer for the show. I tried to get Dad to sign up for it, or at least donate or *something*, but . . . " He winces, and Sarah puts an arm around him consolingly. "He had better things to do."

I raise an eyebrow. Obviously, Oakley's father is a patron of the arts and has some kind of influence that we could use for the show. Rook dips his chin in a silent *I'll explain later* before saying, "That's okay, bud. We're here for *you*."

Oakley flushes, rocking back on his heels as he looks between the two of us. "Me? Are you sure?"

"Of course. You're Mav's favorite student," Rook says, his eyes crinkling when Oakley's mouth falls open.

"He said that?"

"Multiple times. And he loved what he had read of that draft, by the way," Rook says. Oakley beams at him, allowing his mother to ruffle his hair.

"We're still recruiting, but as long as you have enough to fill a ten-minute slot, we'll go ahead and get you signed up. The venue has the capacity for up to fifteen hundred, so you'd get exposure if you want to promote your plays, too."

"Fifteen hundred?" The tips of Oakley's ears redden, his freckles stark against his skin. "I've never had an audience that big."

"We don't have an exact number yet," I interject. The kid is about to hyperventilate at the thought of it, and we *have* to get him to be there. Otherwise, this entire stop was a bust. I gesture toward the rows of benches. "Based on what we saw, I'm sure you'll do amazing."

"Right," he says, sounding wholly unconvinced.

"Think about it." Rook claps him across the shoulder, directing his next words at Sarah. "We'd love to have you both there either way."

She gives him a grateful nod, and he redirects the conversation to the college Oakley will attend starting this fall. They walk and talk, venturing back downstairs to the treehouse. I trail behind, barely following their conversation as anxiety tightens my gut. If Oakley ends up not being able to perform, we'll need to recruit an extra act at the next stop, wherever the hell that's supposed to be. This stop would've been a jarring, emotionally draining waste of time. Except . . . he did say that he reached out to his mysteriously famous and despondent father. If we could get *that* guy on board, people would flock to the show.

I manage to maintain my composure through both the round of hugs from Sarah and Oakley and my purchase of a Branch O' Books tote bag. (Vivian would kill me if I didn't bring her at least one souvenir.)

"What's the story with Oakley's dad?" I ask once we're safely out of the parking lot. "Between the tree-themed store and tree-themed offspring, he's got to be interesting."

"'Interesting' is one word for him," Rook grumbles, turning the blinker on. "He can't help the theme. Trees are in his name."

"Let me guess—his last name is Sequoia," I say.

His lips quirk up, but the heaviness from earlier settles into the crease of his brow. "Not Sequoia. You're on the right track."

"Pine. Spruce. Birch," I say. Yes, my mom made us cut down Christmas trees every year. No, I don't know any species other than those.

"Close, but no." Another beat of silence. Then, "Basswood. His last name is Basswood."

Great. None of my guesses were close.

"Am I supposed to know . . . OH." I slap a hand over my mouth the instant the right neurons fire together. There's no way. "Joel Basswood? As in the author of *Uproot Me, Let Them Fall,* and *Wayward Pines?* As in, the most successful romance writer of his generation?"

"That's the one." His eyes shift to the top of the windshield, far too nonchalantly for this revelation.

"Are you kidding me? We totally need to get him to the show. Imagine how many people would go if they heard he was there."

He ignores me entirely, muttering, "Those clouds don't look good," until I wave my bag in his periphery.

"It's *Joel Basswood*, Rook. How could you not be jumping on this opportunity right now?"

He sighs, leaning back against the headrest until his chin juts out. "Because it's not an opportunity. You heard Oakley and Sarah. Joel doesn't show up for anything."

"But if Oakley can't perform—"

"Oakley will do just fine," he snaps. The words have enough acid behind them to stun me into silence, and I glare at the point on the horizon where dark clouds are gathering. I only agreed to this trip because it would increase the likelihood of successful recruitment. As soon as we find someone with the potential to make the show as popular as Maverick deserves, he decides to turn pissy.

A slight drizzle starts overhead. He still doesn't offer any additional words. Why would he? He's the expert in not showing up when he's needed most—no further explanation needed. The only way he can be sure that Joel will be MIA is because he's done the same.

Lightning flashes, a storm swirling into existence before our eyes. Between the rolling thunder and the obvious delay the weather will impose on our next stop, I almost laugh at the timing of it all.

Almost.

Chapter Ten

"What the hell was it?" I ask. Rook slides back into his seat, glasses splattered with rain. His white shirt is completely soaked through, which I'd usually enjoy if we weren't stuck on the side of the road.

Actually, I can still enjoy it. Very much, despite his most recent assholery.

"An inconvenience," he mutters, throwing something thin and sharp into a cupholder. A nail.

"That'll do it." Two days in, and we've already jumped off a cliff, played strangely rigorous trivia, stayed in a hospital, and watched puppet Shakespeare. Each of these items would individually boost my cortisol levels, but all of them together? Nausea-inducing, to say the least, and that's without considering that we probably didn't secure an act at the last stop. Now we're here, facing yet another delay just when I could almost stomach the delay from the hospital—Rook was right about taking a head injury seriously. But a flat tire in a storm is quite literally the nail in the coffin of any itinerary he was operating from.

Between the way he's slumped over the wheel and the comically loud sound of rain on the glass, he looks as defeated as I feel. Especially as buckets continue pouring from the clouds onto the flooded street, and the car shakes with the thunder rumbling directly over us—

"AHHH!" Dad gathers my shrieking mother in his arms, hiding his smile in her hair as the lights flicker. Lightning flashing through the dining room window, illuminating the Sorry! board on the table. It's a miracle she hasn't flung the thing off with all her flopping around, but Dad always insists we play Mom's favorite game during a storm.

Like that'll make a difference.

"It's fine, honey. We have protocols for this," Dad reassures her. He gestures toward the mountains of candles, flashlights, and lanterns strategically placed throughout the house. You can barely walk without tripping over a light source, which Maverick has proven about fifteen times tonight.

"I know," she whimpers. She pulls back from him enough to pick up a yellow token. But when the next roll of thunder makes the shelves bounce, she launches herself at him again. He chuckles as they nearly tumble backward, and Maverick throws his hands in the air.

"Get a grip, Mom. We haven't even started playing yet." The rain pounding on the roof shingles drowns out Dad's response, but based on how angrily his mustache is moving, it can't be good. It also means he's distracted enough to not notice the thudding coming from the front door, just under the noise of the storm. Like someone is knocking.

With my brother getting chewed out and my mother busy arranging and rearranging game pieces into clusters, I slip off my chair to investigate. It's probably a sign from someone's yard that got blown over, or a stray cat clawing at the wood. Either way, it's better than waiting for Mom to burst another one of my ear drums.

The sturdy wood of the door is almost impossible to budge with the force of the wind, but I finally throw it open just as Dad says, "Where'd Cameron go?"

Through the rain slashing across my face and the strobing porch lights, there's clearly someone on the front porch. Not a sign or a cat. Definitely a human, only a few inches taller than me.

"Hello?" My voice gets carried away on the howling wind. Lightning flashes in the same moment that three other people cluster around the doorway, and it's bright enough to reveal the face of the figure in front of us.

A boy. He looks around Mav's age. Long, dark hair clings to his forehead, and he shivers in his drenched clothes.

"What in the world are you—"

Mom's reprimand is cut short once she gets a good look at the porch. She gasps, then shoves us away from the doorframe while simultaneously ushering the boy inside. "What're you doing out here in this weather? You'll catch a cold."

"I was looking for a flashlight," he replies simply. He stays planted on the small rug inside the entryway, keeping the water dripping off his clothes and hair within its borders.

Dad takes a step closer. Apparently, he had the slowest response time to my disappearance and was far enough back that he couldn't hear. "What's going on here?"

"He said he was looking for a flashlight," Mav repeats, and the adults exchange a look.

"Your parents didn't have any at home?" Mom asks gently. Of all the times to make that purchase, I don't think in the middle of the thunderstorm was the best one.

"We just moved here. My mom wanted me to find one since we don't have power yet." He looks down at the puddle forming at his feet, shoulders dropping. Like the weight of the world sits on them. Or at least, the weight of finding a flashlight. *"I haven't seen my dad in months."*

"I see." Dad shifts his weight, the floorboards creaking under him. *"Where'd you come from?"*

"Parrish," the boy says matter-of-factly.

"But that's miles down the road."

"I got a little lost."

Mav looks at me with wide eyes, and I can practically see the question marks in them. I'm sure I have the same ones. This kid walked miles through a storm to find a flashlight. Who does that?

"Let's get you warmed up, sweetie." With that, my mom is back to her normal, no-storm self. She nudges us toward the kitchen, where Maverick heads straight for the pantry. Leave it to him to prioritize snacks for himself at a time like this.

It's not until he sets five packets of hot chocolate mix on the counter that I understand what he's doing. So does my mother, based on the quiet hum of approval she gives him before backtracking to the hallway closet, where we store blankets and towels. Which leaves Dad, Maverick, and I to stand in awkward silence with the new kid. He squints back like he can't quite make us out, probably from the acid rain in his eyes. Speaking of eyes...

Wow. I can see the vibrant green even when he's squinting, like there's a fire in them. There's something else, too, that shines like copper. It makes my stomach feel all fluttery. Not in a bad way, but definitely in a fluttery way.

"Here you go." My mother returns with an armful of towels, flinging one over the kid's shoulders with a flourish. When he tightens the towel and goes from squinting to staring squarely at the tile floor of the kitchen, she turns her attention to the rest of the room. "Why don't we do some introductions? Kids, this is . . . "

"Rook. Rook Hale," the boy fills in. His eyes are still on the ground, hair forming a protective sheet around his face. I don't blame him. I wouldn't want to talk to a room full of strangers after hiking miles through the rain, either.

Oblivious to the kid's—sorry, Rook's—obvious exhaustion, Mav sticks his hand out and smiles broadly enough to show the entire front row of his braces. "Hi, Rook. I'm Maverick, but you can call me Mav."

Rook eyes the outstretched hand, still bundled in the neon blue towel Mom half-swaddled him with. After a long moment, he takes it, shaking his head enough to flick away the wet hair hanging over his brow. "Mav," he repeats. When he looks at me, the butterflies swarm enough to scramble my brain. What are we doing again? What's my name? I could've sworn I had one a second ago.

"This is Cam. She's very strange, but we decided to keep her around because Dad wants another scientist in the family," Mav says. While I fail to telekinetically launch him across the room, I do glare hard enough that Dad lets out a low whistle.

"Not a scientist. Neurosurgeon. And since I'll only work on people with brains, you're safe," I say. Mav sticks his tongue out at me as he finishes mixing powder into the mugs on the counter. He hisses when a few drops of boiling water spill over the side, and I continue, "My real name is Cameron, but you can call me Cam."

"Or Camel," Dad says.

"Or Camelot," Mav pitches in, handing Rook a mug. *Thanks to the King Arthur musical Mom's been working on, I've been hearing that one for weeks now.*

Rook carefully accepts the mug, and I make myself maintain eye contact without totally losing my bearings again. It becomes harder to do so when he smiles. Not a huge smile, more like a smile-in-training. But it's enough to make my cheeks glow.

"Nice to meet you, Camelot."

"I have a spare in the back. Just give me a second, and I'll grab it," Rook says, voice slightly muffled from where he rests his forehead on the steering wheel.

I blink a few times as the twelve-year-old version of him morphs into the utterly depleted man in the driver's seat, his words catching up with me in real time. A spare tire? There's no way he's messing with that in this weather. And judging by the way he's slumped over the wheel, he's not in the state to. Even if he's been sulky and unreadable, I wouldn't wish that upon him.

"You're not going to change the tire right now, Rook."

He lifts his head up, taking in my expression. I may have a cache of righteous anger, but I don't want him to hurt himself. Especially since I'm partially responsible for getting us into this mess. If I hadn't gone and fallen off a stage, we may have bypassed the torrential downpour.

"We can wait out the rain and then deal with the tire situation," I say.

He glances up at the dark clouds overhead, and I flinch as thunder rolls close enough to reverberate through the car. There have been a handful of times I've gotten a flat tire in my life. Of that handful, none have been during a storm while trapped in the car with my childhood crush turned destroyer of my heart. All things considered, this is territory I would've rather left uncharted.

"There's another option," he says, wiping his glasses off and resting them on the dashboard, "if you're willing to walk a little bit."

"Depends on your definition of 'a little bit,'" I retort. Any distance in this weather would qualify as swimming, so I'd like to keep it at a minimum.

"There's a bed-and-breakfast up there." He points to the right, where a cluster of trees are bending in the wind. "Probably around half a mile off."

I follow his finger to the blur of green. How he can see anything through the slanting rain is beyond me. Unless he has a sixth sense for locating bed-and-breakfasts, in which case we need to figure out how to take advantage of that for the talent show.

I fold my arms. "And you know this because . . . "

"Mav and I stayed there. Got caught in a storm worse than this one. We even made friends with the owners, but . . . " he trails off, brow crinkling in the dashboard light.

"But?" I prompt, sipping from my warm water bottle. Lord knows where this is going. Mav could've ran into an ex. Or broken out into song with the bellhop. Or remembered that he's allergic to forest-bound inns.

"There were some creative differences. Plus, he thought it was haunted," he finishes just as lightning cracks overhead. It's so cinematic, I choke on my water, forcing myself to swallow as my eyes well up.

"He said that?" I get out, thumping my chest as nonchalantly as possible. Why must I always be the one hurting or otherwise embarrassing myself? When will it be his turn?

"I believe his exact words were, 'I'm never doing this haunted shit again,'" he says solemnly. I snort, officially clearing whatever water was left in my system. It's not completely out of character for Mav to say something like that. He was always open to that kind of thing. We must've consumed our ten thousand hours of *Ghost Hunters* by the time he hit high school.

"So our options are haunted bed-and-breakfast or flat tire stakeout?" I sum up. Rook drums his fingers across the top of the steering wheel, then grunts in agreement.

"With any luck, they'll have a couple of rooms open. We can wait out the storm and start fresh in the morning," he says.

Great. We get to trudge through the newly made wetlands of Nowhere, Arkansas, and hope that the spirits residing within the bed-and-breakfast welcome us with open arms. The thought makes me wince, though it might also be from the concussion. Or the cramps that started up in the vicinity of my right ovary. These things come in threes.

After a few seconds of watching water coat the entirety of the hood, I say, "Alright. But I call the pamphlets so my hair doesn't get wet." Sarah made sure we had a few playbills from the show. Upon seeing the atrocious puppet graphic on the front, Rook requested ten more.

"Oh, you're not touching those," he says, the side of his mouth hitching up. "But I do have an umbrella in the backseat you can use. I think I'm a lost cause." He gestures toward the soaking-wet shirt currently clinging to his chest and abs.

I swallow. Strange, how quickly my throat dries these days. "Touché. Now let's get the hell out of here before I change my mind."

• • •

I'm not usually a fan of towering, Gothic-style houses straight from the Edgar Allan Poe Cinematic Universe. But this one has a sort of charm to it.

"This is all very *Rocky Horror*," I whisper-shout to Rook, finger still on the doorbell next to two enormous oak doors. Between his glasses and the film-set worthy amount of rain, he could pull off Brad.

"I'm not in the mood for a dance number," he says back, swiping at the hair plastered on his forehead. The pamphlets were a good idea in theory, as was the umbrella he pulled out from under the backseat, but the wind has blown about three gallons of rain directly in our faces. We're standing in a veritable pool on top of the musty welcome doormat. The only thing between us and a dry bed is whatever kind of person would own a house like this. If we're lucky, they'll be warm and welcoming enough to lodge two waterlogged travelers in the middle of the night. If we're even luckier, they'll have a talent we can recruit for the show to offset the delay from the storm. From the looks of it, that talent would have something to do with contacting the Other Side.

On cue, one door starts to creak open, wide enough to show a sliver of a dark figure hovering over the threshold.

I take a half-step toward Rook, transferring my bag to my other hand so I can lean into him. For his part, he doesn't make a fuss about angling his body in front of mine. It's instinctive, a protective gesture that I can't help but appreciate. The door creaks further, iron hinges straining under the weight of the wood. Rook wraps an arm around my waist as light pours through the crack between the doors, revealing—

"Madame Truffalo?" I ask.

The bespectacled woman blinks at me. She's dressed head to toe in black, from tattered robe to even more tattered nightgown to cat slippers. Must be the uniform here.

"Hush, child. Come here," she hisses, opening the door enough for us to step through. Since when did she get so uptight? I've never heard Truffalo raise her voice. Also, how can she be here tonight if she's running the bookstore? The commute would be terrible.

Rook tightens his arm around me, and I give a start at the contact. A year ago, a move like that would've had me swooning for weeks.

But not now. While I care enough not to have him change a tire during a small hurricane, I'm not completely discombobulated by his touch. Or the ease with which he holds me so closely to him.

Those details are irrelevant. We need to get indoors before we develop trench foot, which would surely prevent us from driving to the next stop. Plus, I need to know when Truffalo started leading a double life in the hospitality industry. I tug at his arm, urging him to move. "We'll be fine."

He shakes his head and looks behind me at the path we trudged through. Almost like he thinks I'd willingly walk back to the car.

"Don't tell me you're afraid of a few ghosts. I'll sage the room, just to be sure." He levels a flat look at me through streaked glasses, and I meet his gaze with as much fire as I can muster. The bags under his eyes have only grown more prominent over the last few hours of driving and wading through water. He has to know this is the most logical option if we're going to get any sleep tonight.

After another five seconds of me shivering in wet sneakers, he lets me pull him through the doorway. The figure shuts the door behind us with an ominous thud, which echoes around the dome that makes up the upper part of the house. It's every bit as large and looming as it looked from the outside. Candelabras line the walls, and the furniture is at least two centuries old, based on my rudimentary knowledge of haunted house interior design.

"This place is huge," I say. My voice ricochets around the dome as we squelch to a stop in the middle of the entrance.

"Stay there," our host barks at us from where she's pattering around the darkness. "You're dripping all over the place."

"Yeah. Huge," Rook mutters. He's occupied with closing the umbrella while spilling minimal water. Meanwhile, my hair drips enough to cover whatever progress he's made, and I crumple the pamphlets into a soggy wad of puppet propaganda at my side.

"Here. Dry yourselves off." She reappears beside us, towels in hand. Despite the spectacles and wild, brilliantly white hair, there's no sign of the Truffalo I know on her face. No smile lines, no indication that she spends her time doing anything other than barking at her guests.

Rook looks at the black terrycloth she holds like it'll bite him. At this point, I'm not entirely convinced it won't.

"Thanks," I say, accepting one with a tight smile. He gives me a sidelong glance, then takes a towel for himself. We pat ourselves down as she stands there, staring, slippered toe tapping on the dark hardwood floor. It's probably Morse code, summoning the creatures she keeps in the floorboards to sic on unwanted visitors.

Rook sidesteps to the right, and the candlelight briefly flickers enough to illuminate his face. A sharp gasp rings out, bouncing off the walls, as her eyes widen. "*You*," she says, pointing a thin, crooked index finger at my companion.

"Me," he agrees. So he wasn't kidding about stopping by here before. No wonder Mav hated the place—the customer service is abysmal. "It's been a while, Opal. Three years, if I remember correctly."

"Yet you have the same sad eyes." Rook stays silent, staring at her like she's a particularly annoying puzzle. Or a malfunctioning fire hydrant. What *do* firefighters get annoyed by?

She curls her lip, shifting her focus to the door behind us. "Where's the other one?"

I pause my hair scrunching. A single visit in three years, and she remembers him. Another stranger that holds memories of Mav only Rook can share. As unprepared as I was to break the news to Dusty, the harshness in her tone makes it all too easy to snap, "Not here."

She narrows her eyes, and I dry my hair more vigorously. There's no way she could know what happened to my brother, but an iota of basic decency would go a long way. Especially when she has the face of the most cherished boss in the world.

"So . . . you aren't Madame Truffalo," I venture. She shakes her head with a sneer, ignoring Rook's attempt to hand her his neatly folded towel.

I suppose that reaction is well-deserved. Because I'm an idiot for not recognizing my boss's *identical twin* in the middle of the woods. At night. In a storm.

"That's my sister. Ridiculous, how she makes everyone call her 'Madame.' We're not even French," she says, the sneer morphing into a snarl.

Rook looks back and forth at the two of us, clearly torn between defending the honor of the French and booking a room. At least, I can only assume those are the options, since he's said all of three words since we got here.

"It suits her," I finally say, breaking our amateur staring contest. I soak up the water pooling at my feet with my towel, which is already oversaturated from my hair. With a sigh, I straighten up, slinging the useless cloth over my shoulder.

"I didn't know there was another Truffalo. What brings you out here instead of Rustin?" I gesture to the woods. Whatever city or town or commune we're near, I doubt that she frequents it.

Opal stiffens in the candlelight. "Our family has been here for the last three generations. It's Genevieve who decided to run off and open some idiotic bookstore, no thanks to your friend here," she shoots back, jerking her chin at Rook.

"She seems well enough," I say with an attempt at a smile. Opal stands with her arms crossed over her robe, not showing a morsel of sisterly joy at that answer. More like shoveling platefuls of sisterly disdain.

"I wouldn't know. Anyone who's willing to abandon a family legacy isn't worth my time," she says, meeting my smile with a flat stare. Her nose wrinkles with enough disgust to make my heart pound, beating louder than the rain on the shingles overhead. My Truffalo doesn't deserve this degree of ill will, much less from her own sister. As far as I'm concerned, Opal can return to whatever hellhole she crawled out of before opening the door for us. She has no idea how lucky she is that her sibling is out there, making their own place in the world, chasing their dream.

She has no idea how lucky she is that her sibling is *alive*.

"I think we've all had a long night," Rook cuts in, stepping in front of me as the lump settles into my throat. How could she say something so cruel about someone she's supposed to care about? What a waste of a perfectly good heart. There's no universe in which I'd let mine turn cold enough to talk about someone that way.

Rook shifts his weight in the corner of my eye, taking his wallet out of his pocket. "Would you happen to have any rooms available? We need two beds, and we'll be out of your hair first thing in the morning," he says. I busy myself with gathering my sopping bag in one hand, rocking on my heels as I stare up at the domed ceiling. A domed ceiling that's not that different from the one in Plot Twist, now that I'm looking at it.

Opal shuffles over to a desk I hadn't noticed in the shadowy space beside the entryway. Keys hang on numbered pegs jutting out behind it. Scratch that—there's one key left, dangling on the peg like the shameless cliché that it is.

"One room. One bed. We get a lot of tourists this time of year, so you're lucky to get that," she says before flinging the key fob at him. He catches it in one hand, managing a grateful smile as he does so. She runs his credit card while I study her face more closely. She might not have the smile lines my Truffalo does, but she does have spite baked into her brow.

"Thank you. C'mon, Loredo," Rook says.

When I don't immediately move, he snatches my bag out of my hand, hoisting it over his shoulder with his own. Opal looks me up and down, from RBF to mangy hair to squeaky sneakers. "Follow him, girl. Wouldn't want me to change my mind about that room."

Rook is already making his way to the spiral stairwell across the foyer, but I lag behind, taking another moment to study this prickly woman. With nothing but shadow around to absorb her jaded spirit behind the counter, she looks so . . . small. Weighed down. Hunched under three generations' worth of expectations. Shuffling around dark hardwood floors in the middle of the night. Alone.

So instead of chewing her out, I place my own folded towel on the countertop in front of her. With Rook barely out of earshot, I say, "By the way, the 'other one' was my brother, Maverick. And I'd abandon a thousand legacies to have one more day with him."

She glances at the entryway my brother once barged into, her face draining of color. I walk away before I'm morally obligated to check her vitals. When I reach the stairwell, Rook falls in step beside me, still hoisting both bags over his shoulders. We begin the ascent to our room, and I take one last look at the other Truffalo.

At where she stands, still staring at the door.

Chapter Eleven

It's not like I've never imagined sharing a hotel room with Rook. What I didn't account for was that the room would belong to my boss's evil twin sister.

Or that there would be so many creepy old pictures hanging on the walls.

"She's really leaning into the Gothic thing," I say as Rook sets our bags down next to the dresser. I take a step back to evaluate: floor-to-ceiling black curtains with black lace trim, off-putting portraits of some family on a farm, no overhead lighting. After meeting the owner, it all makes sense.

"Bit of an overkill, I'd say," he agrees. At least the comforter and sheets are grey instead of straight black. They really lighten up the place.

Speaking of sheets . . . The bed is massive. Forget king or queen—this is the whole royal bloodline.

"What was that you said earlier? About the sage?" he asks, eyeing a particularly sinister painting of a little girl with braids.

"Ah, I'm afraid the rain got to it. It's out of commission," I say as I walk over to my discarded luggage. As much as I'd love to analyze Opal's taste in room decor, I'd love to be unconscious even more. Anything to not have to think about our complete and utter failure today. Without a finalized *yes* from Oakley or any support from his incredibly famous father, a day's worth of road tripping has resulted in exactly no progress. Luckily, it ended with an incredibly rejuvenating, non-triggering conversation downstairs. Sleeping is the only way I can even begin to process the last twenty-four hours.

Which brings me back to the gloriously huge, dry-looking bed in the center of the room.

Rook coughs. "I'll sleep on the floor. Just throw a pillow down there," he says. Before I can so much as blink, he strides across the room, stepping around the bed he won't be sleeping in. A couple of seconds later, the bathroom light flickers on, and the door closes. End of discussion.

I collapse onto the edge of the bed, groaning as the mattress barely gives way under me. You know what? If he'd rather inhale dust mites than be near me for a night, he can sleep on the floor. Fine. I have bigger things to worry about, like whether I have any pajamas that aren't completely soaked from the walk over here.

While the shower sputters on in the bathroom, I force myself to slide off the bed before I get the sheets too wet. It takes almost all my remaining energy to squat down next to my damp suitcase. I unzip it enough to ruffle through the top layer, hands sliding around damp shirts and shorts until I grab a ratty set of pajamas . . . only they're not ratty. In fact, they're the opposite of ratty. Where the hell did all this satin come from?

"You've got to be kidding me," I hiss, pawing through a silky slip that looks just long enough to cover the essentials. Barely. All signs point to the one person who's preached the liberating effects of lingerie-style nightwear for years now.

With a grunt, I slide my phone out of my waistband, where it was mostly shielded from the elements. It's a matter of a couple of swipes, and Vivian picks up my call on the first ring. "Please tell me something interesting happened. I'm so bored."

"*Interestingly* enough, I just noticed that you so kindly packed me unmentionables to sleep in."

A pause, then, "Oh, you mean the lingerie." I exhale loudly, and she says, "Stop breathing in my ear. You know I hate that."

"And *I* hate not being consulted about my nightwear." I pick up an especially lacy top. "This is way too much."

I can almost see her sink further into the living room couch, feet propped up—an unsanitary habit she indulges when I'm not home—on the coffee table. "I don't know what to tell you. You say you want to get back at Mr. Broody Firefighter Man, and I provide the tools to do so."

"The goal wasn't to *get back at him*. It was to *tolerate him* for long enough to get the acts together." I sink onto the floor, knees digging into the bristled carpet as I continue sifting through the clothes. Unfortunately, no sweatpants appear out of thin air. Which means I'll have to wear one of these outfits in front of Rook, exposing my ass to both him and however many ghosts inhabit this room.

"Why do I get the feeling that you've been doing more than tolerating him?" Vivian asks, words dripping with suspicion. I halt my rummaging. Have I been more than tolerating him? I held his hand at Branch O' Books, sure, but that was a moment of weakness. A temporary case of empathy that overruled both logic and any memory of his actions for the last eleven months. I also owed him some sort of favor, since he stayed up with me at the hospital.

The hospital where he said he missed me.

I pick up the first satin slip I landed on, which happens to have the most fabric out of all the available options, and say, "I can handle him."

"It's not him I'm worried about," she says, voice rising in exasperation. The water shuts off in the bathroom, and I wedge the phone between my ear and my shoulder as I pluck my toiletry bag out of my suitcase. She sighs rather loudly for someone who just complained about me breathing in her ear. "I know you've been infatuated with him for half your life, but don't forget what he put you through. I don't care if he nurses you through a hundred more concussions—he can't be trusted."

"I know." The words are automatic, noncommittal even to my half-drowned ears.

"Then put on your big girl unmentionables and suck it up. You've got a show to run and a man to terrorize."

"You have such a way with words." I gather the slip and toiletry bag in my arms as light streams in behind me. She grumbles something about ungratefulness and charity work as a Rook-shaped outline fills the doorway, and I cut her off with a "Gotta go."

Two seconds. I can spare two seconds to collect myself before he fully enters the bedroom. It's not like I've forgotten every point Vivian's brought up for a single second on this trip. For the better part of a year, Rook's actions have been nothing but callous and completely unjustifiable. There's been no explanation for the silence, and I can only keep operating under the assumption that he regretted our night together so much that he couldn't show his face until he absolutely had to.

Vivian's right. He deserves tolerance, which is more than he granted me until three days ago.

By the time I hear his footsteps next to the bed, the latent rage has bubbled to the surface. I'm fully prepared to stonewall him, squinting at his silhouette against the bathroom light, when my brain catches up with other significant visual details:

1) His hair is wet.

2) He isn't wearing a shirt.

3) The only clothing he does have on is a towel. Around his waist. *Low* on his waist.

I straighten, clothes crumpled in one hand, toiletry bag in the other, as he walks toward me. Every step brings a clearer view of the toned planes of his chest, still dripping from the shower. And the deep V-shape of his abdomen.

I can practically feel each region of my brain shut off as he stops about a foot away from me. He holds my gaze, and I struggle not to swallow against the sudden dryness in my throat, nerves a live wire under my skin. The air between us becomes supercharged, a conductor of tension that's been building up since—

"Forgot my clothes," he breathes sidestepping me to where his own suitcase lies on the floor next to mine. I turn to let him pass by, then barrel toward the bathroom before he catches the flush in my cheeks.

By the time I face the wild-eyed, frizzy-haired woman in the mirror, still steamy from the previous occupant, my cheeks have cooled from the temperature of the sun to the temperature of a more reasonable celestial body, like Venus. I take entirely too long to shave my legs, which will be on full display for the night, thanks to Vivian. That's as much effort as I can exert for now. Hopefully, my sleep attire will draw attention away from any remaining crustiness. I exit with a wall of steam and flick off the bathroom light, leaving only the miniature lanterns lining the room.

Rook sits at the end of the bed, a single pillow and blanket laid out on the floor beside him. And because my eyes have adjusted, I can see how his widen when he takes in my especially low-cut slip.

Vivian would want me to do something absurd, like tout my vengeful feminine wiles by tripping and falling onto his lap. Instead, I gracefully and nonchalantly slip under the covers. No need to do anything drastic. I'm here to tolerate him, nothing more.

The thought tides me over for all of two breaths, but when he prepares his bed on the floor, the guilt kicks in tenfold. He did drive for the past two days. And recruited Dusty and Jocelyn when I was unable to do so. And got me medical assistance for my trivia injury.

A couple days ago, I could've justified making him sleep on the floor while I stayed in an obnoxiously large bed, but not tonight.

Ignoring the blood roaring in my ears, I pat the spot next to me. When he doesn't budge, I raise an eyebrow. "Would you seriously rather sleep down there than next to me?"

He shifts from where he's kneeling on the floor, still adjusting his makeshift sleeping pad. I prop myself up onto my elbows to get a better look at him, and he places a hand on the back of his neck. It's a restless gesture, like he's debating whether to accept candy from a stranger.

The stranger thing might be less of a risk. To my heart health, that is.

But no. I told Vivian I could handle him, and I can. I can sleep in the same bed as him and not let it affect me. I can be as blasé as he naturally defaults to.

After a moment of consideration, he says, "Well, when you put it like that."

He stands up slowly, giving me plenty of time to revoke the offer. When I don't, he walks around the bed, peeling the covers back before sliding onto the pillow next to mine. While he's careful not to make contact with my bare skin, his efforts are wasted—the electric current is back, threads of it buzzing between my arm and his.

We lay in silence, and I make an effort to adjust to both the buzzing and the warmth of his body this close to mine. My core body temperature still has three degrees to go before I can fall asleep. As if I'd be able to do that anytime soon.

"So," he says into the darkness, not sounding the least bit tired. In fact, sounding as wholly and utterly conscious as I am. "How're you feeling?"

I close my eyes, blocking out the flickering lights on the walls. Of all the topics we could discuss, he lands on the exact type of question I don't have the brain power to spin lies around, much less present as seductively indifferent.

But maybe . . . I don't have to lie. Not completely.

"I'm just tired," I say, adjusting my head so my wet hair fans out on the pillow beneath me. The room quiets, and there's nothing but our breathing in the semi-dark.

Despite the lingering anger from my conversation with Vivian, I have to acknowledge that this is kind of him. Giving me time to gather my thoughts, that is. I don't have a lot of practice with talking about the weight in my heart, and it doesn't get any easier when he offers to listen. But since he's here with me, quite literally by my side, I can try to show this sliver of myself without revealing how fully he wrecked me.

How everything wrecked me.

"If I let myself sit for too long or have nothing to do, it all catches up with me." The driving, the geriatric drama, the family trauma bookstore—every morsel of extroversion I've managed to squeeze out of my DNA has dissipated, evaporating somewhere into the cosmos. "I should've sucked it up and gotten the lineup together. Now, we're scrambling for acts, and I just keep making it worse. I managed to make us waste a night in the hospital, forced you to drive through a hurricane, and pissed off our host." I exhale, reaching up to coil wet strands of hair around my finger. My limbs are heavy, and my chest aches in that hollow way I usually avoid with excessive caffeine and professional development. "I'm a mess and a terrible sister."

"I was actually referring to the concussion, but thank you for sharing that." My heart skips a couple of beats, and he chuckles as I pull the covers over my face. He tugs at it, pulling it back down to my chin as I resist the urge to sink into the hellhole I assume Opal usually occupies. "You're a great sister. Mav thought nobody and nothing was good enough for you. He told me so himself." His voice drops on the last words, but the emotion disappears before I can identify it. "Give yourself a break. You'll aggravate your head injury. Speaking of which . . . "

The bed shifts, and I automatically scramble for purchase on the mattress as he circles the perimeter of the bed to my side. With a screech that nearly makes me jump out my skin, he pushes the bedside table to the opposite wall. Before I can open my mouth to demand an explanation, he mumbles, "In case you roll off," and makes his way back around.

I blink. Open my mouth. Close it.

Something warm pours into my chest, trickling down to my toes. In the middle of a hellish trip where I've given him barely more than tolerance, he's willing to do something thoughtful for me. Not for Mav or my parents or Dusty the Park Ranger. For *me*.

Offering a shortcut at the waterfall. Staying up with me at the hospital. Sleep talking about missing me.

The trend is there, and not only from this trip. If I let myself sift through the memories, it's been there for years. Considerate Rook. Kind Rook. Someone who's shown me, time and time again, that he feels for me what I've always felt for him. Which means the last eleven months weren't the new baseline data.

They were the outlier.

With the truth of that conclusion reverberating through my bones, I roll over to face him, propping my head on my hand. "Rook?"

"Yeah?"

"You did say something last night." The words hang in the darkness above us. My heart beats frantically in the silence, managing to pick up speed as he gradually turns to face me. His eyes are a careful neutral, illuminated by the flickering light behind me. "I've missed you, too."

His expression shifts, his eyes melting into something soft. Warm. Tender.

There's no room to think about the consequences or the potential catalysts as to why he wouldn't talk to me for all those months. Not when he closes the distance between our pillows and presses his mouth to mine.

His lips are soft, bending to my own as his hands drift to my hair. Each movement is measured. Cautious. But then a low groan escapes my throat, and he's cupping my cheek, angling my jaw to kiss him more deeply. I push against his broad frame, urging him onto his back as I swing my legs on either side of his waist. His breathing speeds up, his heart a wild flutter against my palm. I taste his tongue as his hands roam my bare back, restlessness building in my core as he tightens his grip on my hips.

This is familiar, the way we fit so well with each other. An echo of the one other night we shared, which . . . didn't end well. I tense, and he must feel the shift in my muscles because he pulls back to look at me.

"Is this okay?" he asks, concern tightening his eyes.

Okay? Try cataclysmic. A seismic event that's sure to rip the fissures in my heart wide open.

"Yes," I say, and his lips are on mine again before the word is fully out. Tugging off my slip. Guiding me onto my back. Nuzzling my neck. Whispering muffled words into my skin.

"What was that?" I ask breathlessly. He pulls his head up from where he was pressing kisses between my breasts, eyes glazed over.

"You're so beautiful," he whispers against my skin.

Oh. *Oh.*

There aren't many words after that.

Chapter Twelve

In the light of day, a haunted bed-and-breakfast isn't so creepy after all.

For one, all the candelabras don't cast shadows when sunlight shines through the windows. They're regular wall fixtures, if a bit outdated. Old furniture pieces become vintage rather than eerie, unsettling family portraits become . . . unsettling. There's no saving that one.

"Do you think there's French toast? Or is Madame Truffalo the only one with an affinity for the French?" I ask as we descend the staircase. It's only natural to make small talk after we spent the night in the same bed—I'm still in a liminal space where I can sit with my actions and not face the consequences.

Rook rubs his neck. "If she doesn't like the French, at least we can have the English muffins. Hold on a second."

He halts on the last step, pulling his sweatshirt over his head. For a moment, his shirt lifts too, exposing a taut midriff. Just in case, between last night and right now, I forgot that he works out. Religiously.

We make our way to the breakfast bar, which is overflowing with platters of eggs, muffins, bacon, yogurt, and miscellaneous breakfast foods arranged in a straight line on long, wooden tables. I load my plate up with every possible item and secure us a spot at a tiny table by the window, still streaked with morning rain. Rook follows closely behind, his plate full of colorful, healthy foods. He probably moonlights as a nutrition coach when he's not saving kittens from trees or avoiding my texts. I suppose I can overlook the last one for now, since he definitely wasn't avoiding me a few hours ago.

"So, what's the plan for today?" I ask after successfully swallowing a mouthful of bacon without choking. I can come back from falling off a stage, sure, but public abdominal thrusts? Never.

He sips his coffee and sets the mug carefully down on the table. I'm momentarily distracted by how the natural light brings out the simmering amber in his eyes. How is that color combination fair to the rest of us?

"We're skipping to the final stop."

"What?" My half-eaten muffin lands with a *thump* on my plate. "We need all the help we can get. Why would we skip?"

He meets my gaze without so much as a blink. "We've been delayed too long to hit the other two stops I wanted to take on the usual route. I built in some buffer time, but not enough to cover the miles we lost in the storm . . . and the delay from the hospital."

Shit. So I *did* screw us over with my lack of balance after putting us on a crunched timeline in the first place.

A warm hand rests on my own. "Stop thinking so hard over there. You'll aggravate your concussion," he says gently. I shake my head, withdrawing my hand from under his.

His mouth tightens, but he continues, "The last stop will more than make up for the other two. If we go this route, we'll be back on Saturday like we planned. That gives us a little over three weeks to figure out everything else with Brandi. You've got the venue locked down, right?"

I nod, twirling my spoon in my cup of yogurt. The venue is the one thing I *did* manage to get done all those months ago. Or contributed to getting done, since Aunt Brandi was the one who followed up with the rentals staff at the theater Mav used to perform at.

Rook's eyes shift somewhere above my left shoulder. He pops up, chair screeching, and starts gathering our plates and trash.

"What the hell," I say as he snatches my yogurt. Did he actually see a ghost? If so, can we exploit his mediumship abilities at the show?

He stops next to me, hands full. "Grab my keys out of my pocket. I'm going to get us checked out while you're in the car," he says, nodding toward his waist. I raise an eyebrow, hoping the blood rushing to my cheeks presents as artfully placed blush. Shove my hand in his pants? Here? Teenage Cam would be in hysterics.

"Am I not allowed to finish my breakfast in peace?" I ask. I know we engaged in activities that brought us, in a word, *closer* last night, but it's too early to label my feelings about that into discrete categories. This request feels more intimate, somehow. But that might be because there's spectators around, and the couple closest to us is eyeing Rook curiously. I, too, would continue to openly ogle him in the dining area of a possibly haunted bed-and-breakfast, if the logistics of the situation hadn't just registered in my brain.

"You want me to walk to the car *alone*? I barely remember how we got here," I say, but he's already inching toward the trash can.

"I fixed the tire and brought it round front this morning. You can leave your suitcase, too—I'll bring it out in a second." I crinkle my forehead at the urgency in his tone. I know we're in a time crunch, but separately checking out and walking to the car wouldn't help with that. He catches my expression and pauses his attempt to push his chair in while balancing our breakfast trash in one hand. "I saw your face when Opal was talking about her sister last night. I'd rather we start the day without the two of you going at it."

I look over my shoulder where, sure enough, Opal is shuffling over from the front counter, clutching her black shawl around her shoulders as a guest trails behind her.

When I turn back around, Rook is looking between me and Opal, more alarmed with each step she takes on the whining floorboards. "Please."

"Fine. Just so you know, I never do this," I say before promptly fishing the car keys out of his front jeans pocket. His mouth twitches, and then he's off to intercept her on the opposite side of the room.

I push my chair in and grab Rook's sweatshirt, tying it around my waist. I cross the increasingly populated dining area to the entryway doors, keeping an eye out for the tall, tortured-looking man in glasses striding toward the breakfast buffet.

As I close one of the looming oak doors, my eyes snag on a shroud of white hair next to the bowls of fruit. Opal, looking down at the crumpled flyer Rook must've given her. His back is to me, but I can clearly see her face. How she raises her eyebrows as he makes a sweeping gesture at the surrounding walls, then points at the paper—and the picture of Mav I still can't seem to look at.

The door clicks shut behind me. Squinting against the morning sun, I locate the car in its new parking spot and use the natural light to evaluate my outfit for the day: sneakers, joggers, and a cropped concert T-shirt. While Rook takes the next few minutes to coerce our host, I have time to brave the mirror in the passenger seat, which is more forgiving than I expected. I look like I got a solid quarter night's sleep instead of, say, an eighth. At least I got to put the lingerie to good use—though Vivian might not appreciate the direction that use went.

I definitely went above and beyond *tolerating* him.

When he finally reemerges from the building, I snap the mirror up and take a deep breath to scatter the butterflies in my stomach. They're partially due to the way Rook looks this morning (gorgeous) and partially because I can't help but weigh the odds that he's regretting last night already (not insignificant). By the time he's stashed the luggage in the back of the car and placed two coffees in the cupholders between us, my reticular activating system has ensured that I'm both awake and fully capable of admiring the view of the man next to me.

"What'd you say to her?" I ask, only now registering that he managed to carry two drinks and two bags while crossing the entire parking lot. He grunts an acknowledgment as he buckles himself in, biding his time.

"Thought she'd like to know that Truffalo might be at the show," he says after a few seconds' pause, placing his hand on my chair as he reverses out of the parking spot. It's unreasonably attractive for a purely functional maneuver. "I couldn't tell if it hurt or help, but it was worth a shot."

"Totally," I murmur. Leave it to Rook to revive a sibling relationship across state lines. It's something I would've expected from him a year ago, back before my own sibling relationship was reduced to a single voicemail.

One more stop. I can push through one more stop with the man who's obviously doing everything he can to get the show together.

Whether or not he'll stick around long enough to see the final result . . . that's another matter entirely.

• • •

"What's the strategy for Nashville? I'm assuming it has the highest concentration of *interesting friends* if we afford to skip two stops for it," I say, kicking the two discarded energy drinks at my feet. Between those and the black coffee Rook had at breakfast, it's a wonder how he's not levitating out of his seat.

He gives me a sidelong look, eyeing the coffee I'm clutching as we narrowly avoid a pothole. While he might be able to look rejuvenated and non-jittery after seventeen thousand milligrams of caffeine, I still have a few ounces to go before I feel fully human. "Is that sweet enough for you? Opal wouldn't let me use the entire bottle of creamer, but I did my best."

"I've developed two cavities since you brought it in. One more and I can verify it's sweet enough." I flick his arm but can't help but smile when he chuckles. The chuckle of a man who knows my coffee order is typically more milkshake-like than actual coffee. "Now stop avoiding the question. I need to mentally prepare if we're recruiting *en masse*."

I make sure the words are nonchalant, testing the waters. I've more than earned the right to know what to expect from the route, and I have reason to believe that Rook would be more willing to share that kind of information now than he would've this time yesterday.

He fiddles with his phone where it hangs on the vent. "We need to get gas, and the closest spot is another twenty minutes. Think that's enough time to gain another cavity?"

"Rook."

"Cameron."

I let out an exasperated sigh, putting my cavity-inducing beverage in the cupholder. "Can I at least know how many acts we're expecting to recruit? That'll determine how many phone calls I need to make when we get home." Right around the time Oakley said he might not be able to perform Shakespeare for a crowd larger than the average puppet show audience, I revisited the list of possible acts I could contact closer to Rustin. Maverick's theater friends are at the top of that list, but the idea of talking to Sebastian still makes me borderline ill. Unfortunately for me, Sebastian is the best person to contact for that troupe—when he says, "Ad-lib," they ask, "For how long?"

"We'll recruit however many acts it takes to fill the time slots," Rook says. I frown, and he pats my hand before I use it to pick up my coffee again. "I'm still sworn to secrecy, but nice try. It'll make sense when we get there."

"Right. That makes me feel super assured and not anxious at all," I say. Three days in, and he still refuses to move past the *sworn to secrecy* thing. I'm positive that Maverick wouldn't mind letting that promise expire, given that they made it when they were teenagers. I open my mouth to say so when a giant sign pops into view.

Not just any sign. A stegosaurus-shaped billboard, complete with bubbly letters reading, "Dinos & Drives: 15 miles to the right."

"That's the next pit stop," he announces. I dig my nails in my seatbelt, swallowing a scream. He's using a paleontological marketing campaign to stop talking about key recruitment information, I'll probably need to reach out to Sebastian when we get home this weekend, and the cells in my bladder wall are starting to scream. If only

I started Kegels six months ago when Vivian told me to. I have a feeling right now isn't the time to start that particular workout routine.

He points toward the approaching billboard. "Get a load of these ads. 'Bringing our competitors to extinction since 1995.' Seems vaguely threatening, doesn't it?"

With another scan of the bright green lettering, I say, "Vaguely threatening but also a family friendly establishment? They're walking a fine line."

"What are they competing over, exactly? I thought it was just a gas station, but it looks like they do birthday parties." He leans closer to the steering wheel, surveying the next billboard through his glasses. This one displays a birthday cake with a hyperrealistic rendering of a *T. rex* holding a limp *Triceratops* in its mouth.

"Cam, you've got to see this cake," Maverick says, hovering over the dining room table. I edge closer to where Rook is shielding the bakery box with his body, stepping on my tiptoes to see over his shoulder. After showering off any residual airport grime from my flight back home this morning, I have no reservations about being this close to him. Even if he insists on obstructing the graduation cake he brought here a few minutes ago.

"No, you don't," Rook grumbles, and Mav snickers into a closed fist. They're making enough of a scene that Aunt Brandi, Vivian, and my parents all filter into the dining room with us. When Vivian and I arrived at the house to a "Congratulations!" banner over the front door, I was touched. When Mav let slip that Rook was behind this little celebration, I was ecstatic.

In a nonchalant, not-reading-too-much-into-it way, of course.

"I'm sure it's perfect, Rook," my mother says, laying out paper plates and silverware on the table. On second glance, the pattern on those plates

consists of cartoon stethoscopes and EKGs. Another idea from Rook, since I'll be starting medical school this fall?

"Yeah. And we've been waiting for you to get here for like, two hours now," Vivian adds, eliciting a grimace from both me and Rook. He can't help if he gets off work late . . . or if he had to troubleshoot whatever the bakery messed up.

When he finally opens the box and moves firmly out of interference range, it takes a moment for my eyes to adjust to the blindingly white frosting.

"Oh." I brace myself against the contradictory emotions flooding my system. Shock. Amusement. Confusion. Awe.

Before me, taking up no less than half of the width of the table, is the largest, rococo-est, most T-shaped cake I've ever seen.

Correction—largest, rococo-est, most cross-shaped cake I've ever seen.

While the sides are replete with gold flakes and winged figures made of metallic fondant, the top is adorned with raised letters spelling out "Cameron's First Communion." Except "Communion" has been extended to "Commencement" in what appears to be a child's handwriting.

My mother recovers first, always the "yes, and . . . " type. "This is really lovely, Rook. Very . . . ornate."

Vivian leans over and whispers, "I thought you said you're 'go to church twice a year' Christians?"

"We are," I whisper back.

Rook glares at my brother, who's already taken the designated cake-cutting knife to one corner. "I told you you should've placed the order."

"Hey, you already assigned me to making the playlist." Mav waves the cake-cutting knife at the living room, where a stream of upbeat pop, indie, and country songs has been playing since we arrived. He's also

made sure that Chris Spur's "Head Over Hooves" plays at least once an hour. Because I'm such a big fan.

Mav leans closer to inspect the writing. "At least they got the name right. Though the lettering could use some work."

Rook flushes a light pink, lowering his gel-stained fingers below the table, and I clear my throat. "Is there any particular reason my graduation cake is so, uh, pious?"

Mav starts distributing paper plates as he says, "It's symbolic. An homage to your growing god complex, which is bound to get out of control when you start classes in the fall." Upon seeing my parents' frowns, his smile broadens, and he switches to loading each plate with a slice. "Rook placed the order during work."

"It's possible that I'd been awake for forty-eight hours . . . and said communion instead of commencement," Rook says, absently running a hand through his hair.

Mav tsks at him, shaking his head fondly as he says, "How many times have I told you over the years? You must enunciate. *Also, who says commencement instead of graduation?"*

"Someone who's been awake for forty-eight hours straight," I say, poking at the metallic frosting on my plate. After spending my last semester taking a full course load, publishing a research paper, and working on financial aid for med school, I have a new appreciation for sleep.

Rook, however, is frowning at the fondant angel wing on his plate. "This feels wrong. Should we . . . pray?" All movement stops. Forks pause half an inch from open mouths. Grandma Loredo smiles down on us from the heavens.

After another beat of silence, Mav says, "Nah," and the clattering resumes. Vivian and Aunt Brandi chat about celebrity gossip, sprinkling in their thoughts on the latest stock market trends. Mom and Mav rope Rook into a conversation about their vision for a state-of-the-art theater in Rustin. Which leaves my father, who lets me eat my slice of communion cake in peace.

Or not. "Kid put a lot of work into this," Dad says. He nods across the table, where Rook patiently listens as Mav enumerates five reasons why Rustin is prime real estate for the Broadway of the South.

"He would've done it for anyone."

"Maybe." He doesn't look convinced as he sets down his fork, reaching for the wine Aunt Brandi just set on the table. "Maybe not."

It's an effort to stanch the surge of hope in my heart, especially when I spot Rook's gel-stained fingers from when he attempted to fix the lettering. I'm sure he's dabbling in event planning or had time to kill after work. There's no reason to read into it, even if my socially inept father implied otherwise.

When I finally look up from my disposable dishware, Rook's eyes are already on me.

I register the burning sensation on my lap in the same moment that Rook says, "Either way, they should've gone with, 'Bringing fossil fuels to life since '95.'"

"Oh, shit." I jerk my coffee cup upright, managing to shift the stream of liquid from directly onto my waist to down the front of my shirt. "Shit, shit, shit."

"You're right. It could use some work," Rook says with a glance my way. He does a double take when he notices the spilled coffee and my general disarray. "Are you okay? Here, use my sweatshirt to clean up—we just ran out of napkins."

He reaches over to unbuckle my seatbelt so I'm free to tug his sweatshirt off my waist. Its sleeves are already soaked, but I can use the rest of the fabric to sop up the seventy-five percent of my drink I spilled.

"I didn't like that one anyway," he says, putting both hands on the wheel when I've successfully dabbed all the liquid off my chest. I spread out the sweatshirt to assess the damage. The light grey fabric is now . . . not light grey. At all. "Seriously. Don't worry about it."

But I do worry. Because even though he's been perfectly gracious and insisted that I take over the music in a gesture of good faith, I can't help but wonder what the cost of his kindness will be this time.

Chapter Thirteen

For those of us lucky enough to experience traumatic grie—
"*Six Feet Above?*"

My hands fly off the keyboard as Rook appears over my shoulder. After a night at Opal's bed-and-breakfast, the motel we've settled in for the night is underwhelming. The wall art consists of generic landscapes, not a creepy family portrait in sight, and the two beds have the default white comforter and sheets. And while I don't usually use the desk of a hotel room for anything more than overflow from my suitcase, I am using it for its intended purpose right now.

Apparently, using the desk as a workspace makes me more jumpy than a literal haunted mansion. Though that could have to do with the content of what I'm writing. Rook backs up, hands raised in the universal gesture of surrender. "Hey, I tried to get your attention five times. I didn't realize you were working on something personal," he says. I spin in my chair, not bothering to hide my scowl as I take in his attire: a very loud, very bold, very prehistoric Dinos & Drives logo on the sweatshirt I purchased for him.

"Do you have to keep wearing that thing? I feel bad enough that I ruined the other one. This one is just . . . overstimulating."

"No, really, this is the perfect souvenir. Everyone knows that Dinos & Drives is way better than Raptors & Raves." He holds a hand up when I scowl harder. "Plus, I think jaundice yellow is my color," he says, his dry delivery betrayed only by the slight tic of his mouth. When the last fragment of my ego falls in a heap at my feet, he puts his hands on the back of my chair, leaning over to squint at the words on my computer screen. "What're you working on?"

I instinctively lower the screen, blocking the words with my body. When I stowed my computer under the latch in his trunk at the beginning of this trip, I hadn't expected to have time to write. I also didn't think through the logistics of writing when Rook would be close enough to hover.

But I owe my twelve faithful readers an article.

"I needed a larger screen to contact my friends and many suitors. The phone didn't cut it," I say. His jaw clenches in a satisfyingly disgruntled way, and I try not to crumple at the relief it brings me. Logically, if someone cares about you enough to be jealous at the mention of other suitors, then they should also care about you enough not to go MIA when you need them most. And I'm definitely going to need him to get through both Nashville and the execution phase of the talent show.

Ignoring the minor flip of my stomach, I tilt the computer screen back to its original position, where he can clearly read half a sentence, all I've managed so far, on an otherwise white screen.

"It's nothing, really," I say, spinning back toward the desk. I haven't told anyone about my writing habits. It seems a little juvenile in the grand scheme of things, but I like my blog. It helps me organize grief into bite-sized chunks that I can refer back to.

"It doesn't look like nothing." He points to a citation on the screen, close enough that I can feel the warmth emanating from his body. "Is that from your lab in undergrad?"

I search his expression for any criticism, but there's only curiosity. This is the Rook I've known for most of my life—kind, considerate, willing to listen. If I can focus on the now version of him and not the one that didn't talk to me for almost a year, it'll be easier to share this part of myself. The jaundice-yellow sweatshirt doesn't hurt with the whole vulnerability thing, either.

I take a breath, letting the oxygen inflow settle my nerves, and say, "It is. I always liked neuroscience, but the rat guillotine was a bit much. In my future work, I'd rather not be the rodent executioner."

He nods, like this comment is perfectly reasonable and not alarming. "It looks like you have a lot of knowledge on the subject. Have you considered extending your research on it? Exploring it any further?" he asks.

I scrunch my forehead. "Like a PhD?"

"Like a PhD," he confirms with a nod.

Huh. I've never thought of it that way, mostly because this was never meant to be a formal area of study. More like a cute little hobby that's cheaper than therapy. Plus, it's not like I have a huge following—most of the visibility comes from the forum. People make notes on my content or share their personal stories if they feel comfortable. Someone might point out a flaw in my APA citations while another might talk about how hard it's been since their best friend passed away.

I shake my head. "No. I've wanted to be a doctor my whole life. That'd be like training for a marathon and then hiking Mount Everest."

He nods again, tilting his head. Thoughtful. "What about the MD-PhD route? I had a friend in college who got into a program on the East Coast. He was interested in the pharmaceutical side of things." What a nice way to say he sold his soul to Big Pharma. "The selection process sounded brutal but also like the best of both worlds. You know, become a physician while mostly working on research. With your writing skills, you could definitely get the word out. Make this kind of information"—he points to the diagram of a hippocampus on the screen—"accessible for a lot of people who are grieving. Not that it makes anything easier, but it could help someone."

I lean back in the chair, letting it roll back a fraction of an inch. He's not wrong. Over the months, all sorts of people have interacted on the forum. Grieving parents, siblings, friends. And I've heard about the MD-PhD path. Mostly in hushed whispers because, like he said, it's incredibly competitive. I doubt that an amateur blog could be a potential line of research. But . . .

"If I had the right funding, I could look into neuro-based intervention programs for grief. It could be tiered, depending on the relationship with the deceased, whether the grief is complicated, time passed since the event. A combination of psychotherapy and the most effective practices neurology-wise." A light flickers on somewhere in my rib cage. "A place where medicine and compassion meet. How could they not? You're dealing with people at their absolute worst, experiencing trauma that affects the very epigenetic configuration of your DNA—" I pause at his expression. "What?"

"Nothing. I just haven't seen you this excited about something in . . . a while," he says.

I chew on the inside of my cheek, urging the rest of my face to remain blank while I consider the truth in his statement. It's been a long time since I felt anything other than dread at the thought of starting medical school. Ever since The Accident, the whole thing has felt like another reminder of the future I'll never get to experience with Maverick. I've been so focused on the fact that I couldn't save him that I haven't considered all the people I could help.

Will help, once I officially start classes in a couple of months.

I toss my hair over my shoulder, aiming for nonchalant rather than completely and utterly overwhelmed. "You obviously weren't looking when I saw the bacon this morning." At that, I feel more than see him shake his head behind me. "Speaking of which, does the last stop include food? Or am I not allowed to know that, either?"

He steps back, settling onto the white comforter. "We'll get food before. I wouldn't trust whatever they'll be serving."

I pivot enough to arch an eyebrow at him. "And what's the dress code for this place of questionable food?"

He glances down to my bare thighs on the chair, eyes quickly returning to my face. "Whatever you're comfortable in," he says. With that, he retreats to the chair in the corner of the room, where he's already laid out the novel he purchased at Branch O' Books. I refocus on the blinking curser on my screen and try to shake off the lingering feelings from our MD-PhD conversation. There's no way I would be able to turn a blog into an entire line of study. Besides, if I haven't been able to get a talent show together without significant help from a third party, I wouldn't be able to handle a program of that caliber. I don't know how I'll be able to get through medical school, much less a med school-research hybrid.

I need to focus on why we're here in this hotel room, having this conversation in the first place. There's too much at stake if we don't recruit enough acts tonight:

1) Life-threatening doses of embarrassment.

2) Wasted time, money, and emotional labor.

3) The complete decimation of my pride along with any hope I had to honor Mav's name.

While Rook had good intentions, I can't afford to fixate on a future that I shouldn't even be excited about, since Maverick won't be around to share it.

After avoiding the talent show for all these months, I can't afford to fail now.

• • •

We're at a honky-tonk. I know this because a neon yellow sign approximately seventy feet across the front of the building nestled between a pizza joint and a tattoo shop reads, "Honky-Tonk."

"Remind me how this works again," I say, blinking against the unnatural glow as I adjust my cleavage. I didn't account for how much of this trip would be spent on nightlife. My personal wardrobe is more Adam Sandler-esque than age-appropriate going out attire. Without the schemes of Vivian, who encourages me to be the best worst version of myself, I'd be screwed. Tonight's jumpsuit drops down in deep V moment in the front, and the back is open to feel the summer breeze. The midnight blue fabric is smooth and breathable, cinching my waist and making my ass look fantastic. I know this because Rook has stared at it approximately seven times in the last five minutes, looking away whenever I try to catch his eye to call him out on it.

If I'm expected to keep my shit together for one more night, I can at least have a little fun with him. It's not every night that you get to recruit for a memorial talent show on the Nashville strip.

"Mav liked to think of it as improv practice. We have to go with whatever schtick the other person starts to get as many free drinks as possible," Rook says, stepping aside as he holds the hefty door open for me.

I raise an eyebrow, adjusting the purse strap on my shoulder before walking through. I've never witnessed Rook have more than a single beer. Based on my brother's stories, Rook was always the buttoned up one that drove them home after a night out. It's only to be expected, given his father's alcoholism. And Maverick always did appreciate having a built-in designated driver as a best friend.

Hopefully this time around, Rook's out-of-character behavior is contained to being a lush for a night and not giving me the silent treatment for another eleven months.

I shove down the uneasiness in my gut, focusing on the sprawling bar in front of us rather than the implications of last night. It's not hard to extrapolate those implications when I vividly remember what happened after the last time we spent a night in the same bed, even if Rook has been nothing but a gentleman for the past twenty-four hours. There's no reason to mull over the probability of him falling back into the silent treatment, not when we have a mission to complete tonight. No, this is our last opportunity to recruit for all the remaining talent show slots. Based on the amount of "Tennessee Whiskey" covers we heard on the walk over here, Nashville promises to deliver.

Honky-Tonk turns out to be worthy of its generic name. This place is the prototype for honky-tonks everywhere. The hazy '90s country aura is palpable, and the menu posted over the bar overflows with drinks like, "Man! I Feel Like a Whiskey Sour" and "Watermelon Crawl Mojito." Between the sea of cowboy hats and boot-clad couples on the dance floor to our left, all that's missing is a John Deere tractor.

"Whatever the other person starts, you say?" I ask, my tone impressively flippant and teasing. See? I can act like I'm completely convinced that Rook will stick around long enough to see the show. I can convince myself that everything will work out perfectly, that my heart will stay intact long enough to collect top tier talent and make the drive home.

For Maverick, I can pretend for one more night.

"Within reason." Rook stops next to me, broad shoulders tugging at his navy-blue shirt. His sleeves are rolled up, showing the no-nonsense watch on his left wrist.

Damn him and his sexy forearms. How am I supposed to take control of my internal spiraling situation when he looks like that?

I head toward the perimeter, away from him and his irrationally attractive forearms, where a cluster of pool tables offers a better vantage point. He follows, and we claim a small round table at the junction of billiards and dance floor. "So what scenarios have you used before? Give me something to work with."

"Let me think . . . " He zeroes in on the bar, taking a deep breath as he accesses whatever memories Mav isn't around to weave into stories. "We've done tourists from out of the country. Mav spoke fake Dutch for five minutes straight."

That earns an exhale through my nose. Mav should've gone with fake German, the language he actually took in high school for three years.

Rook continues, "The shtick was that we lost our wallets and passports. That worked pretty well."

"This is starting to sound like socially acceptable role-play," I say, forcing an easy, nonchalant smile. The most chalant of smiles.

"Role-play, improv. Whatever you want to call it, it's tradition," he answers, eyeing my smile suspiciously. Okay, so I'm not the best thespian. Along with any semblance of vocal talent, Mom's acting genes somehow went entirely to Maverick. "I'll grab some water while you think on it." He rises from the chair and hesitates. "Cameron?"

"Yeah?" I chirp. He looks at me quizzically, probably because my voice is about three octaves higher than usual. Super nonchalant, I am.

"Please don't try to get a traumatic brain injury while I'm gone." With that, he leaves, albeit a little hurriedly.

I wait until he's deep in the crowd to sit down and cover my face with my hands. Right now is *not* the time to completely unravel. We still have over half of the talent show to fill, and I can't get through a single minute without losing my mind—

"What a wonderful night," a voice croons from my right. I nearly jump out of my skin, then settle back into it when I realize it's a petite older lady with Reba red hair. She's perched on the seat next to mine, sipping on something dark and potent. "Cameron, was it? Lovely name," she says, raising her glass.

She hums happily, sipping her drink long enough that I have time to slap on my willing-to-talk-to-a-stranger-during-a-micro-breakdown face. When she does come up for air, she leans over with a sly expression and says, "He's quite the looker."

"I know it," I mutter, tapping my heel against the metal footrest of my chair. Under the bar lighting, Rook's side profile is all hard angles and evening scruff. Of course his appeal spans generations.

"My Bobby used to look at me like that," she sighs, looking wistfully at her ring finger. *Used to.* My foot stops moving at approximately the same time my heart descends into my abdomen.

Shit.

"Look at you like what?" I ask, careful to turn toward her. She smiles, gazing somewhere in the distance beyond my head.

"Like the sun and the moon and the stars all rolled up in one."

A startled snort escapes my throat. "Oh, no, we—"

I catch myself when her brow wrinkles in confusion. This woman clearly thinks we're together. Given the optics of us spending the night out, I can't exactly blame her. There's no way I'm going to subject her to an explanation of our . . . relationship? Friendship turned hookup of convenience? Trauma bond?

It doesn't matter. Tonight's a night of make believe. The simpler the better.

"This Bobby person sounds very special to you." I swallow, conscious of the weight of the lie on my tongue when I say, "I'm sure we haven't been together long enough to come close to what you had."

"Trust me, girl, I know a lifelong love when I see one. That man would lasso the moon for you."

The words flutter around my heart, not quite settling in. If this woman could say something like that with such surety, then maybe I've been worrying for nothing. Maybe he really does care, and the chances of him running away with no explanation are minimal. Maybe I should be able to believe that he would lasso the moon and not regret it.

"I know that look, too. He's done something to hurt you. Hurt you deeply, even."

My head snaps up. What's the likelihood that the first person I spoke to tonight would have mind reading capabilities? And is she willing to display those capabilities on a stage in three and a half weeks?

"It's okay to sit in your hurt," she says. Her smile is nothing short of devious as she daintily gathers her carpetbag purse in her lap. "Don't worry, dear. Love is worth all the hurtin' parts."

Before I can begin digesting that, she hops off the chair and walks purposefully toward the crowded bar.

"What was that all about? Looked like y'all were having a real come-to-Jesus talk over here." Rook sets two iced waters on the table. So glad he arrived at this moment and not, say, twenty seconds ago.

"I think I just had a chat with me from the future. Possibly from the past. Unclear," I answer, accepting the water. He sips from his cup as he considers my words.

"You never know who you'll meet in Nashville," he agrees. "So, what's it going to be tonight?"

Shit. I was supposed to be brainstorming an improv bit, not engaging in moderately unsettling conversations with sagacious gingers. Since Rook made it clear that we needed to stick to the improv tradition rather than only recruiting, there's no way around it.

"Let's walk and talk," I offer. "I need inspiration."

"If all else fails, we could play up the concussion." He chugs the rest of his water, snagging the empty glass as I slide off the chair. "Maybe you're in the throes of amnesia and can't remember where you put our wallets."

"I have a purse."

"Ditch it."

He falls into step next to me as I wander, aiming for the outskirts of the bar itself. To our left, couples spin around on the dance floor to the music of the house band, something lively and twirl-inducing. It doesn't matter if they're dating, married, or trauma-bonded childhood friends turned hookups — anyone could pass for a real couple down there. And, as the encounter with Future Me proved, Rook and I wouldn't even have to dance to sell it. Thanks to dopamine, everyone's a sucker for a good love story.

I steel myself against the dread clawing its way up my throat as I fish around my purse. It takes a few seconds, but eventually I procure the faux engagement ring I keep on standby in the side pocket.

This is it. This is how we're getting free drinks *and* recruiting acts for the show . . . if I can get my own act together for the entire night.

"Sweetheart, you're always saying the darnedest things," I say, throwing in an obnoxious giggle as I lightly slap his chest. Rook's bemused expression morphs into confusion, forehead crinkling from where he leans against one of the four pillars framing the bar.

Ignoring the increasing clamminess of my palms, I grab the front of Rook's shirt, throwing my other arm around his neck until we're in what's ostensibly a lover's embrace. When he's nice and close, I hover by his ear.

"I think I've got our shtick."

Chapter Fourteen

Rook didn't love this idea. Apparently a zealous believer in preserving the sanctity of real proposals, he threw around words like *unethical*, *disparaging*, and *egregious*.

"Then what do you suggest? Because as far as I'm concerned, playing up my concussion is more *unethical* than getting on one knee a couple of times," I say. He frowns at me, folding his arms across his chest, highlighting the hard angles of the muscle under the fabric of his shirt. There's no time for me to admire him and his firefighter physique when I should be spending my energy on more important things, like getting his ass into recruitment mode.

I hop off the chair, planting a hand on my hip as I force him to acknowledge me. "You two schmoozed your way into free drinks for years now. Why is this any different?"

I wait for an answer, but he seems content to furrow his brow and keep his mouth shut. Typical. Just when I find the perfect solution to an otherwise outrageous request, he clams up.

"Look," I say, leaning across the table until he has no choice but to meet my eye. "I'm not the one who insists we stick to tradition. We could head out and recruit plenty of performers on the street right now.

I'm ninety-five percent sure I saw Willie Nelson on the way over here. Or someone who could pass for Willie Nelson in low enough lighting," I add. His lip twitches, but it's not enough to pass as the "yes" I need it to be. It's not like I want to be in this position, borderline begging for him to fake propose to me. If anything, I should be the one in distress here—I only fantasized about our future of blissful matrimony for over a decade.

"Face the facts. This is the one way we can maximize our visibility, secure free drinks, and get people to like us enough to consider crossing state lines for a random talent show," I say. He grimaces as I tick off each point on my finger, like the prospect of fake proposing is more painful than complete and utter failure would be.

But I do need this. I need to get these acts so that the show has a chance at being as grand as Mav deserves. Even if the thought of returning home to figure out the logistics of a show that large makes me nauseous, it has to be done. And I need Rook to make it happen.

I need him to pretend with me for one more night.

"Please?" My voice comes out smaller and more pitiful than I intended. But maybe pity is what finally cracks him—his eyes soften, and his lips press in a tight line as he takes in my expression. He weighs my words and the desperation in my voice, his expression shifting from pained to resolved before my eyes. After a long moment, he releases a slow stream of air.

"I still think the concussion route would be easier." He extends a hand to me, a begrudging smile on his lips. "Care to dance?"

Without letting my jaw drop all the way down, I let him lead me onto the dance floor, where the house band is playing a cover of—wait for it—"Tennessee Whiskey." To be fair, the lead vocalist is hitting those runs better than anyone we heard on the way to Honky-Tonk. To be even fairer, I'm not the harshest music critic when Rook is this close to me. It's entirely possible the lead singer is butchering it.

"They're killing it up there," I say, waving at the band. A necessary distraction. Rook has resigned himself to the shtick, eyes crinkling in the corners as he half-smiles. It's enough to put me on the verge of a spontaneous myocardial infarction.

"They are." His glasses slide as he looks down at me, and I push them back up before he can remove his hand from my waist. I need to make sure he keeps dancing while we still have momentum, though he has been holding his own for the few minutes we've been two-stepping. All those years of the Tennessee Trail, and I never considered that Rook would be dancing in a club or country bar like this. I assumed he would sit on the sidelines and make sure my brother didn't do anything stupid, like flirt with two girls from the same friend group or get on stage.

Scratch that—get on stage without warming up first.

"You've been holding out on me," I say as he spins me into his arms. I catch his smile in the corner of my eye, and we seamlessly transition into a half-step.

"Don't act so surprised, Loredo," he says. He hugs me tighter as we narrowly avoid an enthusiastic pair on my left, and I laugh into his chest.

He's absolutely right. I shouldn't be surprised. As in every other part of his life, Rook Everett Hale is quietly, unexpectedly amazing at dancing.

We blend in well with all the other couples, smiling and laughing as I step on his toes again and again. He does a stellar job of acting like he's genuinely enjoying himself.

Which is why it looks all too natural for him when he gets down on one knee in the middle of the dance floor. For my part, it's no effort at all to throw my arms around his neck as the dancers clap and the possibly shitty singer says, "Let's get a round for the happy couple!"

• • •

Possibly shitty singer's "round for the happy couple" was shots. Once Honky-Tonk's other patrons caught onto the faux celebration of love, one shot turned into three.

The first round burned. The second was a little more bearable. The third went down like water.

We made friends in the few minutes or hours or years that we stayed at Honk-Tonk. Lots of friends. Another couple came over to congratulate us. They turned out to be from Texas, too, over by Houston. Personally, I wouldn't wish that upon anyone, but they've been nice enough. A particularly enthusiastic line dancer offered me a body shot to celebrate. While I declined, I appreciated the gesture.

I don't remember the entirety of the walk over to the next stop on our crawl, a dueling piano bar, but I *do* have the distinct impression that I got a piggyback ride along the way. Hopefully from Rook, and not from the dozens of live singers that we passed. In restaurants, on outdoor stages, crawling out of storm drains—it wouldn't be a night in Nashville without a gaggle of aspiring musicians. I believe that I told at least half of the aspiring musicians we encountered to join us for the talent show.

Now, with tastefully ambient lighting in my eyes, I sit on a piano bench, pounding out my own rendition of "Great Balls of Fire." *Top*

Gun style. It's a phenomenon that defies physiology. Alcohol is a depressant, after all. I should not be this in tune with my fine motor skills.

With a zest I usually reserve for writing blogs and psychoanalyzing my own actions, I play the chorus, articulating each lyric clearly and coherently. Thematically, Rook is Carole Bradshaw, but position-wise, he's Rooster, sitting on top of the piano. His head is thrown back, laugh roaring over the keys as I triumphantly lay down a final chord.

With that last trill of notes, I slide off the bench and give the crowd a bow. Rook hops off, still clutching his side while the crowd laughs along with him. My dueling opponent sits slack-jawed across from us, and Rook pulls me into a hug.

"Bet you didn't know I could play like *that*," I say into his ear.

"No one knows what *that* was. You were just banging on keys for five minutes." His giggle echoes through my head, bouncing around between my ears. It might be the most beautiful sound I've ever heard.

Oh, yeah. I never did learn how to play the piano.

When he pulls back from our embrace, his cheeks are flushed, eyes blazing green.

"Hey," he says with a lopsided grin as the crowd applauds. I grin back. "Hey."

"Ready for a proposal?" he asks, cracking his knuckles.

Lord, help me.

"Take it away."

• • •

I'm standing on top of a pool table. This is a new bar with a life-sized cutout of Dolly Parton in one corner. Is it just me, or does she look worried about my ability to balance without falling?

"Cam, you've gotta get down from there!" Rook says, but he's slurring his words. It's only to be expected—the piano bar was successful enough to land us both margaritas. And because all drinks in this city are inherently inspired by Jimmy Buffett, the ratio of alcohol to non-alcohol was wildly off. I only got halfway through mine, which Rook finished for me after his. Proof, once and for all, that chivalry isn't dead.

So it makes sense that Rook's words sound more like, "Cam, you'vegottagetdownfromthere."

"I'm just getting my sea legs," I assure him, holding out my arms like I'm surfing. Which is impossible, because I'm on land and in Tennessee.

He reaches for me, laughing his beautiful laugh while his teeth gleam in the overhead light. Why are we even here right now? Oh, right. Tradition. Speaking of, he hasn't proposed in a while. I already politely requested that the bouncer lift heavy things at the talent show, since his biceps were the size of my thighs, so we've gotten recruitment taken care of.

Might as well take advantage of the high ground while I'm up here.

"Listen up, everybody! I have the most special of announcements!" I shout. My voice doesn't carry, but the place is crowded enough that people within a two feet vicinity can hear me. Cowboy-hat clad heads jerk toward me. Rook rushes to my feet, grabbing at my hand.

"What're you doing?" he whisper-shouts. I shush him with a finger to his mouth.

"Tradition," I say by way of explanation. I draw myself to my full height, narrowly missing the light hanging over the table.

"Tonight, I'm here with my favoritest person in the world. The solids to my stripes. The chalk to my tip." Rook winces. I would've, too, about three shots and half a Jimmy Buffett marg ago. "We met a year ago today, on this very table." I sweep my hands over the table as if we did, in fact, meet while standing on a pool table. "Make me the happiest man in the world and be my bride?"

Rook laughs so hard he's crying, wiping tears from his eyes as he accepts the ring from my extended hand. He shoves it on his pinky finger, the only finger it'll fit on.

"The perfect fit!" I scream, and he drops to the floor. Literally. Rook is on the floor, clutching his ribs from laughing so hard. Not the silent laugh he used to make when we were kids, back when his shoulders would shake and no sound would come out. No, this is a full belly laugh, the sound deep and rich over the confused mutterings of pool players around us.

It's quickly becoming my favorite sound in the world.

• • •

Fortunately for my blood alcohol content, Rook suggested that we take a break from drinking and get some food. The burger joint he and Mav used to stumble into was still in business, had a questionable health and safety rating, and was greasy enough to instantaneously clog at least one major artery. I must admit that the combination of protein and carbs has done wonders for improving my cognitive functions—the night got iffy for a moment there. I've now recovered enough to realize that, despite the fact that he's proposed multiple times at this point, Rook has yet to kiss me.

"Here it is," he says, pausing in front of a nondescript building. It's faded brick all the way up, and the only entrance appears to be the single door. A bald security guard looks at us with enough impatience that I instantly ruffle through my purse, pawing at various receipts and chapsticks and tampons, and finally settle on my wallet.

I present my ID, and Rook does the same. Security looks at the cards for all of two seconds before waving us through to the dark tunnel in front of us.

"If we don't see light soon, I'm running," I mutter into the darkness.

"They don't call this place *Descent Into Hell* for nothing," he replies, and I smack his arm. Or try to, at least. I end up making more of a light graze.

There's rumbling in the distance—like music and chatter—but it's far enough away that my heart flutters. Completely unrelated to the hand Rook now rests on my lower back, heavy enough to let me know he's there . . . and light enough not to convince me that he wants to be. We had a couple hours of fun, sure, but why hasn't he kissed me?

The tunnel finally opens up into the main draft room. As my eyes adjust to the light, I spot the massive sign lined by fluorescent lightbulbs on the far wall that reads, *Bareback Rodeo*.

"Wow" is all I can manage. Rook's hand falls away as I do a full three-sixty to scan the place. Walls, artfully decorated with borderline pornography, from the classic bikini models to shirtless cowboys. A bar in the center. A stage on the right, shrouded in synthetic fog. All that's missing is—

"Please tell me you've ridden that thing," I say with a nod toward the mechanical bull. Look, it even has a sign that says *Bruce*. Cute.

Rook cringes. "It wasn't my favorite activity."

"Ah, yes. Mechanical bulls—the number one cause of testicular torsion in America."

He chuckles, edging us toward the bar. "I'll need to see the literature on that."

I pivot to tell him that I don't think the word "literature" has ever been uttered in this place, but I'm quickly distracted by the dodgy lighting, which only seems to emphasize those high cheekbones and strong jawline. In his glasses and rolled up sleeves, Rook looks a little too Hercules meets dark academia for my residually tipsy state. Thanks to that state, I turn directly into him and catch myself on his chest. Even through the mustiness of this bar, his scent goes straight to my head.

You don't get to be hot *and* confusing *and* smell good. Damn MHC-1 molecules.

"Whoa, there. I haven't even proposed yet," he teases, but his expression is strained. There's no alcohol to buffer him anymore—or the regret that seems to be brewing just under the surface.

Before I can overanalyze the clench in his jaw, the lights bordering the stage start strobing, and stream of high-pitched squeals attacks my cochlear cilia. Probably because of the bachelorette party that just rolled in, all wearing matching light up cowboy hats wrapped in pink feather boas. And the other bachelorette party by the mechanical bull. And yet another at the pool tables, but I think their boas are purple. While I'm happy for the brides-to-be, my chances of being able to hear by the end of the night are dwindling by the second.

"What's happening?" I shout, covering my ears as "Save a Horse (Ride a Cowboy)" blasts through the speakers.

"We're recruiting," Rook shouts back in the same instant that a shirtless, oiled up performer struts on stage, tipping the brim of his hat at Pink Boas as Purple Boas try to get his attention on the other side.

I blink rapidly. *These* dancers? At Mav's memorial show?

He catches my alarmed look and huffs a laugh. "Don't worry. I'm sure we can explain that it's a family function. Can't have Lonesome Dick up there traumatizing anyone. Which reminds me"— he snaps his fingers, scanning the room until he locks in on someone in the dark wing of stage right—"I need to find their stage manager."

"Stage manager?" I yell back, but I'm interrupted by another round of high-pitched squeals. The lights dim, and the bridal parties manage to shriek louder. Without another word, he bolts off, dodging bedazzled cowboy boots and drinks alike. Leaving me to secure seats for us on my own because, for whatever reason, I won't be included in the Bareback Rodeo recruitment cycle. Smoky tendrils spread across the stage, which juts out into the crowd in a surprisingly long strip. The floor closest to the stage fills with feather boas and lingerie-turned-corset tops.

Luckily, the performance involves enough gyrating, twisting, and thrusting to capture my attention for a few minutes. The stamina alone is impressive, not to mention the audience engagement. Performing a routine while screaming audience members are chomping at the bit to shove bills in your assless chaps? That's more cardio than I attempt in an entire month.

Rook slips into the seat next to me just as the song winds down, and a small, stout man in a cowboy hat emerges from the side of the stage.

"I hope you've enjoyed a hot, sweaty Bareback welcome," his baritone voice reverberates throughout the room. Accompanying that cowboy hat is the thickest, most voluptuous mustache I've ever seen. "Before we get down and dirty, I want to express my appreciation for all you beautiful women out there. After all, it wouldn't be ladies' night without you. Go ahead and give yourselves a hand."

I flinch at the rise in decibels. We're swiftly moving past ear-splitting.

"We have a very special show for you tonight. Do I see a Caitlyn in the crowd?" Mustache panders, placing a hand on his brow to scan the audience. Pink Boas start screaming, jumping up and down as Caitlyn stays put in her chair of honor. "Nice to see you, darling. How about Natalia? Is there a Natalia somewhere around here?" Now he's got another group I hadn't noticed walk in—their hats are replete with tiled mirrors, stage lights bouncing off them in every direction.

"You okay?" Rook murmurs in my ear. Sometime during Mustache's intro, I twisted a napkin into oblivion in my lap.

"Are you kidding me? I'm pretty sure I've dreamt of this place. Naked cowboys and all," I say with a light slap on his chest. Avoiding his reaction, I scan the wall of framed photos of shirtless men next to us while Mustache continues jabbering something with tasteful innuendos about rodeos and one last night of freedom.

Was Mustache the stage manager Rook decided to talk to without me, or are emcees a standalone position?

I turn my head, ready to ask, when the image of a bright red helmet catches my eye on the wall next to us.

I squint. Blink. Cock my head to the right. Yeah, that's definitely him.

"Is that you?" I ask, the queen of subtlety. He follows my line of sight to the picture.

"Probably not."

If we hadn't been sitting at this exact spot, I wouldn't have noticed it. It blends in so well with the millions of other shirtless men in various positions and outfits. But I'd know that face anywhere.

Rook's hair is mid-length, just a half-inch or so shorter than it is now. He has his firefighter uniform on—at least parts of it. Looks like a suspenders-with-no-shirt situation, but he has the bottoms on. A helmet is tucked under one arm, and a black cat is perched on his other shoulder.

"Liar. That's Midnight, right there on your shoulder."

Yes, I helped name my parents' cat, and that cat was named after a Taylor Swift album. No, I don't regret it. I try to see Rook's expression in my peripheral vision but end up turning my entire head instead.

He throws his hands up in submission. "You got me. I've been modeling on the side for years. I didn't want you to find out this way, especially since I exploited your cat for it." He laughs when I roll my eyes. "Okay, fine. I lost a bet. They never noticed—and they haven't recognized us in the years since."

"Huh."

"Folks, you're in for a *big* treat tonight." Mustache shuffles toward the right side of the stage just as the lights shut off. In the darkness, the crowd rustles and chatters with anticipation. Someone loses an earring. Someone else finds it.

"Why am I suddenly nervous?"

A tremor runs through him as my lips brush his ear. So he *is* still attracted to me. Or a stream of cold air just hit him from . . . somewhere in this windowless place. Maybe he hasn't been kissing me because he's self-conscious of his drunken kissing style.

Yeah. That's it.

"They won't bite. Unless you ask," he tacks on. I press my lips together to keep from laughing, and his gaze catches on the movement before shifting back to the stage.

"Say hello to Big Country!" Mustache's voice echoes across the floor, rolling with the fog as the opening bars of Tim McGraw's "Real Good Man" play. A silhouette appears in the fog. The profile of a man sitting on a stool, touching the brim of his cowboy hat. Just as the beat drops with heavy guitar, a spotlight reveals Big Country himself. He rises from the stool, thrusting it to the side with a mighty kick of his non-bedazzled cowboy boot.

It's quickly apparent where the stage name came from. This is a mountain of a man, farm-raised and corn-fed. He flashes a smile at Pink Boas, and they descend into hysterics. He's just getting warmed up, and bills are already flying.

Thank God they dunked him in a vat of oil backstage. Otherwise, we never would have been able to see the hard angles of his chest and abdomen, so perfectly emphasized by the low lighting. And would you look at that? He brought a whip.

An image of Rook, equally shirtless and muscular, standing in the waterfall flashes in my mind. He could easily make a killing here, if he ever felt called to abandon a life of public service for, well, another kind of public service.

A spotlight pops on, scattering the memory and illuminating a lone saddle in the middle of the stage.

I have a feeling it won't be empty for long.

• • •

Personally, my favorite was Big Country. He set the bar high from the start. But Young Buck, The Sheriff, and Lonesome Dick were also impressive.

We haven't been completely immobile. I got up once to deliver some bills to Big Country. Like I said, he was my favorite. Rook just watched for a moment, bemused and broody, before adding another five to the mix. Other than that, he's been watching the performances alongside me. A couple of times, I found myself turning to see his reaction, when a performer executed a particularly skillful move or a bride-to-be got too handsy.

The newest performer—who landed on the underwhelming stage name of *Bryan*—is on all fours, making the most of those last few notes of a "Chattahoochee" remix. Even without the music, we've watched enough of these things that I can tell Bryan's routine is winding down. Besides, Purple Boas ran out of cash ten minutes ago.

I drum my fingers along the table. "Do we still need to do the whole proposal thing if you already talked to the stage manager? If not, there's that club I saw earlier—"

"I hope y'all enjoyed the show tonight. Let's get another hand for all these fellas," Mustache cuts me off. The dancers jog out from backstage, bowing to the crowd. How they manage to make a bow erotic, I'll never know. "Before you head over to the bar to visit our lovely staff"—said bar staff waves for emphasis—"we have one last surprise."

The dancers shuffle to the sides of the stage, smoldering at each other knowingly. What's this about? We still have at least two more acts to go before we can reasonably call it quits.

Mustache twirls the microphone in his hand. "Here at Bareback Rodeo, we favor the bold. And tonight, we have a special request from a bold new friend."

The upbeat music fades out, and the opening chords of Chris Spur's "Head Over Hooves" start playing. God, I hate this song. Always have. I turn Rook to tell him so—and stop cold at his expression.

He's watching me. Smirking.

My stomach sinks to the bottom of this sticky floor. Mustache continues, "One young man has chosen this fine establishment to ask a very important question."

My blood turns to ice. He wouldn't. There's no way Rook Everett Hale would agree to something like this. Fake proposing on a dance floor is one thing, but fake proposing on a stage like *this* is something else entirely. Except . . .

Maybe he would. Because I *did* say we needed to be as visible as possible to increase the likelihood of securing free drinks. For the sake of tradition and the show.

"Is there a Cameron with us tonight?" Mustache asks. A spotlight blinks on, swerving through the crowd.

"Are you shitting me right now?" I whisper-scream into Rook's ear. He's still wearing that terrible, sexy smirk. "Haven't we established that I shouldn't be on a stage?"

"You asked for this, *future fiancée*," he replies. We stare each other down, our noses inches apart. There's no way in hell that he expects me to go through with this. No, that would be a whole other level of *egregious* and *disparaging*.

Little does he know—I've been watching the bachelorette parties all night. And might just have enough thespian genes for method acting after all.

"Right here!" I shout, maintaining eye contact before scooting off the chair. One minute, Rook is staring at me, wide-eyed. The next, I'm blinded by the white light searing holes in my retinas. I jump up and down, like those bridesmaids when Big Country first came out.

Mustache finally spots me. "There she is. Come on up."

I strut over, making sure to sway my hips like Vivian does. A couple of appreciative whistles carry over from somewhere behind me. I'm all smiles, waving at the drunk women swaying on their feet as they cheer for me. Now that I'm approaching the stage, I'm not quite sure how to hop up there in a sexy manner.

But Mustache is way ahead of me.

"Why don't we help her up here, boys?" He snaps his fingers, and two oily, shirtless men climb down to the floor. When I reach them, they smile and promptly lift me onto the stage. Princess-style.

"Well, howdy, little lady."

Now that I'm within spitting distance, Mustache isn't actually so short. He's got a few inches on me, but his mustache is still larger than life. He folds his arms and looks me up and down like I'm a prize cow at the county fair. He lets out a low whistle, eyes roaming freely over my jumpsuit.

"Our friend is one lucky man. Isn't he?" He turns to an onslaught of whoops and hollers. I blush, swatting at him playfully. That's more socially acceptable than kicking him in the groin.

"Speaking of our friend, there he is. Bring it on over here, Rook."

Indeed, my fake fiancé appears on stage right next to a set of steps I hadn't noticed. He's doing a good job in his role, too. Ambling up the stage, waving at the crowd. When he gets to me, he wraps an arm around my waist and plants a kiss on my cheek.

I blink, both against the lights and that PDA. I can't decide what's more unlikely: Rook orchestrating a schtick at this caliber or casually kissing my cheek like he's done it a thousand times before.

Mustache turns to the crowd, wiggling his eyebrows. "Looks like Bruce won't be the only one getting a ride tonight," he says, earning a few more hollers and whistles. I've got to give it to him—the endless stream of innuendos can't be easy.

"Now, I think you have something to say?" He extends the microphone to Rook.

For as long as I can remember, Rook has mastered the art of keeping his composure. Even when Mav would throw him into a last-minute accompaniment for a show, he never so much as broke a sweat. But right now, while everyone sees a shy smile, I see the seeds of panic in his eyes as he accepts the mic.

"Thank you so much for that introduction," he says, his voice wobbling slightly. It's enough that a stranger might assume it's a case of the normal pre-proposal jitters.

But I'm not a stranger. It's clear that being up here with me has pushed him over a line I can't see. Like he accidentally called his own bluff when I upheld my end of the tradition and remembered who should be here to carry on the tradition with him.

Right now, it's not so hard to pretend that this is the Rook I've been in love with my whole life. The Rook who'd rather break a bone than be in the spotlight. The scared boy on my porch trying so hard to be brave.

It's nothing at all to slip my hand into the free one at his side. I look into his eyes, their brilliant green showcased by the stage lights. I nod in encouragement, squeezing his hand.

He squeezes back. In his eyes, the panic dissipates by a few degrees, and something new appears. Something teasing and light.

"I met my Honeybun here a year ago today," Rook starts with an exaggerated southern twang, resting his free hand on my waist.

Now, we grew up in a fairly urban part of North Texas. People didn't have an accent, and if they did, it was slight. But the spirit of the South has possessed him—he's laying it on *thick*.

He points across the room. "There she was, right there, riding Bruce like a pro. That's when I knew she was the one for me."

A few gasps escape from the audience. I cover my mouth with my free hand to hide my smile. What a dork.

"You lassoed my heart a year ago, and I haven't been the same since." He drops to one knee, pulling my creep-proof ring from his pocket. It looks convincing enough in these lights. "So what do you say, Snickerdoodle? Will you ride with me in this rodeo we call life?" My breath catches in my throat. I know he's only doing this bit to make sure we uphold tradition. But the unbridled joy on his face? It's nice to pretend that it's for me.

"Yes, Sugar, I'm all yours," I reply, extending my hand. I let the tears forming in my eyes spill over. He slides the ring on, and the crowd goes wild. I'm talking screaming, crying, bra-tossing, the whole works. Rook stays kneeling, his hand lingering now that the ring is in place. With his eyes on mine, so heart-wrenchingly vibrant in this light, I realize the next logical step in this progression: we need to kiss.

Not a peck on the cheek. A lip-to-lip, proposal-worthy kiss.

The thought seems to cross his mind at the same time. Maybe because someone in the crowd shouts, "Kiss her already!"

The crowd is waiting. If we don't do this, they won't buy it. Cue pitchforks and torches.

So I let myself imagine a world where this is real, where I have no doubt that Rook cares about me as much as I've cared for him for over half of my life. Where we spent the last eleven months holding hands, going to movies, attending local Ted Talks on sustainability. Where he stayed.

I open my eyes to that world. Rook stands in front of me, a question in his eyes. I wrap my arms around his neck, and his hand rests on the exposed small of my back as I pull his lips to mine.

As cataclysmic as last night was, this kiss is a worthy rival. Maybe because I'm allowing myself to live in this fantasy where Rook is *actually* in love with me, where this proposal is real. I'd like to stay in this world, with the light pressure of his hand on my back. The reassuring warmth of his lips on mine. A whisper of mint on his tongue.

"When you get home, now that'll be the best eight seconds of your life." Mustache's reedy voice cuts through our bubble. Right. We're not alone. No, we're on the stage of a lewd country bar with drunken bachelorette parties and oiled-up dancers on standby.

Rook pulls back, eyes glazed over. I do the same, dabbing my cheeks with the corner of his shirt. They're wet from the tears that won't stop streaming down my cheeks. A new-made fiancée would be crying this much, right?

"Congratulations! In honor of the very first proposal on our stage here at Bareback Rodeo"—like we could forget where we are for a single second—"why don't we treat the lovely couple to a few drinks?" The crowd roars in response.

Rook wraps an arm around my shoulder, and I raise my hand to proudly display my new, zero carat engagement ring. He leans over to press another kiss to my temple, which feels a bit of an overkill. And like it's making my stomach do backflips. I'm coming apart at the seams, here.

But this is the last act we need, if they agree to drive out to the show. I can hold it together long enough to recruit them, and then we'll be on our merry way back to Texas, where Rook will help me remember how many other acts we collected on our escapades tonight.

Hopefully.

Chapter Fifteen

Maybe it's the success of our schtick tonight. Maybe it's the alcohol from an untold amount of drinks. Maybe it's the position of the moon or the current alignment of our chakras. But by the time we get back into the hotel room, we can't keep our hands off each other.

Granted, it's because my feet hurt enough that I forced Rook to bridal carry me down the hallway and into the room.

"Time to lie down," he coaxes, depositing me carefully on the bed.

"Thank you, good sir," I say with a pat of his hand, and he adjusts my position on the pillow.

Really, I'm fine. We had two cups of water at Bareback Rodeo, which should be more than enough to wash down the pint of beer they gave us. I could still list all twenty canonical amino acids, but I don't think Rook will be quizzing me on that particular piece of information tonight.

"There you go," he says as I lay on the bed, fully clothed with my shoes on. He looks incredulously at my platform sandals. "Need help with those?"

"I still have some degree of dexterity, thank you very much." I pull one leg up enough to tug the strap off my right ankle, nearly falling off the bed in the process. He folds his arms as I wriggle the other strap loose. Only then does the adrenaline begin to wear off, making room for an equally potent wave of fatigue. I can't wait to enter a small period of hibernation, even if it brings the inevitable ride home that much closer.

I reach across the bed, pulling the blanket all the way across until it covers my body. I won't get under the sheets with my street clothes on. I'm not a monster.

Rook chuckles as I nestle into my pillow, hogging the entirety of the comforter. "Ready for bed?"

I hum into the pillow. After three days of chaos, I'm due for a good bout of unconsciousness. Though technically, we're still on a strict timeline when we get home. I need to double-check on the venue, finalize a list of the acts, finally look at the RSVP list . . .

"If we're lucky, I'll wake up before noon," I grumble, sinking further into the pillow.

"My alarm is set for 8:30," Rook says. He sits at the end of the bed, watching as I swipe at the half-loose strap on my left ankle.

"As soon as I get these things off and find my phone, I'll set one for 8:29," I say, giving it a final tug before flinging the entire sandal onto the floor. I don't think these shoes were made for dancing or standing atop pool tables, but they held their own for the night. Whether the rest of me held up is up for debate.

Rook jerks his chin at the TV stand, where I dropped my phone off on the way to bed. "I've got this one. Please hold."

I manage to shake the other, half-loosened sandal, wincing as my ankle cracks with the movement. Rook grabs my phone and holds it close enough for me to type my password from where I rest on the pillow. Luckily, it's angled enough away from him that he won't be able to notice that I'm typing in his birthday. (Damning evidence of my lifelong crush on him.)

The lock screen dissolves into an entirely too bright onslaught of apps as he swipes through, the blue light illuminating his face and suppressing his melatonin. I look down my nose at him, not willing to sit up. My temples started throbbing when I laid down, so it's probably best that I stay in this position anyway.

"What's this?" He waves the phone around, grinning from ear to ear. "A *voicemail*? On Cameron Loredo's cellular device—"

A bolt of pure fear shoots up my spine, and I straighten, catching myself on the bed before swiping for his hand. There's no way we're opening that voicemail right now. It belongs in the limbo of my phone, where I know Mav's words are safe and tucked away indefinitely.

Rook's teeth flash in the light from the bedside table while I claw at the air, swallowing the panic rising in my throat. He raises his hand higher and higher. Impossibly high.

I suck in some oxygen, wrestling my features into nonchalance. To him, this is a golden opportunity to tease me about my otherwise spotless track record of answering every call, text, and email as they come. And we've been fake fiancés all night—this could be his version of post-engagement flirting. There's no way he could know my lungs are shriveling by the second. With an impressively even tone, I say, "I've never known you to be a thief."

"And I've never known you to have a notification."

"Give me that." I make another pitiful attempt at claiming my own possession, and he wags a finger at me, twisting to shield me with his back.

I can hear the smile in this voice as he teases, "Let's see. A voicemail? Who could've possibly broken your lifelong streak of notificationlessness—"

My breaths become shallower and shallower as his finger hovers over the red notification icon. He can't press that button. I'm not ready—

"Seriously, Cameron, it's like I'm not even here." Vivian emerges from the dressing room, pouting in the full-length mirror, where she's modeling a black corset-style top. How she managed to find that piece in the shopping center of Rustin, Texas, I'll never know. But she insisted on shopping local for her post-graduation visit to my hometown. If the communion cake didn't scare her off, I guess I shouldn't be surprised that she showed no signs of intimidation at Rustin's overflowing, understaffed thrift store.

"Sorry," I say. I make a show of looking her up and down. "You look fantastic. Sexy vampire vibes."

She beams at that, her ruby red lips turning up. Success.

"That's more like it. I'll get it for Halloween or something," she says. She eyes me, sitting on a bench in the background of her reflection. "But I said that your phone has been going off for, like, ten minutes now."

"It has?"

She nods, extending her purse to me. I fish my phone out. Sure enough, there are seven missed calls from Dad, five from Mom, and a voicemail from Mav. The one day I ask Vivian to keep my phone away from me, and suddenly everyone needs to contact me. That's what I get for trying to have some self-control and not check for a text from Rook every five seconds. I'd rather enjoy my post-hookup bliss than drive myself crazy waiting for him to say something, especially when I lost my underwear to

*the dimension usually reserved for socks, car keys, and chapstick. Oh, and
the green bracelet I somehow lost after a decade of wearing it every day.*

*A phone buzzes in her back pocket, and she answers it mid-eye roll.
"Vivian speaking." Before I can ask who would possibly be calling her
when texting exists, she strides toward my spot on the bench.*

*"It's your dad." She extends the phone to me. "He says he's been trying
to call you."*

I frown at her, accepting it while she returns to the dressing room.

*"Hello, Father." I cradle the phone between my ear and my shoulder
as she returns to the body length mirror. "What's up?"*

*"You need to come home right now. I'm sending Brandi to pick you
girls up."*

I pause at his tone. The ragged edges of his voice. Like he's been crying.

"Why would Aunt Brandi have to pick us up? What's going on?"

"I don't want you to drive." He pauses. "It's Mav."

"What do you mean?"

*Vivian is asking something from her spot a few feet away. But all I
can manage to focus on is my leg, the knee bouncing up and down. Up
and down.*

He inhales deeply on the other end.

"He's gone, baby."

My body goes still. Everything goes still. I can't breathe.

"Gone?"

*Vivian is in my face, asking me questions, but I don't hear them. I
don't hear anything except my father's unbalanced breaths through the
radio waves.*

*"Just stay where you are. I have your location. Brandi is two minutes
away . . . "*

He continues as Vivian grips my arm, leading me out of the store. As I blink against the sudden light of day, not a cloud in the sky. As a blue Porsche pulls up to the curb. As Vivian tugs at my hand, guiding me to the passenger side of my aunt's car.

Some primitive part of my brain makes sure my heart is pumping, my lungs are moving. But my legs are no longer shaking. I can't feel them anymore, anyway.

"... driving home early this morning... "

Vivian reaches across me. My arms don't seem to work. Some connection is severed. Something is wrong.

"... the other car ran straight through the red light... "

Everything is wrong.

"... struck on the driver's side... "

Somewhere far, far away, there's a faint click. Or maybe it's right here by my non-shaking legs, where Vivian must have buckled my seatbelt.

The car is moving. There are other cars nearby, also moving. Some honk as we cut them off, narrowly missing a collision in the intersection. Aunt Brandi mutters to herself, ugly words directed at strangers we'll never meet.

But there are uglier words.

"... autopsy... "

The ugliest words have no alternate interpretations.

"It's Mav."

They leave me with no room to speculate. To analyze. To calculate.

"He's gone, baby."

For once, there is just silence.

"Hey." Rook's voice is gentle, and it's only when I feel the cool touch of his finger on my cheek that I realize that I'm crying. The bed shifts under us as he slides closer to where I'm doubled over, knees tucked into my arms, the tears freely falling onto my legs. Maybe if I hadn't been so focused on Rook, I wouldn't have missed Maverick's call. Maybe I could've spoken to him before The Accident. Maybe we could've had more time.

Instead, I spent that time obsessing over a man who couldn't bother attending my brother's funeral. He doesn't deserve to be anywhere near that voicemail, much less waving it around like it's worth nothing at all.

"Give me the damn phone."

Rook freezes at my tone long enough that I finally snatch the phone from him, cradling it against my chest as I curl into a ball near the pillows. These words belong to me and me alone, not tossed around in the hotel room by someone who abandoned me during the worst months of my life.

"What's wrong?" Rook asks. His eyes are wide, fixed on the object I'm clutching hard enough to turn my knuckles white.

Of all the questions he could ask his dead best friend's little sister on the road trip they used to take without her, this is the one he lands on. Where do I begin? That I had been so occupied with Rook that I missed my brother's last call to me? That so many individual things had to go wrong for Maverick to end up in that intersection at the exact time someone else would go barreling through it? That no matter how many miles we drive, I can't seem to shake the sound of my father's voice when he told me Maverick was gone?

I settle on, "Nothing."

Rook weighs the word in silence while I squeeze my eyes shut—like the darkness and deep breaths will drown out the panic still echoing through my chest. It's purely physiological, what's happening right now. I need enough time to pass that my heart rate can slow, and then I'll be able to think straight. It's the last night of the Tennessee Trail, and Rook is my ride home. I'll calm down enough to pretend like I'm fine, and he'll let the subject drop so we can get enough rest to make the drive back tomorrow.

I focus on the feeling of the pillowcase under my fingers, waiting out my galloping heart as Rook monitors me closely. Just when I think all will go to plan and he'll let me handle this on my own, he says, "Obviously, it's not nothing."

His fingers are still tracing the tears running down my face, but a surge of heat, blinding and hot, floods my system at his words.

Obviously. As in *Obviously* there's something wrong with me if I'm reacting this way to a simple notification. As if, after all those stops, I still can't face those last new words from my brother. *Obviously,* I'm not ready.

Obviously, I'll never be ready.

The wave of fire in my veins sharpens into a physical weight in my chest. It's a heaviness I've borne for the eleven months all on my own, hoping if I ignored it for long enough, it'd go away. And for the majority of this trip, it's been possible to play make believe with Rook during those moments where it felt like the weight got a little lighter. Like I could share it with him and know he wouldn't let it fall back on me.

But after three shots, half a Jimmy Buffett marg, a pint of beer, and terror at the prospect of hearing Mav's voicemail, it becomes clear that Rook should've never been trusted with a fraction of that weight. He couldn't possibly understand how much his absence destroyed me, not when it was so easy for him to walk away in the first place. I never needed his help with the talent show, and I don't need his judgment now.

Which is why it's suddenly easy for me to sit up straighter, blink away the tears from my eyes, and say, "It's really convenient that you choose moments like this to pretend to care."

His finger stops where it was caressing my cheek. A part of me screams at the pause in contact, willing him to say, "Of course I care. I always cared." But his eyes harden in a way that's not conducive to that comment. When he does speak again, his voice is low. "What's that supposed to mean?"

"Exactly what it sounds like." I shake off his hand in the same moment I release a sound that lands between a laugh and an exasperated sigh. This is it, the breaking point Vivian tried to warn me about. I never should've entertained anything more than tolerating him. It's too much for my overworked, overtired limbic system. I've exhausted all avenues of spinning these feelings into something manageable, into something that made sense. There's nothing left but the truth.

"*Obviously*, you're only here out of guilt or some misguided sense of obligation. But don't worry—I don't need your help. You've already made it abundantly clear that you regretted our night together last year, and I'm not stupid enough to think last night was any different."

"You think I'm only here out of guilt?" He twists the words into something incriminating, as if I'm insulting him by even mentioning it.

I don't respond, sliding off the bed to put my shoes in my suitcase. A simple task that does nothing to stifle the roaring in my ears.

He runs his fingers through his hair, growling with frustration as he says, "I don't get you, Cameron. You're cold with me one minute, then insisting that I propose in front of a bunch of strangers the next."

I spin around to face him, folding my arms. From his wide eyes to his open mouth, every sign points to pure bewilderment. "It's confusing when someone's actions don't line up with their words, isn't it?"

Not waiting for his response, I go back to shoving stray clothes into my suitcase. A sock here, a sandal there. Anything to not have to look at him when he spent months acting like I wasn't worth his time.

He gets off the bed and takes a step toward me, close enough that I can feel the warmth of his body on my back. "What do I have to do to convince you that I'm here for you?"

The words make me pause, synapses firing and sputtering out. In the past few days, I've deluded myself to the point where I could almost believe that his words do, in fact, align with his actions. Waiting up with me at the hospital. Kissing me like he cared about me. Twirling me around like he'd still be there when the world stopped spinning. Data points that showed he could still be the Rook I've known and loved for most of my life.

In an alternate universe, I see myself turning around, sinking into his chest as I play Maverick's last words out loud. Not alone.

But that's not the universe we currently reside in, and all I'm left with is the bitterness of the last eleven months on my tongue. No, he's not allowed anywhere near that piece of me. Those words are mine to listen to or ignore for as long as I like. I should've known better than to trust Rook with any part of my heart—especially the parts he helped break in the first place.

I scan the area for any belongings I left strewn on the floor. When I find nothing but chevron-patterned carpet, I resign myself to standing up. When I do face him, I make sure to square my shoulders and look him in the eye when I say, "And how long are you here this time?"

He inhales sharply, an outstretched hand dropping to his side as I continue, "Honestly, I'm impressed you lasted this long. I thought for sure you would've bailed back in Arkansas."

"I would never—"

"Bail on something for Mav?"

He freezes, eyes wide. "That's not fair. You have no idea—"

"No idea? Right. Because I can't *imagine* what you must've been going through," I say, no longer able to hide the venom I've accumulated for almost a year now. "Evidently, you think that being here could make up for not being *there*."

I don't have to elaborate. He knows I mean the funeral.

His back straightens, eyes narrowing incrementally as they meet mine. "I'm trying. Which is more than you could say up until about four days ago."

His statement lands like a hammer to the jugular. It's almost comical, the way the air is sucked out of my lungs. I was trying to get the show together before he decided to come back around. I thought about this damn show every single day as I *tried* to keep going about my daily life, like everyone expected. Whether it was my family or the thought of my future patients, I've always known I'm the one who's supposed to take care of other people. I'm the one who's supposed to have everything together. He truly isn't capable of understanding the depths of hell I've had to navigate alone if he can say I wasn't *trying* until four days ago.

It's a full beat of silence before I manage to say, "That's rich, coming from you."

He shakes his head, more disappointment than hurt on his face. "I thought you liked facts, Cameron. The fact is, if I hadn't dragged your ass out here, there wouldn't *be* a show."

"You're right, Rook. I do like facts. Let's look at the rest of them." I need to keep talking. Anything to not linger on the truth his insult is coated in. "Mav is dead. Gone. My parents can barely hold themselves together. You were the only one who might be able to understand what I'm going through, and you were too much of a coward to stick around."

"You missed one. In all that time you had before I showed up, you didn't get a single act for the show. Not one." His words are quiet, suspended in the space between us before landing squarely in my chest. "If I'm the coward, what does that make you?"

The moment he shuts his mouth, I see the regret in his face. But the question is still there, floating around in the ether, where neither of us can dance around it.

It doesn't matter that each day since The Accident has felt like a new variation of drowning.

It doesn't matter that I've spent every waking moment trying to maintain the facade of normality.

It doesn't even matter that we've managed to get acts together on this trip.

All that time Rook was avoiding me, I was avoiding doing the one thing that might bring my parents closure. And that does make me worse than a coward.

My chest crumples at the thought, and I choke out, "Thank you so much for that, Rook. I knew I could count on you to be here for me, just like you were *here* for me the last eleven months. Like you were *here* for Mav's funeral."

He puts his hands up in surrender, giving up on me. Again.

Tears blur my vision, and I swat at them with my wrist while getting up to retrieve my computer from the desk. I can't be here for a moment longer, not when his silence sucks any remaining air out of the room.

He stays quiet as I crouch back down to my suitcase, which has conveniently chosen this moment for a zipper malfunction. When I hitch it over the obstructive bump, I force myself to look at his shining eyes. Some internal struggle plays across his features, scrunching his brow and twisting his cheeks. He opens his mouth . . . just to close it a second later.

I don't know what I expected. He hasn't offered any explanations for the past eleven months. No reason to start now.

"Guess I can't blame you," I say. "Like father, like son. Right?"

Without lingering on the hurt contorting his face, I grab my half-zipped bag and head for the door.

Chapter Sixteen

In the movies, when the protagonist storms out in a display of female rage, you get a nice montage of the would-be couple getting back to their normal lives. She smiles a smile that doesn't quite meet her eyes, sipping away during endless mimosas at brunch with her friends. He absently squeezes a football behind his desk, gazing out the window of his corner office in a high-paying job you never quite figure out the title of.

They get to fade out to the next scene, while I'm stuck figuring out what the hell I'm doing tonight. Which is difficult, considering the throbbing in my head, the compound fracture in my heart, and the fact that my ride home is the one person I can't stand to be around right now.

And can't stand to be around me, based on how horrified he looked at my last comment.

I kick a towel someone left outside the door of their room, sending it a full three inches to the left as I barrel toward the elevator at the end of the hallway. The room numbers blur in what remains of my angry tears, and I wait until the elevator doors close in front of me to pat my face dry with the bottom of my shirt.

Now's not the time to lament how delusional I've been or debate whether the guilt I feel at bringing Rook's father up outweighs my hurt at his words. No, now is the time to figure out how I'm fleeing the premises. As much as I would love to teleport back up to the room and swipe his keys, he'd probably intercept me before I could make the return teleportation to the car. Plus, I'm not in a state to make a ten-hour drive. Or any kind of drive.

The elevator doors open as I resolve to take to the skies. Ignoring the lingering gaze of a man fully clad in pleather, I pause next to a couch in the lobby and pull up flights from the nearest airport. I guess fate decided to toss me a bone—there's a red eye home if I leave right now. Thanks to the adrenaline that overrode the most potent alcohol in my system, the ticket is booked in record time. The shuttle to the airport isn't running, but a rideshare can be here in less than five minutes.

I don't let the exhaustion seep in until the white sedan pulls up in front of the hotel. The driver nods a greeting and places my suitcase in the trunk while I slide into the backseat. He doesn't say anything about my disheveled, bleary-eyed appearance, though I suspect he sees his fair share of equally disheveled, bleary-eyed folks around here in the middle of the night. His polite silence gives me plenty of time to mull over the events of the last several hours, from the proposal in the middle of the dance floor to Rook's declaration of my incompetence. As turbulent as my gut is at the memory of his words, I don't dare imagine how the conversation with my parents will go when I reveal how catastrophically I failed. There's no way Rook will help me gather information on all the acts we collected tonight, which means the entire stop was a bust. Which also means we've had a blow to the number of acts in the show and little to no time to recover from it. And while I was spearheading our recruitment efforts along the Nashville strip, Rook maintained the bandwidth to actually get contact information from the people we talked to.

Our best chance of saving those acts is the man in the building I just stormed out of . . . and I wouldn't be surprised if he skips out on the talent show. This time around, I wouldn't blame him. Not after seeing the broken look on his face at my parting words in the hotel room.

"Do you know that guy? He's been staring at us for a minute." The driver breaks my streak of rumination, and I become conscious of the fact that the car is still barely pulling out of the hotel parking lot. I turn around and peer through the back window, where Rook stands in the middle of the hotel's automatic doors, haloed in the lobby light behind him. Based on his position, directly blocking anyone who would be exiting or leaving at this hour, it's clear that he felt guilty enough to follow me out here . . . and then couldn't make himself take the last few steps to fully exit the building.

Despite the ache in my heart and the embers of rage in my veins, a small part of my chest crumples at the evidence that he physically couldn't bring himself to be near me again.

Eyes still on the figure lingering between the doors, I say softly, "Not anymore."

· · ·

"That *dickhole*."

Vivian plunges her chopsticks into her California roll like the fake crab on our kitchen table is a suitable stand-in for Rook's chest.

"A little graphic, but I'll take it," I say, picking at my own plate of sushi. Towns this far away from a large body of water should steer clear of seafood, but Vivian insisted it'd make me feel better. Now that we're in the soothing familiarity of our kitchen, sitting at the bar stools of our granite countertops, I can admit she had a point.

We've already gone through the mortifying highlights of the past week: how I cliff jumped at the waterfall, tripped into an overnight hospital stay, *Rocky Horror*-ed into Opal's haunted house, and finally got fake-proposed to at the improv bar crawl. How after all that, he gave up on me.

Again.

I let out a long breath. "I wasn't very nice either."

Like father, like son.

Vivian snorts. "So what? The man had daddy issues. Get in line." Ah, yes. Vivian has her fair share of those. "He still could've fessed up to why he stopped talking to you in the first place. It sounds like he was giving mixed signals this whole trip. Playing games because—"

"He's a man," we say in unison. I poke at my seaweed, not convinced. Rook isn't the type to play games. Even after mulling it over during my emotional hangover this morning, it's all jumbled and messy. Too many variables at play that I can't begin to identify.

"To be fair, I was the one who suggested the fake proposal thing for Nashville," I say. She waves me off, mouth full of shrimp tempura.

"You only did that because he was dead set on sticking to the improv role-play thing. Which is freaky as hell, by the way," she says through bulging cheeks. Seriously, she's got to dislocate her jaw to eat so much at once. It's impressive. "But it sounds like he was doing boyfriend things the entire time. And then *he* kissed *you* at the haunted witchy place."

I shrug. What am I supposed to do? Maybe he briefly did care about me when we were there. I just wish he wouldn't have given me hope again before re-shattering my heart.

She takes in the gesture with a roll of her eyes and says, "So what's the plan now that you're not talking to shitbag again?"

Crawl under the covers and molt. Avoid seeing my parents. Eat a few gallons of ice cream. Most likely all of the above.

"I'll never be able to get ahold of all the people we met on the Tennessee Trail" — I doubt Rook would answer my calls even if I asked for their information, anyway— "so I'll have to visit local spots. I'll just explain that I struggled putting the show together and could really use some last-minute acts. Rook was right—it's harder to say no to someone's face," I say, pushing away my plate. She fake-gags at my admission. Or is that a real gag? "Blink twice if you're choking."

She rolls her eyes, taking a sip of her lemonade before swallowing. "Yeah, well, he still sucks." She chews on her straw, narrowing her eyes into a near squint. "You know I love you, right?"

I nod. "Since you first laid eyes on my periodic table poster."

"Don't speak of that thing in my presence. You know it ruined the color palette of our dorm." She tilts her head, twirling a coil of hair between her fingers. "You know I'd do anything for you?" I grunt an acknowledgement. "Including put together a talent show for your brother's one-year memorial."

"Thanks, Vivian." I smile as the seaweed sours in my mouth. "But it's cancelled. I told Aunt Brandi to get the word out."

Her eyes widen large enough that I look down, spearing another sushi roll through the center. This one's a stand-in for *my* chest. After all, I was supposed to be able to handle this. I had months and months and an interstate road trip to create a proper tribute to Mav. And I failed.

"Cam." She sets her glass down, eyes softening with a rare show of vulnerability. "A talent show would've been theatrical and all, but I think Maverick would understand."

Maybe it's how gentle her tone is, maybe it's a lesser-known side effect of imitation crab poisoning, but my eyes well up with tears. I know she only met Mav a handful of times over the years, but she says the words with such surety that I can almost believe that he would understand why I failed him so miserably. He would give me shit for it, sure, but he would get over it and forgive me.

But he's gone, and now I have to break the news of my colossal failure to my parents. After what they've been through, I can only imagine how they'll feel when they realize how much of a disappointment their daughter turned out to be.

I angle myself toward the fridge, swiping a tear as it spills down my left cheek. "Yeah, well, I guess we'll never know." Tugging at the freezer door, I pull out a gallon of ice cream. If I could put off recruiting for the talent show for eleven months, I can put off that conversation with my parents for another day or two. "Now be a good friend and eat this entire thing with me."

Part Three

If I've said it once, I've said it a million times: With great loss comes great opportunity to get your shit together. And when it comes to grief, getting your shit together means a full system reboot.

The process is called "post-traumatic growth," and it sucks.[5] You're figuring out what being yourself means now that you've lost someone, which also means your brain is figuring out what the world looks like without them.

The good news? This is your chance to completely change your life for the better. All of it.

—Cameron Loredo, Blog Post #42, *Six Feet Above*

Chapter Seventeen

Forty-eight hours. It's been forty-eight hours since returning from that godforsaken road trip, and Vivian's idea of distracting me from *stewing* has been hauling me to her shift at Plot Twist, getting a tarot reading from a psychic, and buying sickening amounts of ice cream.

She nearly backed out of her date with Lucy, one of the *Cats* cast members, tonight. She had planned it back when I was supposed to be home and not in crisis mode. Luckily, I'm incredibly persuasive . . . and also have all the passwords to our streaming services as blackmail. Now, I'll have all night to stew, drown my sorrows in dairy, and binge irreverent British comedy series before sleeping off my emotional hangover.

"Do everything I wouldn't," I say, hopping out of the passenger door of my own car, which she'll be borrowing for the night. She winks through the open window, executing a cartoonish skid down the street as soon as my feet hit the sidewalk.

The sun casts a peachy glow on Aunt Brandi's two-story colonial. She had originally suggested Vivian and I stay in the main house during my gap year, but I already felt guilty enough about not paying rent for an entire year. The guest house turned out to be the perfect faux apartment for us, accessible through the stone path leading across the lawn to the back gate.

I take my time walking from stone to stone, coming to an abrupt stop when I reach the padlocked gate, which is . . . open, for some reason.

Blood thrums in my ears, and I hike my purse strap up my shoulder. I am *not* in the mood for a home invasion. My pace quickens until I'm at the guest house door. The knob turns easily, and I swing the door open, prepared to attack whoever picked the lock—

And find Aunt Brandi sitting on the couch, TV blasting the AI-generated background music of a reality show. Between the dark, coarse hair that's like mine (except clean and styled) and the chic pantsuit combo, she appears to have waltzed directly out of a meeting and into the living room. She turns her head at the sound of the door, grabbing the remote from the coffee table and standing up to greet me in one swift movement.

"Why are you here?" I shriek as she pulls me into a hug. Unlike my father, she has no qualms about hugs and outward affection.

She gives me a light squeeze before leaning back to scan my face. "Why am I in my own guest quarters?"

"Why are you not in Japan?"

"Ah, yes. You see, I got a really interesting text from my niece." She pats her pockets for her phone, holding it five inches from her face as she scrolls. "*We're cancelling Mav's show. Please notify the world of my complete and utter failure as a sister at your earliest convenience.*" She returns the phone to her pocket, folding her arms across her chest. "And here we thought Maverick was the dramatic one."

My face burns. "Was I wrong?"

"Yes." She makes her way back onto the couch, patting the cushion next to her while moving the decorative pillow to make room for me. Next to the remote, a half-eaten gallon of chocolate ice cream is already sweating on the coffee table, along with a spoon and box of tissues. She certainly came prepared. "What happened on that road trip, exactly?"

"That's a great question," I hedge. She rests a hand on my arm, and I force myself to meet brown eyes that are only slightly darker than my own. She did fly halfway across the world for this conversation, after all. Aside from the flight time, she's also my landlord—I should make an effort to keep her happy. No matter how raw my heart still feels after forty-eight hours of convalescence.

I exhale, letting the airflow take some of the tension out of my neck. Here goes nothing. "Things did not go well. I mean, they started off okay." As okay as a trip with your kinda-ex can be, visiting places your dead sibling went without you. "We did get some acts for the show. Singers, dancers, possibly the son of Joel Basswood." She looks at me like I spontaneously recited the entire periodic table, and I allow myself a small smile at the shock in her eyes. She's not as big of a Basswood fan as my mother is, but she's read enough of his books to know how bizarre that is. "We had some . . . delays, so we skipped to the last stop in Nashville. We'd go bar to bar and improv a situation to get us free drinks. It's Tennessee Trail tradition."

"That sounds like your brother."

"Believe me, he must've been in his element there," I say, picturing the blunted horns of Bruce in the dungy walls of Bareback Rodeo. There was so much material for him to work with, and even more when he convinced Rook to put a picture of himself on the wall. I'm surprised he didn't invite his cast mates to go to Nashville and do the same thing to refine their improv skills. "Anyway, Rook and I decided to do a fake proposal for our shtick. We'd show up, he'd propose, we'd get free drinks. It was great. He even drank more than one beer."

"Wow," she says. She knows as well as I do how much Rook prefers to be the calm, cool, and collected one at all times.

"I know. But when we got back to the hotel . . . " A malfunctioning zipper. Tears on my suitcase. Those terrible, cruel words. Aunt Brandi doesn't know everything about what happened between Rook and I last year, but she knows that he never reached out to me after skipping the funeral. I clutch the ice cream spoon tighter and say, "I know he felt obligated to bring me along on this trip, but there were so many moments when it felt like he understood me. But then I figured out that maybe he never did, and I was just projecting some version of him I wanted to see."

She rubs slow circles across my back, and I let my head fall into my hands. "This whole week has been a confusing mess. It's all too much. I just know that it hurts."

The circles stop as Aunt Brandi grows still next to me. I keep my eyes on the ground, not willing to see whatever emotion is on her face. I've already made a fool of myself a thousand different ways this week. I don't think I can bear another.

"Let me ask you something, Cameron. Look at me for a second." Her words are firm enough that I do look up, but it's not pity or disappointment I find. By the way her eyebrows draw together, it's concern. Undiluted. "Were you ever going to ask for help before Rook took you on that trip?"

"You helped with the advertising." She gives me a flat look, and I resist the urge to fidget. "No. It was my responsibility to—"

"Have you asked your parents or best friend or favorite aunt for help since you've returned?"

My silence stretches long enough to be an answer. I asked Aunt Brandi for help with the marketing at the beginning, and Vivian let me rant to her over sushi. It didn't occur to me that I could pull my parents into the mix rather than cancel, not when I was supposed to be the one taking the weight of the responsibility off of *them*.

Brandi sighs next to me and says, "Cameron, I'm sorry that you've been dealing with all this on your own. This week, and the last eleven months." I turn my head enough to give her side eye, and she smacks me with a pillow. "Don't give me that look. I know why you wanted to stay here. To have your own space, sure, but I suspect you didn't want anyone to see you hurt. You shut everyone out, honey."

My blood turns to ice at those words. All these months, I've been furious with Rook for running away and shutting me out, and I've been doing the exact same thing. Even at the end of the road trip, *I* was the one to run away. Not Rook. Me.

Aunt Brandi waits patiently as I drop my head into my hands, willing them not to shake. She continues, her voice soft, "You hold onto your pain too tightly, enough to hide it from everyone—even yourself. But it's still there, even if you're not looking at it. It will sit there and grow until there's no room for anything else."

Whatever portion of my heart survived thus far crumbles away. Truth reverberates through you, even when you don't want it to. Which is why I need to voice the thing that's been eating at me for the last eleven months, eroding my heart and lungs under the sarcasm and attempts at pretending like I'm whole.

"What if the pain is all I have left of him?" I say, my voice breaking. "Once I face that, he's really gone."

There it is. Because it doesn't matter if I know exactly where this pain stems from, how many neural networks have to fire together for me to feel this way. I've tried so hard to figure out the formula for grief, I never let myself sit with it. Beyond the gathering of data and dissecting and analyzing, what I do know is how badly it hurts to want my brother to be here again.

She pauses for a long moment. Long enough that I look up, and tears cling to her lash extensions. When she speaks again, one falls onto her cheek. "It's okay to let go a little. Maybe not all the way, but enough to turn the pain into something else."

I snag a tissue from the table, blowing into it like an especially sad elephant. "Like what?"

She takes a long breath, leaning back on the sofa. "Something that brings light to others, like your brother did," she says. "Something good."

Something good. For so long, I've felt alone. Alone in my grief, alone in planning my future, alone in finding my place in a world that doesn't spin the same way anymore. But maybe some of that loneliness was self-imposed. As terrible as the road trip was in so many ways, it was nice to have Rook along for the ride.

"Why don't you call your parents? I know they miss their son, but I suspect they've missed their daughter, too," she says, interrupting the image of Rook adjusting the dial on the radio.

I recoil at her words. "They're going to be devastated about the show . . . " I trail off as she arches an eyebrow at me. "You didn't tell anyone it was cancelled, did you?"

"Absolutely not." With that, she gives me a final pat on the arm, lifting herself off the couch without so much as crinkling her pants. One day, I'll figure out how to move through life with the confidence she seems to. Or at least, with the style she seems to.

"How much do I owe you for the therapy session?" I ask, smiling through puffy eyes. She's already halfway to the door, but she tosses a smug smile over her shoulder.

"You could never afford me."

• • •

I haven't been to the water tower in over a year now, but everything looks the same. Same jagged hole in the chain wire fence. Same "No Trespassing" sign with various phallic objects drawn on it.

The only thing missing is my trespassing companion.

"Could've used your credit card right about now," I grumble, snatching my severely overpriced gas station haul from the passenger seat. Mav and I spent a small fortune on snacks over the years—the least they could do is give me a pity discount.

The water tower (appropriately) towers above me. There's no wind, nothing to rattle the rusty rungs. Or to distract me from the specter of the person who climbed them with me.

"Easy does it," I whisper, forcing myself to approach the base of the ladder. I take a moment to shove my chips and Mountain Dew into the drawstring bag Mav forgot in the trunk of my car.

I fiddle with the straps, shifting on my feet as I evaluate the bars in front of me. The moon is full enough to illuminate them in their unobstructed, historical landmark glory.

There's nothing to it, really. Just another round of method acting. I can channel the surety he had in his grip, his conviction that no forces—tetanus or otherwise—would get to him.

"One of these days, you'll realize the best stuff is on the other side of fear."

With Mav's words ringing in my ears, I haul myself up to the first rung, closely followed by the second. And the third. By the fourth, I've found my rhythm, a slow and steady pace that allows me to focus on the next steps, making progress a few inches at a time.

This time, I don't look down.

Somewhere between a million years and no time at all, I arrive at the platform, hauling myself up by the guardrail. I don't let stop moving until my feet are firmly planted on the crisscrossed wiring below, every limb accounted for. Only then do I lean against the body of the water tower itself, looking out at the lights twinkling in windows of homes far below, the snaking S of the main road through the heart of town makes the whole thing looks more charming than suffocating.

Some people feel their loved ones best at a cemetery, sitting on the plot in front of a headstone. Mav has one. A nice one, too, right under a cypress.

I should've known I would feel him better from up here.

"I have to say, shit has gone *down* since you left," I say to the empty spot to my right. His spot. "I tripped and fell off a stage, found out Mom's favorite author was a scumbag, and watched cowboy strippers dance in the span of like, forty-eight hours. It was madness." I sigh. "You would've loved it."

Nothing says "talking to your dead brother" quite like a Mountain Dew. I glance to my right as I unscrew the cap, half expecting him to be lying there.

But his spot is still empty.

"It's Mav."

It will always be empty.

The stars become silvery blurs overhead, the soda bitter in my throat. That darkness between the stars is somewhere in my right atrium, making its way to my aorta.

Everything is so heavy. My arms, legs, the fingers still holding the bottle cap. This is what it comes back to. Every night in the dreams I try my best not to have. Every time I see a friend post their brother's birthday. Every advertisement for a play or musical.

An endless, burning ache.

"It's okay to let go a little. Not all the way, but enough to turn the pain into something else." Aunt Brandi's face appears in my mind.

Something else. For now, words will have to do.

Ignoring my galloping heart, I lower myself down until I'm lying on my back. There. This was his view of the stars, too.

"I've done all I can to avoid you, you know. It's so much easier to pretend like you're still here. Like one day I'll head to Mom and Dad's and you'll be at the table again, eating all the bacon." I chuckle, a small, sad sound that scrapes out of my raw throat. "I don't know what to do in a world without you. There's no procedure for this kind of thing."

The guardrails creak in a breeze I didn't notice picking up. I should head down soon. No need to tempt fate when it took a small miracle to get up here.

But I need to say it. To talk to him again, even if it's like this.

"Trust me, I tried to figure it out. I read all the books, did the research."

"He's gone, baby."

There are no more words to an open sky, nothing at all. For once, I let myself sink into the crack in my chest. Long, heaving sobs echo in the treetops. I tuck my legs into my arms, rocking myself like a child. A large, highly educated child. But a child nonetheless.

I gasp for air, crumpling the bag of chips in my fist. There's nowhere else for this to go, this terrible, unrelenting feeling. I pound the mesh wire until the platform reverberates, the top of the ladder rattling.

My big, beautiful brother. Gone. Dead. Expired. Nothing left of him. A finite ending to someone unquantifiable. No matter how I try to stretch and reframe the data, the result is the same.

Except . . .

There is something left. Maybe even a lot of somethings left. A reptile-loving park ranger, willing to look the other way when two best friends swim in a secret waterfall. The musically inclined couple, who host the most rigorous game of trivia I've ever encountered. An absurdly intelligent Shakespeare scholar, preparing reimagined versions of his favorite plays. The jaded owner of a haunted bed-and-breakfast, looking at the front door like she's remembering how he had burst through it. My parents, who have a shrine of theater programs they face every single day.

Mav is still everywhere, from our childhood home to the most uncouth corners of Tennessee. There's no forgetting him. He insists on being remembered.

The crack in my chest recedes, closing into something more manageable. Still throbbing, but in the darkness, there's a point of light.

Of hope. Because I don't have to let go, not all the way. Just enough to turn the pain into something else.

I stand up, brushing specks of dirt and rust off my sweatpants.

"It turns out, when you push everyone away so that you can deal with things on your own, you have to deal with things on your own *and* suffer the consequences of self-imposed solitude. Who knew?" I ask the night sky, shoving the half-full Mountain Dew in my bag alongside the crumpled bag of chips. "I'm sorry I fucked everything up with your show. Like, really bad. An über fuck up. To the giga degree."

I take one last look at the stars.

"But I think I know how to make it right."

Chapter Eighteen

Three Weeks Later

Between the color-coded checklist on my lap, the blood relatives on the couch across from me, and the red-headed fiend sitting with legs crisscrossed on the carpet, I'm starting to believe that the talent show won't be a bust after all.

If only we didn't still have a million tasks to get done before tomorrow.

I clear my throat, tapping a pen on the metal rod of my clipboard. "Eyes up here, everyone." The side conversations dwindle, and I straighten in the wicker basket chair of my parents' back patio. It's a rare summer day where the sun and humidity are offset by a breeze, though the industrial-sized fan my father brought out might also have something to do with that. Plus, getting some Vitamin D wouldn't hurt during this conversation. "You're probably wondering why I gathered you here today."

"The calendar invite said 'Maverick Loredo Talent Show Logistics Check-In.' I think we have an idea," my father says, the corner of his mustache twitching upward.

"Right, right. Then let's go down the list. Vivian, how's the food situation looking?"

Between her exceptional track record of price negotiations and aggressive charisma, Vivian was the natural choice for haggling local businesses into donating food. She taps her phone a few times, scrolling through her notes. "We've got burgers and tacos for sure, still waiting on the beignets and coffee," she says, catching sight of my wrinkled nose before I can neutralize my expression. "You can't ask me to work miracles and then complain when I do. There's, like, two restaurants within fifty miles of here. We're lucky the beignet bus is sticking around town for another week."

"No, it's perfect. I actually prefer my tacos with a side of powdered sugar." I scoot my chair as I turn my attention to my mother. It's a conscious effort to unravel the knot of guilt in my gut—my body doesn't seem to understand that she willingly contacted Rustin High's new theater teacher. In fact, when I asked my parents to help revamp talent show recruitment efforts, she *offered* to do so. I'm passably upbeat when I ask, "Status on the *Glee* kids?"

She dips her chin, giving me a stern look under her recently threaded brows. I would know because Vivian did them in the bathroom about thirty seconds ago. "We've been over this, darling. The glee club is entirely different from theater." She releases an exasperated huff that's so similar to Mav's, I have the sudden urge to make fun of her. "But they'll both be there. One number from the spring show, and one song from the glee students."

I give her a short golf clap before pointing my pen at my father. After years of attending every single one of Mav's lacrosse games, I figured those teammates would rather hear from him than me. "The jocks?"

"'Jocks' is generous. But you were right—half of them said they remembered the skit, the other half promised they'd watch the footage." I smile down at my freshly inked checkmarks. I was only a sophomore at the time, but I still witnessed the senior homecoming skit Mav made his lacrosse teammates do in the name of *team bonding*. The theme? "The Best of Britney Spears." Rook carried the backdrops, of course, but the rest of the players were impressively committed to the choreography. "The goalie started DJing last year, so I went ahead and gave him a slot, too."

I shuffle across the living room carpet to give him a high five, penciling in "Disc JOCKey" under "Rustin High Lacrosse" when I return to my spot.

Scanning the remaining blank spaces, I say, "I've got Mav's theater groupies, two improv groups, and the a cappella group from his alma mater covered. I'll call the fire station this afternoon to make sure they're ready to go." While I'm ninety-five percent certain that Rook said he convinced their coworkers to perform, I haven't exactly been on speaking terms with him to make sure. I was lucky he responded to my text confirming that he took care of traffic control for the amount of people we'll have at the theater, and it did look like he updated our ongoing document of acts for the talent show with some Tennessee Trail participants. But my attempts at actually *talking* over the phone were foiled—after getting sent to his inbox three times in a row, the last leaf of my olive branch was incinerated. I got the message loud and clear, even if all mine went to voicemail.

"That leaves advertising. Aunt Brandi? Did we secure the blimp?"

"In my experience, blimps aren't the most effective strategy for this kind of thing."

I mime crossing something off the list, mouthing *no blimps*, and she chuckles. "Mav's favorite record store, the bakery across town, and the antique mall agreed to have a booth. Along with Plot Twist's pop up, of course." For someone who had just heard about my encounter with her estranged twin, Madame Truffalo was enthusiastic about this event. It may have had something to do with the fact that Maverick turned out to be the one who encouraged her to open Plot Twist in the first place. He was the one who planted the seed of moving to Rustin, Texas, in her ear, where buying a brick and mortar might be more affordable.

He always did have a knack for helping people dream.

Aunt Brandi checks her phone. "We're up to seven hundred and fifty RSVPs, so I'll double-check the parking situation."

"Seven hundred and fifty?" My mind stalls, and I drop my pen on the carpet two feet below. Seven hundred and fifty living, breathing people indicated they would show up to this thing. After months of agonizing over recruiting the acts, I hadn't had the bandwidth to think about the hundreds of potential audience members Aunt Brandi could reach with her marketing strategy.

"The theater has a capacity of fifteen hundred. We have to account for people who will show up without letting us know." She raises an eyebrow, as if to say, "The goal was to show up and show out, wasn't it?" Which is correct. The goal was always to go big, to put on a show worthy of having Mav's name on it. With these numbers, it's more likely by the minute.

"Good point." Even if we ended up with only an hour and half's worth of acts, we can stretch out intermission with vendors and food. With hundreds of people attending, we'll fill up the time slot that was disseminated on all the flyers.

Probably.

Once I've made note of the RSVP status updates, I set down the clipboard, looking around the patio. At my parents, giving each other the sort of knowing look that only twenty-five years of marriage seems to bring out. At my aunt, who's smiling with the confidence of a marketing whiz turned informal therapist. At my best friend, who's currently drawing spirals on the corner of my checklist.

"Well, team. It looks like we might just pull off the best memorial talent show fundraiser this town has ever seen."

• • •

Aside from the title of the upcoming show on its marquee, the theater looks just as I remember it: original, yellow-tinted tiling on the walls on either side of the ticket booth, the exterior deceptively plain for the borderline lavish interior. There's a reason Mav would drive all the way over here for shows.

Vivian offered to make the drive with me tonight. Aunt Brandi did, too, for that matter. But after allowing them to help with the talent show these past few weeks, this is the one thing I wanted to be able to face alone before tomorrow.

I put the car in park, breathing through my nose as I study the marquee's newest message, framed against the dark, starless sky: "Maverick Loredo Memorial Talent Show."

He always wanted his name on that board. I just wish it wasn't like this.

"Cameron?"

The voice startles me enough that I slam my forearm into the steering wheel, and the horn blasts through the otherwise quiet night. A few people are streaming out of the theater doors, but one figure stands off to the side, chortling as I scramble to get off the wheel.

I rub the afterglow of the marquee lights out of my eyes and open them to a curly-haired man, rocking on the balls of his feet on the curb just next to my passenger side window. If it were anyone other than Sebastian, I'd book it back home.

But it is Sebastian, and guilt isn't a good enough reason to not roll down the window right now. So I do.

He leans down to look through the window, nodding his head pointedly toward the wheel. "Some things never change," he says with an easy smile. The gesture is so normal, so Sebastian-like, that tears spring to my eyes before I can properly avoid his.

Aunt Brandi was right. As mad as I was at Rook for shutting me out, I spent all those months doing the same thing to everyone else. Including the one person who was nearly as close to my brother as Rook was.

I was planning on talking to Sebastian tomorrow, when I'd be forced to see him and the rest of Maverick's theater friends. Tonight was solely reserved for moping and calibrating my brain to the reality of Maverick's name on that board. But I can't very well skid off into the distance while Sebastian eagerly waits for me to say something. As tempting as it is to sit here and ruminate in real time, I owe him an apology. More like a session of begging for forgiveness at his feet, but we can start with a simple "I'm sorry."

I exhale, pulling my keys out of the ignition. He tilts his head, watching me carefully as I get out of the car. In true Sebastian fashion, he's wearing joggers and a silky button-up. Maverick always did give him a hard time for his conflicting aesthetic choices.

I stand a few steps away from him on the sidewalk, checking that I parked in an actual parking spot before asking, "What're you doing out here so late?"

"Rehearsing. We wanted to make a proper tribute to Mav and everything."

"What'd y'all decide on?"

"*One Day More.*"

I wince, and he chuckles again. "I know. Pretty morbid, right? But *Les Mis* was his favorite."

My recovery isn't quite as smooth as I'd hoped, but I do make a conscious effort to smile. "It's perfect. He loved an ensemble piece."

"I know it." He scans me, from my socks and sandals to the oversized hoodie I stole from Mav back in high school. He nods toward the theater. "Walk with me?"

As much as I adore Sebastian, my heart drops at the thought of following him through those doors. The last time I walked through them was to watch Mav perform.

But, if the Tennessee Trail was any indication, these types of trips down memory lane are better with someone next to me. Tonight was reserved for self-inflicted exposure therapy, anyway.

So when he starts walking in, I follow in step behind him. To his credit, he doesn't make a huge fuss about how slowly I walk, or how I audibly choke when I cross the threshold. He does stay close, a silent, reassuring presence while I focus on the red carpet underfoot.

We march down the hallway, its walls filled with posters from past shows, articles, accolades—

"Mav," I whisper. Right in the frame in front of me. His hair is meticulously styled in a swoop above his forehead—he must've taken this picture during the run of *Hairspray*. He's smiling in that toothy way of his, the same exact way he did in all his yearbook pictures.

"We had the plaque made right away." Sebastian hooks his thumbs into his pockets, stationing himself next to me.

"It looks nice," I say, tracing the engraved lettering on the dark wood: "In memory of Maverick Loredo." Sebastian grunts in agreement, and we stand in silence. All those years Mav roamed this place, just to land a permanent spot.

After what feels like a respectful amount of time, we resume our stroll to the auditorium itself. Rows and rows of seats across two levels, and the velvet curtains are closed—until approximately sixteen hours from now, at least.

I take a seat in middle of the first row—not far from where Rook and I sat together at Mav's last show—and Sebastian hoists himself on the side of the stage. The stage he shared with Mav at that show, come to think of it.

Sebastian swings his legs, perfectly content to sit here indefinitely with the person who couldn't bother to talk to him for a year. Guilt floods my system, and I clear my throat. "Look, Sebastian, I'm really sorry. It was incredibly shitty to not respond to your texts, and even shittier to ask my mom to be the one to talk to you about the show. I know Mav's been gone for a while now"—he flinches at the words, but I force myself to soldier through—"and I should've said this a lot sooner, but I'm glad that he at least had his last night at rehearsal with you."

Sebastian dips his head forward, resting his forehead on his hands. We sit in silence until eventually he straightens up, his eyes glistening when he says, "Don't ever apologize for having me talk to Mama Loredo. You know how much I love that woman."

I heave a relieved sigh. Of course he loves my mother—she's the one that introduced him to theater, right alongside Mav, in her eclectic, severely underfunded classroom.

"I figured you were working through your own stuff, you know. You've always been too hard on yourself. Mav knew it, too. Said you reminded him of Rook that way," he says. My heart rate spikes at that name, and I scramble for something to do with my hands. Readjusting my bun will have to do for now. "Glad you two made up in time for the show—I *told* Mav you were a cute couple."

My brain short-circuits, and I force a dry laugh as I tug stray hairs into my hairband. "Rook helped me get the show together, which I'm sure my mother told you, but we aren't a couple. Never were. Just"— two people that broke each other's hearts before promptly resuming a mutual vow of silence—"friends."

"Right. I also forget my belongings in the beds of my *friends* sometimes," he says with a wink, swinging his legs like he didn't shift the tectonic plates of my life with a few words.

"Belongings?" I repeat.

"Mav definitely mentioned finding some underclothing in Rook's room." I flush a brilliant red. Maverick found my *unmentionables*? Plus, Rook had a shift the morning after we hooked up, so what was Mav doing in his room in the first place?

"Those could've belonged to anyone . . . " I say noncommittally.

Sebastian flashes a knowing look before closing his eyes, pressing a finger to his temple as if it'll help him remember their year-old gossip session. With the placebo effect, it just might. "He also found that ragged little bracelet you used to wear all the time. It was all very incriminating. Textbook smoking gun."

My brain dissolves into a liquid, sliding somewhere down my esophagus. Underclothing could've belonged to anyone that visited Rook's room, sure, but the *"ragged little bracelet"*? Mav definitely would've recognized that. All these months, I never considered that he could've found out about what happened That Night. A key piece of data. A confounding variable in the case study of Rook's silence.

When I regain the ability to speak, I ask, "Did Mav say anything to him about it?"

Sebastian taps a finger on his chin thoughtfully. If he remembered the bracelet, I'm positive the rest of the conversation stuck with him. "He was really torn up about how Rook didn't trust him enough to tell him about you two. Poor guy was at work—got an earful over the phone about how he hadn't given Mav time to 'emotionally prepare for the repercussions.' Told him to stay away from you until he could make peace with the idea." He rolls his eyes and chuckles, albeit sadly. "So dramatic, that one."

"So dramatic," I echo flatly, but all I see is the hurt on Rook's face after I slammed the hotel door on him in Nashville. He must've had the same expression during that call.

His last day on this earth, and my brother spent it yelling at his best friend.

Sebastian's brow furrows in concern, and he hops off the side of the stage. "Did I say too much? I thought Mav called you, too. Or Rook would've told you already—"

The radio silence. The sweet gestures. The pained looks every time we'd get close to an authentic interaction. He hasn't been an unfeeling, grief-immune monster, playing games or tossing me aside like a random hookup.

No, Rook Everett Hale has been doing the good, loyal, honorable thing and following Mav's last request.

"I just remembered, I have to wake up early to pick up our order of approximately eight hundred play bills." I spring up, patting my pockets for my phone and car keys. Sebastian doesn't look convinced, so I slap a smile on. "Thank you so much for everything. You've helped me . . . more than you know."

The "Unfortunately, I don't have the wherewithal to stay here for another second" is implied.

"Of course," he says while I practically sprint back up the aisle.

"You're the best," I throw over my shoulder. "See you tomorrow."

Chapter Nineteen

When I originally pitched the talent show as Maverick's one-year memorial, it was all about grandeur. Every act would be locally sourced but somehow novel and extraordinary, and people would flock from all over for a chance to see. Then reality set in, and I didn't let myself hope that anyone beyond Maverick's theater buddies would show up.

One peek behind the curtain shows a veritable sea of people. Today is the day to . . . "Sink or swim" isn't a theater term, is it? Let's go with "break a leg." Or however many legs it takes for today to go well.

Vivian leans close enough to peer through the same sliver of curtain and lets out a low whistle.

"Not bad," she allows. I can't stop staring at the crowd. My parents in the front row. Our teachers—and Mom's coworkers—from Rustin High. People Mav went to school with, taught, and performed for. Along with a few hundred people I've never seen before in my life. Between the police officers helping direct foot traffic out front and the dressed down firefighters monitoring the exits, we've made good use of Rook's professional connections.

While he's technically not on duty, Rook does stick to the perimeter, regularly checking in with coworkers and attendees alike.

The latent guilt wriggles its way out of my gut and into my chest. After all we've been through, all the years he stood by Mav's side through thick and thin, and I'm the one to push him away for good.

"You're doing the constipated thing. Cut it out," Vivian asks, following my line of sight.

I rearrange my features into something less pained, looking her and her bright yellow pantsuit from head to toe. "Strong words for a sentient highlighter."

"Please," she says with a wave of her hand. "Have you talked to him yet?"

"About permits and evacuation plans, yes." Despite my intense fixation on counting every hat in the crowd, I can still feel Vivian's eyes boring a hole in my forehead.

It's my own fault for trying not to *stew*. After I got home last night, Vivian and I stayed up for hours rehashing my conversation with Sebastian and dissecting Rook's actions all over again. The months where he didn't stop by Plot Twist, the communication he kept up with my parents and not me, every stop on the trip . . . The data was definitely skewed, and now I have to figure out how to tell him how wrong my conclusions were.

"He's busy. I'll talk to him after the show." I clear my throat, letting the curtain drop just as Aunt Brandi's clacking high heels sound behind us. We still have twenty minutes until the official start time, and she's the one getting the acts organized behind the scenes. If she's finding us already, then something must be wrong. I forgot to contact someone or they missed my email or got towed and can't perform anymore—

"Before you ask, everything is fine. I just wanted to check in before you find your seat," Brandi says, pulling me in for a hug before I can get a word in. I try not to breathe too hard on her perfectly curled hair as she squeezes me, which, ironically, does make breathing a little easier. She leans back enough to ask, "How're you holding up?"

"I'm . . . " Terrified that Rook will never forgive me for being so callous. Relieved that we pulled enough acts together to make this a real, Maverick-worthy show. Extraordinarily, astronomically overwhelmed by all the people who are here to support my brother. How could I possibly condense a million contradictory feelings into an acceptable response? " . . . fine."

Her eyebrows draw together as she scans my face. Whatever she finds there passes her inspection enough for her to turn to Vivian. "How's our emcee? Almost ready?"

For her part, Vivian looks entirely unbothered at the prospect of speaking in front of almost a thousand people, flipping her hair like it's another day at Plot Twist. "Of course."

A few scattered shrieks echo from somewhere backstage, and Aunt Brandi rolls her eyes. "If I have to ask Big Country to stop lassoing the other performers one more time, I'm going to lose it."

"He does that," I say sympathetically. She gives me an exasperated look before repositioning her clipboard in the crook of her elbow. She taps the schedule with her pen, trailing it down the list. A list of acts we managed to pull together in time through the power of friendship, desperation, and repurposed trauma.

I raise my eyebrows at Vivian, and she bobs her head in confirmation. Yes, this is really happening. A fever dream come to life.

In a couple short hours, it'll all be over. We'll have done the thing I spent months dreading, and then I'll . . . have to do those other things I've been dreading. Like speak to Rook for more than two seconds.

"Do me a favor?" I hadn't realized that Aunt Brandi was still lingering next to us. She's poised to walk away, but her eyes are carefully monitoring my face. "Enjoy the show. You deserve it."

With that, she struts toward a cluster of performers, breaking them up with a wave of her manicured nails.

"She's my hero," Vivian says dreamily. When I hum in agreement, she gives me a sidelong look. "She was also right. You deserve to sit back and enjoy it all. Just think of how much shit Maverick would give you for being an uptight nerd during his big show."

I tweak the curtain enough to survey the crowd again, which only seems to have multiplied since we checked a few minutes ago. "Are you sure? I can help you practice the intro or double-check the A/V setup—"

"You've already done your part. We've got this." Her tone leaves no room for discussion.

While part of me wants to force more discussion, to stay back here for a few more minutes and pace around until the last possible second, the larger part of me recognizes the truth in her words.

I did my part. It's time to let go.

"Thank you," I say, my voice only wobbling the tiniest bit. She takes my hand, giving it a brief, comforting squeeze, and then swats me away.

"Get your ass down there. And if I catch you making the constipated face again, I'll make you emcee the rest of the show."

I wrinkle my nose, and she laughs as I finally take my cue to leave. It's a matter of a few seconds before I make my way down the stairs of the stage wing closest to me, and another few seconds before I find one of two empty reserved seats in the front row.

"Camelot," my father greets me, and my mother reaches across him to pat my arm.

"This is already spectacular, sweetie. You know how he loved a full house," she says, tears already welling up in her eyes. I swallow the rising lump in my throat.

Shit. How am I supposed to make it through the whole show if I'm already sympathy crying?

We flip through the program, and I regale them with tales of Shakespearian puppetry and drunken karaoke until the lights flicker overhead. The room's echoing chatter lowers incrementally, and a singular baby starts wailing in the back.

"There he is! Rook, come sit over here," my mother stage whispers across our row, where Rook was pivoting down the aisle to a seat a couple of rows behind us. To my horror, he acknowledges her with a wave of his hand, redirecting his course to the front row.

Every nerve ending lights up as the lights lower, and he approaches the empty seat next to mine.

"Mind if I sit here?" While I was expecting it, the sound of Rook's deep voice sets my skin aflame, and I scramble to move off the armrest.

"Go for it."

He settles down next to me as the perimeter lights fade to nothing, the crowd's residual noise fading with it. Vivian appears from stage right, and cheers fill the air as she struts over to take the mic. I clap with them, focusing on the phenomenon of coordinate skeletal muscle contractions rather than the man sitting next to me.

"Hello, beautiful people! So glad everyone could make it. My name is Vivian, and I'll be your host for the day," she says, smiling like she knows she's already got her polished claws in the hearts of everyone here.

"We have talent from near and far—seriously, some of these folks crossed state lines to be here today—and they're all here to raise money for the Maverick Loredo Memorial Fund. You can scan the QR code in your program to donate at any time, and all donations will go toward the renovation of Rustin's own community theater."

I breathe a small sigh of relief at the announcement. I only reminded her about the QR codes about a dozen times this morning.

She clasps her hands together. "Now, our first act is from Arkansas, so let's go ahead and give a warm Texas welcome to Jocelyn and the Tumbleweeds."

Jocelyn is all smiles when she appears on stage, and Vivian makes sure to give her a thumbs-up before disappearing behind a curtain. Her blonde ponytail bobs almost as much as it did from behind the counter at the Bar Owl. The others—who I can only assume constitute the Tumbleweeds—take their spots at the drum set, keyboard, and second microphone stand. While I don't recognize the drummer or guitarist, I do huff a laugh when I spot Sam taking extra care to avoid the cord connecting the keyboard to the amplifier.

I instinctively lean toward Rook and say, "I think he learned—" before catching myself. The words were lost in applause, anyway. Which is for the best, given that Rook is sitting rigidly enough to warrant a double take.

Right. Because the last time I saw him in person, I insulted him and attacked his character. Of course he doesn't want to sit next to me—yet another obligation he has to fulfill on top of being here to make sure the place doesn't catch on fire during a performance.

There will be time after the show to apologize. To tell him that I understand why he did the things he did and that I should never have said those terrible words.

But right now, my job is to enjoy the talent show we managed to put together to honor one of the people I love most in the entire world.

So I do.

Chapter Twenty

"What's been your favorite act so far?" I figure I should lob a softball question to my parents rather than "Is your heart also painfully full at the fact that all these people are performing in honor of Maverick?" After almost a dozen acts, the room buzzes with the usual sounds of intermission: people rising from their seats, stretching, and dispersing to the hallways.

My dad strokes his mustache, looking at the stage as he considers. "I liked the fella with the snakes."

"I could've done without those," Mom says with a shiver.

"Dusty had them under control," I say. It really was a sight to behold—Dusty without a park ranger uniform, first of all, and also Dusty donning a two hundred-pound Burmese python around his neck like it weighed nothing at all.

I sneak a glance to see Rook's reaction, but his seat is empty. A quick scan of the room reveals his broad shoulders retreating to the back, helping direct foot traffic as the audience floods the theater hallways. While I'm sure he legitimately planned to help out, I wouldn't blame him for wanting to avoid me during the few minutes we don't have to sit in silence next to each other. Aside from a couple of accidental knee touches, we've had minimal contact throughout the first act.

My parents devolve into conversation with our neighboring audience members, and I take the opportunity to escape. I duck my head, managing to avoid most curious eyes that may or may not recognize me as Maverick's sister before successfully making it into the hallway. Aside from the usual food vendors in their designated booths that are built into the hallways, there are tables lined up against the far wall from the local vendors Vivian and Aunt Brandi managed to convince to attend in the last couple of weeks. Mav's favorite vinyl store and thrift shop brought a few of their own displays and racks of clothing, which are being swarmed by anyone who isn't waiting for food, drinks, or the mile-long bathroom line.

I follow the flow of people to the right, where Madame Truffalo is perched on a folding stool by the stairwell beside a few signs we use for author signings and carts of books. Plot Twist seems to be holding its own thanks to its tactical position by the stairwell, where Truffalo can catch any bystanders as they explore other levels. And, just next to Truffalo on another stool, is Opal. Though she still has a small thundercloud hovering over her head, her glowering has turned down a few notches. When she watches Truffalo offer book recommendations to a pair of middle school girls, she almost cracks a smile.

Almost.

"There you are." One moment, I'm admiring the reparation of sisterly bonds in real time. The next, I'm being spun directly into Vivian's face. "I've been looking all over for you."

"I should've been looking for you. You're killing it out there." My stomach flips as I take in her pinched eyebrows. "What's wrong?"

"Brandi didn't want you to be worried, but we don't have much time before intermission ends." She tugs me to an unoccupied spot near the wall, outside of the flow of people streaming past. "Your little Shakespeare friend is supposed to start the second act, but he disappeared."

"Oakley?" I confirm, and she nods.

"Apparently, he was doing fine when intermission started. Brandi's been looking all over the place. Do you have any idea where he'd be?"

I stand on my tiptoes to look over her shoulder, as if Oakley will magically appear next to the cocktail bar at my will. "Did you already check the Branch O' Books booth? I heard Sarah had signed copies of Joel Basswood's latest release, *Weeping by the Willow*. Maybe he stopped by to help?"

She shakes her head and pulls her phone out of her back pocket, squinting at the screen. "He isn't over there, and we have less than fifteen minutes until he's on."

"Shit." He'd told us he hadn't been in front of a crowd this large. I should've checked on him before the show. Based on the few minutes we interacted on the Tennessee Trail, I can tell he'd never forgive himself for not giving this performance for Mav.

I roll my shoulders back, straightening enough to hold my own in a crowd that's gradually returning to their seats. "Keep looking. We'll find him."

Vivian nods and heads in the opposite direction, her bright yellow pantsuit a beacon as she beelines to where the vinyl and thrift booths are. I turn left, waving at Truffalo and Opal as I race up the stairs next to them. Only a few people mill about on this level, where there's nothing much beside a couple of balconies. Even during Mav's shows last year, I hadn't spent much time up here other than getting lost trying to find our seats.

Oakley has to be around here somewhere. He probably got lost, too. It's not like he'd completely ditch us in the middle of show—

" . . . there's nothing to be sorry about." Rook's voice wafts down from somewhere on my left, and I stop in my tracks. "We can talk to Brandi right now. The Loredos will understand."

I follow the sound to a small glass door, cracked open enough to reveal the setting sun outside. Careful not to trip on the flat ground, I creep toward the door until Oakley's dark curls are visible through the vertical slit. He also has a white button-up and dress pants, clearly prepared to be on stage. Or at least, he was when he arrived here.

"They might," Oakley says. His voice is muffled, like he's biting the inside of his cheek. "It's just that he believed in me, you know?"

I wince as his voice cracks on the last word. He sounds as miserable as I felt for the last year, like I was letting everyone down before I properly got started. Based on the track record of Oakley's dad, he can't be a stranger to disappointment. But being the one doing the disappointing is another matter entirely.

Someone else shuffles just outside of my view, shifting his weight. Rook, measuring his next words for the impromptu crisis situation. "He did. He believed in himself, too—except for when he didn't."

"What do you mean?" Oakley tilts his head, and I copy the movement from the other side of the door.

Yeah, what do you mean? For as long as I can remember, Maverick went into everything headfirst. Every high school play he helped direct, every song he sang, every performance he gave. There was never any room for doubt, at least from where I was sitting in the audience.

"Most times, right before he went on stage, I could tell when he was feeling a hundred percent. The best of the best. He'd say it to my face, sure, but it was how he carried himself as he got up there. On those days, he had all the confidence in the world." Rook pauses, like he's sifting through a few memories. A lifetime of memories, even. "But sometimes, he didn't feel great or talented or all the things he actually was. Sometimes, he was just as afraid as you are right now."

"Really?" Oakley perks up, his profile outlined against the glowing pinks and oranges of the sky.

"Really." Rook chuckles sadly, the sound hollow enough to pierce a small hole in my own heart. "He had this thing he'd like to say. 'The best stuff is on the other side of fear.'" I jolt at the familiar words. I thought they'd only exist in my memory, but to hear them in Rook's voice? It's another part of Mav that I don't have to carry alone, wondering how soon I'll forget it. "Maybe because he was dramatic and wanted to seem wise, but it got him through moments like these."

I swallow, willing myself not to cry while standing in the hallway, eavesdropping on the private conversation between my brother's pupil and best friend. Maverick had me fooled, but I should've known—his courage was never from a lack of being afraid. The acting must've extended beyond the stage for more than I realized all those years.

Rook continues, "You don't have to do anything you're not ready for, but don't let fear be the only thing getting in your way."

Oakley leans back, considering this, and I check my phone. Five minutes until intermission ends.

We're running out of time, but I can't go out there without them realizing I overheard their conversation. So I stand, rocking on the balls of my feet, drying stray tears with my sleeve until Oakley clears his throat.

"Then I guess it's time to give my monologue."

• • •

The second act goes by in a blur. With his gaggle of puppets on full display, Oakley only stammered through the first couple of lines in *Romeo and Juliet*'s balcony scene before he got into the swing of it. His transitions to upper register vocals were surprisingly smooth, and he modified some of the lines to be more comedic than dramatic. That, mixed in with impromptu slapstick where Juliet nearly fell over the balcony, and the kids in the crowd were fully engaged for his ten-minute set.

Mav's favorite improv comedy club lifted the crowd out of the depths of Shakespeare and into fully modern language, after which we had a nice stream of musical acts from the Nashville strip. To my relief, Bareback Rodeo's troupe was significantly more *Step Up* than *Magic Mike* and were a crowd favorite, based on the sheer number of whoops and hollers they received. Big Country only lassoed two audience members during their set, which I'll count as a win.

Somewhere between a cover of "Tennessee Whiskey" and now, Vivian announced the last act—Sebastian and Mav's theater friends performing "One Day More." Besides obliterating my mascara, hearing Sebastian sing without my brother alongside him also managed to extract any remaining salt in my body. Which is why I originally attributed the lack of Rook next to me to my blurry vision. It's only reasonable, given the extended crying sessions.

It isn't until Vivian takes the stage for closing remarks that it hits me. We did it. The show is over. And Rook is too disgusted with me to be here for it.

"Thank you for being such a wonderful audience tonight," Vivian declares, smiling through tears of her own. Like a true professional, her voice doesn't waver in the slightest as she says, "However, we do have one more act ready to take the stage. You won't find it on the program because . . . well, because he decided to perform five minutes ago."

I look at my parents questioningly, as if they would know something I don't after sitting directly next to me during the entire show. They shrug, clearly as out of the loop as I am.

"Everyone, put your hands together one last time for Rustin's very own Rook Hale, performing an original piece on the piano," she says, starting to clap with the microphone still in hand.

Before I can scream or cry or disintegrate on the spot, a tall, dark-haired figure makes his way across the stage to the piano on the far right. The savant himself, dressed in the same navy-blue button-up he wore for our night in Nashville. I hadn't noticed that detail earlier. Then again, I was focused on my ability to breathe when he was sitting next to me.

Whether they know his status as Maverick's best friend or are just excited for another performance, the audience members clap. Rook nods to Vivian, who narrows her eyes but maintains a stage smile. Even after we rehashed my conversation with Sebastian, Vivian couldn't completely get over Rook's whole vow-of-silence phase. We'll have to fix that dynamic at some point. One mangled relationship at a time, Cam.

Rook flushes slightly as the spotlight follows him, ducking his head in a semi-bow as he maneuvers himself onto the piano bench. Adjusting the microphone so it's at mouth level, he says, "Hello, everyone. Thank you for letting me take the last spot. I'm sure you're all ready to get home"—an apologetic smile when a few people cheer— "but Mav always wanted me to play my own stuff, so here we are."

It's not until he lays out a few pages of sheet music that it hits me— he's playing the piano. Right now. In public.

While I've since repressed the most embarrassing parts of the road trip, I do remember the conversation we had with Sam at the Bar Owl (pre-falling off the stage). Rook claimed a wrist injury and opted not to play the keyboard, shortly before the cord led to my public demise. Either the injury mysteriously healed itself in a few hours, or he was looking for an excuse not to play. Then there was the dueling piano bar in Nashville. At the time, it wasn't strange to me at all that Rook was sitting on top of the instrument rather than playing it.

"I started writing this about a couple of years ago on a trip Mav liked to call the Tennessee Trail." He smiles a sad smile at the keys, his shoulders slumping incrementally. He's doing a great job of looking calm—except for the fingers tapping on his sheet music and the slight dip in his voice when he says Mav's name. He turns to adjust the stand, lining up that music in a neat row. "It didn't start out as much of anything, but he liked the melody. Said it sounded like *Moulin Rouge* meets Beethoven."

What a nonsensical, Mav way to describe that.

Rook pauses, collecting himself, and then hovers over the mic again. "To me, it always sounded like him." With a final deep breath, he quits fidgeting with the sheet music. "This one's called 'Maverick's Melody.'"

Soft and light, the opening bars fill the stage as he paints the scene: A butterfly fluttering through green leaves, flying lazily until it settles on a mossy rock beside a secret waterfall. Nearby, a couple of scrawny teens splash around, smiling as they take turns climbing up the waterfall and jumping off again.

His fingers glide along the keys like a warm knife through butter as the flowery intro shifts, descending into something deeper, darker. Something slow and creeping.

Dark clouds gathering up ahead. Sheets of rain blowing sideways with the wind. Thunder booming across the sky.

It's the night of a summer storm. Lightning flashes to reveal the boy on my porch, the one with a calm face and scared eyes. I blink. The boy dissolves into the man at the piano, his eyes closed as the tension builds.

Notes keep pouring in, knocking the two teenage boys back as they trudge through mud and weeds toward the looming house up ahead. Wind howls, the storm crescendoing into an unbearable onslaught of rain—

A baritone melody sings triumphantly across the thunder, cutting through the chaos. The clouds break, and sunlight streams in.

It's my brother's baritone as he belts to the crowd, raising his arms to a sold-out theater.

I blink the tears from my eyes as Rook's fingers gradually slow, the triumphant melody finding a soft place to land.

On a hill, under a cypress.

He lingers on the last note, and the entire hall remains silent. In a building full of adults, older adults, children, and younger children, it sounds like nobody is breathing at all.

All at once, the crowd erupts into applause. My mother cries from her spot tucked under my father's shoulder, and Aunt Brandi dabs at her mascara in the left wing. Even Vivian looks stunned, her eyes shining in the stage lights.

Only when she walks over and taps him on the shoulder does Rook raise his head, blinking rapidly. Like he's pulling himself out of a trance. He pushes himself off the bench, eyes searching the front row.

"Thank you, Rook, for the beautiful song," Vivian says as he searches the crowd. While I know that the lights are blinding and he probably can't see the first row, there's a moment where our eyes meet. When time slows to a dribble, and it's just the two of us bearing a mountain of grief and memory and hope together.

And then the moment ends. Vivian takes her place behind the mic, motioning for the room to quiet down.

"Well, we've had some truly exceptional performances tonight—and a surprise guest! Who knew," she says with a pointed look at where Rook still hovers at the piano. "In fact, if you participated in the show today, please come up here on stage with me."

She puts a hand to her forehead, scanning the audience for performers who took their seats with us once they were done with their set. Oakley, Sebastian, and the comedy improv group saunter over from where they were waiting in the wings. Gradually, every dancer, singer, actor, and snake-wielder we watched over the last two hours makes their way on stage again, where Vivian lines them up in a row.

"Please put your hands together for everyone who made the Maverick Loredo Memorial Talent Show possible," she declares with a sweeping gesture behind her, from Jocelyn on one end to Rook on the other.

Chairs squeak and rustle around us. Row by row, people stand. The applause is thunderous, echoing off the walls. My mother gives up any semblance of holding herself together and openly sobs into my father's shoulder. He's not shaking like she is, but a single tear escapes from under his glasses. It's not until I spot Aunt Brandi making her way down to us that it becomes real, and warm tears start dribbling down my own cheeks in earnest. I don't choke down the emotion anymore. How could I?

One last standing ovation. All for Mav.

Aunt Brandi wraps an arm around me, and I lean into her side-hug as Vivian thanks everyone for their donations and urges them to get home safely. The performers disperse, and the audience gets shepherded through the pre-planned exit routes in neat rows.

"You two were amazing up there," a waterlogged voice says. My mother, complimenting Rook and Vivian as they approach us from one side of the stage.

Vivian says, "Only the best for Mav" at the same time Rook says, "I'm glad you enjoyed it."

Mom laughs, and Rook offers her a weak smile in return. We stand, nearly shoulder to shoulder, watching as the last of the performers— Dusty, massive snake in tow—clears the stage.

Dad smiles under his mustache. "Good work, kids."

"Mav would've loved this," Mom says, sniffling next to him. We stand together, absorbing the truth of her words. She's right—Mav would be ecstatic right now. Regardless of how much we earned in donations, he would've enjoyed both the performances themselves and bringing people together. I can't think of any other person who could manage to get Opal and Big Country to attend the same event.

After months of feeling like an isolated, burnt out, procrastinating failure as a sister, it's only right that an extravagant, chaotic, barely assembled-in-time talent show would prove me wrong. Against all odds, we created a show worthy of Maverick's name. Not just me, suffering in silence, or even Rook, who also suffered in silence but under more mysterious circumstances.

It took all of us to assemble the pieces Mav left behind for us to find.

Chapter Twenty-One

While security and various public servants helped direct the masses to the parking lot, Vivian completed a final sweep of the vendor booths. My parents left the building to recuperate at home, and Aunt Brandi said something about calculating donations before disappearing back into the auditorium. Which left Rook and I in the foyer to say goodbyes to the performers I spent so many months avoiding.

"I didn't know you could play like that," Oakley says, and I redirect my attention from Jocelyn's retreating ponytail to his gold-rimmed glasses. He gazes up at Rook with pure admiration—a look I don't doubt he gave Maverick a time or two, back when they were rehearsing lines or figuring out the logistics of Shakespearian puppet costume changes.

"Yeah, well. Mav wouldn't be happy with me if I messed up his favorite song," Rook says. I can't help but imagine Mav pacing beside the piano, distraught as Rook hit the wrong note. He'd probably say something like, "You dedicate a song to me and then desecrate it with dissonance? Unbelievable." So dramatic, that one.

Rook plucks a play bill from his pocket, holding up the page with the second act so Oakley can see his name on full display. "He'd be proud."

"You think so?"

"I know so." Rook smiles, giving him a pat on the back of his shoulder. Behind him, the theater doors open briefly to show the cluster of Bareback Rodeo dancers, posing for a picture in front of the marquee. If we're lucky, that one will get framed and put on their wall of obscene decor, right next to Rook's.

A blur of silver hair and floral print flashes in my peripheral, and Sarah comes striding over to claim a spot next to her son. She rubs his shoulders in that maternal, slightly overbearing way that immediately makes him say, "Mom, c'mon."

"What? A mother can't be proud of her kid?" she says, but she does drop her hands. With a toothpaste commercial-white smile, she looks between Rook and me. "We sold out of our inventory, by the way. I'll wire you the revenue when we have time to run the numbers with our bookkeeper. I think a hundred percent of the proceeds should go to the memorial fund, don't you?" she asks Oakley, who enthusiastically nods his head in agreement. Before I can formulate a word or the beginnings of a negotiation—we didn't expect anywhere near a hundred percent of their revenue from today—she says, "Do you have a date picked out for next year yet? We'll get it on our calendar."

"Next year?" I repeat. Maybe I heard her wrong. It almost sounded like they expect this to be an annual thing—

"Of course! Look at how many people showed up tonight. I've never seen anything quite like it." She inspects her watch, which has just enough carats to cover my med school tuition. "It is getting late, and we still have to pack up the backdrop." Oakley groans, and she shushes him with a wave of her hand before looking Rook and I in the eye. "Send me the details for the next show as soon as you have them. And feel free to stop by the store more than once a year—don't be a stranger."

My head buzzes with at least three variations of *There's no way in hell we can pull this off every year*, but Rook cuts them off with, "Of course. Thank you for everything." He straightens, looking over Sarah's head at a pair of kids attempting to slide down the stairwell banister. "Excuse me."

With the three of them dispersing to their respective cleanup and safety duties, I dig my heels into the popcorn butter-stained carpet. Along with his ability to avoid eye contact with me, Rook is excellent at stepping in when my brain short-circuits. There were so many moving parts to make tonight possible, I couldn't even begin to create a plan outlining every step of the coordination process. I definitely couldn't create a folder with every performer's contact information for future reference or ask Sebastian to help us rent out the theater for a night next summer. Holding a talent show at this scale on a year-to-year basis would be a tremendous amount of work and planning that I couldn't possibly commit to for an indefinite amount of time—

"So did you talk to Mozart or what?" Vivian asks, armful of bags in tow. From the looks of it, she raided every single booth on the premises. Twice.

Across the room, Rook sits on the bottom step of the stairwell with the kids, miming what would happen if they fell off the side of the banister. I let out a long breath, heart clenching when he gives the kids a high five. "Not exactly."

She rearranges the bags enough to fish something out of the pocket of her pantsuit. "Well, you're going to have to talk to him at some point. He left his jewelry on the piano bench."

"What . . . " I trail off at the flash of green string poking out of her curled fingers. A faded green. The kind of green you get after wearing that string on your wrist for ten years.

Or the kind you lose in your brother's best friend's room.

"Definitely has interesting taste," she says, shaking the bracelet out onto my palm. I hold it up to my eyes for inspection, examining the weathered knots. This is really it. The supposedly lucky, raggedy, incriminating bracelet that Sebastian confirmed sealed Rook to a one-sided vow of silence.

If she found it on the piano bench, he must've had it with him tonight when he was performing. And if he's held onto it all this time . . . maybe there's enough leeway in his heart to accept my apology.

I spin to face Vivian, my hair nearly whipping her in the face. "New plan. I need the car, and you need to get a ride home with Aunt Brandi."

She eyes me suspiciously. "Does this have anything to do with the crusty string?"

"It's not *crusty*. It's *weathered*," I say. Beyond the glow of Vivian's yellow outfit, Rook is wrapping up his pediatric safety lesson. I'm running out of time to plan a proper apology, and I'll be damned if a walking glowstick holds me up at the last minute.

"Should you be driving? You have that weird look in your eye."

"I'm fine." I stuff the bracelet in my pocket just as Aunt Brandi pops her head out of the auditorium. "Perfect timing. Brandi can take you home while I . . . "

Apologize? Confess my love? Melt into a puddle on the sidewalk and get swept into a nearby storm drain?

"Do your thing. Brandi and I have some catching up to do, anyway. You should've seen the way the snake guy was looking at her backstage. He looked almost as pitiful as you do right now," Vivian says. I flick her arm, but in a loving, affectionate way. She was the best emcee this talent show has ever had, after all.

With a final smirk my way, she sashays off into the distance, where my aunt is waiting with an expression equally wary and amused. It's not until Vivian whispers something in her ear, casting furtive glances in my direction, that I sense the man approaching me from the stairwell. The same man that drove through three states, one storm, and countless moments of emotional turmoil to make tonight possible.

I swallow when he plants himself next to me, folding his arms across his chest in that broody way of his. Old habits die hard, I suppose.

"So," he says.

"So," I repeat. Off to a great start here.

He nods down the hall, where the Basswoods have nearly finished breaking down their booth. "It's not a bad idea to have this every year, now that we have a solid lineup. I can help keep it going while you're busy with school."

I deflate at the implicit, "You're no longer needed." Of course he wouldn't want me to help out in the future. When it came down to it, he was the one who recruited most of the acts on the Tennessee Trail. I was quite literally just along for the ride.

But, whether I will be involved in talent show planning or not, I do owe him an apology. I've been able to maintain my composure for ninety-five percent of the time I've spent in this theater, but I'd rather not test my luck. This is the kind of apology that needs to be aired out, so I ask, "Walk me to my car?"

He stills, studying me down the bridge of his nose. I feel like an amoeba under a microscope, except human-sized and under the flat stare of my former road trip companion. It's an effort not to squirm, and even more of an effort to stay grounded. All these years, and those eyes still get me. Vivian was right—it's pitiful, how easily his presence inhibits my ability to act logically. For example, it wouldn't be logical at all to sob into his chest and beg him to forgive me. He'd never be able to understand me, with the tears and whatnot.

So instead of succumbing to the whims of my limbic system, I gesture for him to follow me outside. I keep a couple of paces in front of him, unwilling to look at him again until we've crossed the street. Audience members and performers alike linger around their cars, chatting as the stars pierce through the light pollution overhead.

This is it. If Rook could revisit a road trip of memories for the sake of helping with the show, I can get through a single apology. I take a breath of humid parking lot air, as if inhaling asphalt particles will help me get my thoughts together, and say, "I'm sorry." There. That seems standard. I brace myself against the anxiety tightening my gut, and the next words come out in a single breath. "I'm sorry that I even implied that you're like your father. You're nothing like him, and I never should have said that. I'm sorry that I ran out on you in Nashville, and I'm sorry that I treated you like shit when all you did was help. I know what it took to play that song tonight—"

"Cameron." Rook's voice is low, pleading enough to make my heart rate spike. I don't look at him until we reach my car, directly under a lamppost at the back of the lot. "You don't need to apologize. A song could never make up for missing the funeral." I wince at the echo of my own words, back when I thought he was a heartless asshole.

He may have moonlighted as an asshole at times, sure, but he was never heartless. He was hurting just as badly as I was, in his own way. He's only human.

I reach for his hand, but he pulls it back with a wince. "I wanted to talk to you, to be there for you. But I knew if I saw you, I wouldn't be able to . . ." The pain on his face is too raw. And too familiar. "There's no excuse for not being at the funeral, but please believe me when I say I thought I was doing the right thing. I've been trying to make it up to you—"

I throw my arms around him, unable to handle his borderline self-flagellation for a moment longer, and breathe in the clean, woodsy scent I know so well. He tenses, unsure of what to do with this burst of physical affection.

I pull back to find eyes so wide with shock, I can't help but laugh. This man, shocked that I hugged him after all he's done to make this show possible. All he's done to show me that he cares, even when he thought he owed it to Maverick to stay away from me.

"Thank you. For everything," I say. My heart swells with fourteen years' worth of repressed, bottled, centrifuged love so concentrated it's a wonder I can bear it.

And then his arms are around me, solid and steady on my back, and every nerve ending is on fire. He cups my neck with a hand, lowering his cheek to mine.

"I thought you still hated me," he murmurs. I hug him harder.

"I thought *you* hated *me*," I say. He chuckles, leaning back enough to look at me. "What changed?"

"I moped for a couple of days, had an intensive therapy session with my aunt, and then ate about three gallons of ice cream." I bite the inside of my cheek, looking at the incandescent lights of the marquee, shining just as brightly as they did when I parked in front of them last night. "And Sebastian told me about the fight you had with Mav."

"Sebastian knows?" He jolts back.

"Yeah. Maybe I should've led with that. Sorry." I swallow. "He overheard Mav yelling at you on the phone, and then Mav told him about what he found in your room."

Though it's impossible to tell in this low of lighting, I swear that Rook's cheeks flush at that comment. He looks away, but I catch his chin in my fingers, forcing him to meet my eye. "You were right about me, that night in Nashville. The show wouldn't have been nearly as successful if you didn't force me on that godforsaken road trip. I didn't understand why you weren't at the funeral, but now I know you were just being a good friend. The best friend Maverick ever had." I had hoped that those would be the magic words, that Rook would realize he's the kind, stubbornly loyal person I've always known him to be. But I can see in the slight downward turn of his mouth that I've done too much damage with cruel words and accusations—he still doesn't believe me. He spent so long trying to convince me he was here for me, and now he won't let me return the favor.

Except . . . there is one thing that might convince him. I never gave anyone else a chance to help shoulder the mountain of grief until I absolutely had to. If Rook could put his heart on full display during the show, I can try to do the same.

I drop my hand from his face, and he looks at me questioningly as I swing my keys around my finger. "We're going for a drive."

• • •

"He really made you climb that thing?" Rook peers up at the water tower through the windshield, respectfully not commenting on the small swarm of bugs it accumulated on the way over here. I follow his gaze to the platform at the top, where Maverick would bow with all the fanfare of a seasoned performer.

"*The best stuff is on the other side of fear.*" Phantom words carry on the wind in the surrounding trees, and I take deep breath.

"I never climbed it with him. Didn't make it up to the top until a few weeks ago, actually," I say. From inside the car, the rungs of the ladder look even more rickety than usual. The moon is full enough to illuminate them in their unobstructed, historical landmark glory.

He raises an eyebrow. "And you want to climb it right now?"

"No, I just thought it'd put you at ease to have familiar equipment around, since you're a firefighter and all." He gives me a flat look, and I laugh loud enough for the sound to ricochet off the glass and back into my face. Once my ears stop ringing, I pull my phone out from the cupholder. "I thought it'd be easier to do this out here."

For whatever reason, this ancient, alarmingly deteriorated water tower was one of Maverick's favorite places in the world. If there's anywhere I should listen to his voice for the last time, it's here.

Rook looks at me, curiosity in his eyes, as my finger hovers over the red icon. My last voicemail from Mav. After the day, and weeks and months, I've been through, I can finally bear the thought of listening to it—as long as I don't have to do it alone.

I clear my throat. "I have something from Mav. A voicemail."

"A voicemail?" he asks, brows furrowing in his default expression.

I nod. "I've never listened to it. It's from that day."

I don't need to clarify. He knows I mean the day Mav died.

A fissure opens in my heart, more abruptly than expected, and I tighten my grip on the phone. There are a million reasons I could come up with to continue avoiding listening to it, including the pain radiating throughout my chest, and all of them would be perfectly acceptable. But if I'm ever going to convince Rook that I can show up for him the way he showed up for me when it counted, this is the way to do it. It's letting go, but not completely—just enough to make room for *"Something good,"* like Aunt Brandi said.

"And you brought me here to listen to it with you?" Rook's voice is low, reverent. I don't trust myself to speak, so I bob my head once in affirmation. He reaches for my hand, stroking the back of it with his thumb. The sensation alone is enough to make me cry.

God, I've missed him.

I lift my phone, finger once again hovering over the red badge on the phone icon. The same damn notification I've stared at for the past year. The last new words from my brother.

"Whenever you're ready," Rook says. Concern is etched in his brow, but his eyes are calm, steady. Reliable Rook. Honorable Rook. He'll still be here when my heart falls apart again, just like I'll be here when his does.

I press the button, and we sit back as my brother's voice fills up the car for the last time.

"Hey Cambucha. It's your favorite, smartest, most handsome brother, Maverick." Rook inhales sharply next to me. It's Maverick, alright. In all his self-assured, not-a-care-in-the-world glory. Speaking like he's right here in the car with us, hiding in the back seat.

I squeeze Rook's hand as Mav sighs over the speakers.

"Look, I messed up. Actually, *you* messed up. Big time. I know Rook's had a crush on you forever, but for you guys to sneak around behind my back? Treason, to the highest degree."

Sebastian's muffled voice cuts through Mav's monologue with, "I told you they'd be a cute couple."

"Hush," Mav says. He must've been out with his castmates, celebrating their last rehearsal. Based on the clattering in the background, he was still at the diner they'd go to for a late-night breakfast-for-dinner. His next words are clearer, like he cupped his phone with his hand. "I said some things to him . . . Let's just say I knew it was bad when he didn't drive out here tonight. I mean, I told him not to, but I didn't expect him to actually *listen*." He laughs, a dry chuckle that brings another wave of tears to my eyes. Never thought I'd hear that laugh again.

"Anyway, you could do a lot worse. He's a big, broody hunk, and I love the guy. But can you blame me for being pissed? You know I need time to emotionally prepare for something as major as my little sister basically stealing my best friend overnight." Someone cheers, and silverware clatters louder than before. "Gotta go—our food just got here. See you later. Love you, Cam Bam."

The car falls silent as I evaluate myself. My face is numb, along with every appendage. If I couldn't feel Rook's fingers clenching mine, I would posit temporary paralysis. Shock.

Mav was just doing the big brother thing. It's only natural, given the situation. He didn't mean those ugly things he said.

Maybe we're more alike than I thought.

Rook sits stiffly in the passenger seat, his hand still clasped firmly around mine. While I was worrying about how Rook felt about me, he's been bearing the burden of Mav's last words *and* my attitude. No wonder it's so hard for him to accept my apology—he's been wired to give himself hell for the past year.

"I think he forgave us," I say gently, bringing his hand to my lips. He stares at the sky through the windshield, jaw flexed in a hard line. We sit for a long moment until, gradually, he relaxes. I see the exact moment the admission hits him. His shoulders drop, and every line on his face eases. Finally, his gaze shifts from the car speakers on the dashboard to me.

"I suppose he did." His smile is small and more than a little broken, but his eyes are clear. At peace.

I extract my hand to pull the keys out of the ignition. It's been a long day, full of emotional upheaval, surprise performances, and a cameo from Maverick himself. In other words, it's the perfect time to sit back, process, and plan out future periods of emotional upheaval.

"If we're really going to do the talent show every year, it's in our best interest to keep taking the Tennessee Trail. I mean, the show will only get more popular in the years to come, and we'll have to keep recruiting fresh talent." I take a breath and look over, where he's listening to my mini rant with smile that's not so small anymore. That's promising and also disarming enough to make me lose my train of thought. After a brief buffer period, I recover smoothly and say, "What do you think? Are you willing to follow me into the depths of despair every year to keep this show running?"

"I'd follow you anywhere, Cameron," he says, his words soft but firm. Warmth rushes through my system, the byproduct of an influx of dopamine—

You know what? It doesn't matter what neurotransmitters and hormones have to be released to make me feel the way I do. I sink into the comfort of Rook's presence by my side, looking up at a water tower that once seemed impossible to climb. Every moment of the last year has seemed impossible to get through.

Maverick was right—the best stuff was waiting on the other side of fear. I should've known we'd get here together.

Epilogue

Two Years Later

The evening air is a hazy kind of warm, burning off the last dregs of a summer day. I sit on the patio of my suite at Opal's bed-and-breakfast and stretch out my long, pale legs—the direct result of spending every waking moment in lecture or studying. Outside of this road trip, I'm not sure I'll have a chance to tan in the next decade, unless they install sunroofs in the labs and lecture halls.

The wonders of being an MD-PhD student.

"What's that you're reading? Looks like a Tolstoy."

The sliding glass door whistles behind me, closely followed by Rook's heavy footsteps as he sidles into the chair next to mine. I purse my lips when he nods at the novel in my lap, and I pick up the book so the front is on display: a bright pink cover featuring an animated couple fully making out. Leg pop and everything.

"Tolstoy got rather romantic in his later years," I drawl, clutching the book to my chest like it's something precious. Which it is—this is the one week a year I get to read something other than lecture slides, textbooks, or research papers, courtesy of Branch O' Books. "Honestly, though. This author rivals Tolstoy in pure imagination."

He half-smiles, reaching over our chairs until his hand finds mine. Our fingers intertwine against Opal's jet-black patio furniture. Yet another confirmation that her interior design taste bleeds into her exterior design taste, though the suite we booked this year is significantly less haunted-looking than the dusty room from our first visit. Think Vaguely Unsettling Gothic rather than In Need of Exorcism.

"Let me guess. There's something insurmountable that drives them apart, they surmount it, and everyone lives happily ever after," he says. I make a show of frowning, casting his hand aside like it burned me.

"You're missing all the nuance. Sometimes, there are multiple insurmountable somethings that drive them apart. But there's always a significant encounter, just to kick things off."

"There is?" he offers, eyebrow arching above his glasses. God, I love how he looks in those things.

"Yes. There's a meet-cute. On some form of public transportation, in a bookstore, the occasional publishing house. Or they have a long, complicated history, and the forces of the universe push them together again." I grab my spiked lemonade, lifting myself out of my chair and onto his lap in one fell swoop. I take a long sip, and his eyes follow where the straw meets my lips.

"This is sounding familiar," he murmurs, his hands tightening where they rest on my waist.

I lower my voice. "Are you implying that we have a generic love story?"

"Never." There's a playful glint in his eye, but his delivery is serious enough. I trace his jaw with the tip of my finger, and he leans into my touch.

"I, for one, think the whole grief road trip thing disqualifies us from being generic. We're generic-adjacent, at most," I say.

"Took the words right out of my mouth."

He rests a hand on my thigh, and I momentarily lose focus. I should be used to his touch by now, habituated after years of moments like this.

Once my skin stops tingling, enough synapses fire for me to remember the topic of conversation, and I add, "Some of the elements are there. I hated you for a little bit. And myself. We're borderline enemies to lovers."

"Don't forget childhood friends to lovers."

"Exactly. Who doesn't love that?"

Behind those glasses, his eyes are wide and open. I gaze into their vibrant green, the specks of amber. When I inhale, he lays another gentle kiss on my cheek.

We don't get a lot of moments like these anymore, not when he's busy saving kittens from trees and I'm knee deep in medical jargon. Most of our time is cobbled together—a long weekend here, a few date nights there. But we do manage to carve out a week in the summer, dedicated solely to driving the Tennessee Trail. Besides, between the final phase of renovations on Rustin's theater and the scholarships we started handing out last year, *someone* has to keep Mav's memorial fund going. If *someone* happens to be Mav's sister and her childhood friend slash enemy to lover, so be it.

Thunder rumbles, and I frown at the dark clouds. "Do you think we'll be able to work around the storm?"

Lightning cracks through the dry air not five miles away, lighting up the tender smile on his face. "Cameron, love, you know I added enough buffer time for a night at the hospital, a flat tire, *and* a storm. We'll be just fine."

I pull away to peck his cheek, and he grins while I settle back into his lap. As we wait for the approaching storm, I take it all in. The solid weight of him under me. The bright pink book cover. The dark clouds that aren't so dark, just weighed down.

I can't help but feel, in more ways than one, that I've found my *Something good.*

Acknowledgments

I'm lucky enough to have a veritable novella's worth of people to thank for the completion of *Love En Route*, so here we go:

First and foremost, thank you to my late brother, Nathan. Among many, many other things, you taught me how to dream big—big enough to make this book a reality.

Thank you to my editor, Austin, for helping me bring the soul of this story to life. Between your editorial eye, passion for storytelling, and work ethic, I can't wait to see what the next chapter (ha) of your career holds.

Thank you to my parents, who laughed with me over margaritas when the talent show-grief road trip extravaganza was first spoken into existence. Through nights of writing and brainstorming and celebrating every milestone, I'm so very grateful to have had you along for the ride.

Thank you to my sister, Joanna, for believing in my writing abilities and providing makeshift lap desks, countertops, and real desks for me to write at.

Thank you to my sister, Lorena, for being not only my beta reader but my perpetual cheerleader. If anyone can validate my scattered bouts of creativity and general delusion, it's you.

Thank you to the rest of my sisters, cousins, nieces, nephews, and various relatives who have been nothing but supportive as I have written, rewritten, queried, and ultimately self-published this book.

Thank you to Canali, who endlessly encouraged my creativity whilst making me cackle. Thank you to Denise, who helped me dream when grief was getting the better of me. Thank you to Athziri and Michiah, who celebrated every query reply and manuscript request I had.

Thank you to Cassidy and Savannah, who have lived at least three different lives with me at this point. You'll always be home to me.

Thank you to my beta readers, Connie and Kelsey, for your literary expertise. Thank you to Morgan, who printed my first official copy of the manuscript and never doubted my manifestation abilities.

Thank you to Leila. I don't know if I could've gotten here if you hadn't believed in me more than I believed in myself.

Thank you to Josie, who made me laugh and contributed to the joy I ultimately used to refine the themes of this book.

Thank you to Paige Lawson, who made the first round of developmental and line edits on this manuscript.

Thank you to Lex Salazar, who created the cover of my dreams. Seriously. I don't know how you translated my hodgepodge ideas into actual art, but I can't thank you enough.

Thank you to the Fort Writers and Crawdaddies, my reading and writing friends I love so dearly. These months and years discussing books, writing, and life with you have kept me afloat in the shitshow that is your (my) twenties. Special shoutout to Julia, who is both a Fort Writer and lover of acknowledgements. Thank you for reading this far (because I know for a fact that you did).

Thank you to my favorite indie bookstore, The Plot Twist. While I never dreamed I would find a bookstore so similar to my own Plot Twist (of Madame Truffalo fame) when I started writing this in 2022, thank you for existing. It was the serendipitous push I needed to publish this thing myself. Your genuine support for local authors is deeply appreciated, and I'm so glad the stars aligned enough for us to cross paths.

Last and certainly not least, thank you to anyone who has taken the time to read this book. Loss comes in many forms, and none of them are especially fun. But I hope that, despite Life's best efforts, each and every one of you finds your *Something good.*

Six Feet Above References

1. Eisma MC, Stroebe MS. Emotion regulatory strategies in complicated grief: A systematic review. *Behavior Therapy*. 2021;52(1):234-249. doi:10.1016/j.beth.2020.04.004

2. Shear K, Monk T, Houck P, et al. An attachment-based model of complicated grief including the role of avoidance. *European Archives of Psychiatry and Clinical Neuroscience*. 2007;257(8):453-461. doi:10.1007/s00406-007-0745-z

3. Duffy M, Wild J. Living with loss: a cognitive approach to prolonged grief disorder – incorporating complicated, enduring and traumatic grief. *Behavioural and Cognitive Psychotherapy*. 2023;51(6):645-658. doi:10.1017/S1352465822000674

4. Battaglini E, Liddell B, Das P, Malhi G, Felmingham K, Bryant RA. Intrusive memories of distressing information: An fMRI study. *PLoS One*. 2016;11(9):e0140871. doi:10.1371/journal.pone.0140871

5. Johnsen I, Afgun K. Complicated grief and post-traumatic growth in traumatically bereaved siblings and close friends. *Journal of Loss and Trauma*. 2020;26(3):246-259. doi:10.1080/15325024.2020.1762972

About the Author

Originally from California, Cassie swapped mountains and beaches for the Buc-ee's and concerningly loyal Cowboys fans of Texas. With a bachelor's degree in biology and graduate degree in science education, she considers herself a woman in STEM with a penchant for prose.

About the Author